TOO LATE
IN THE AFTERNOON

TOO LATE
IN THE AFTERNOON

One Man's Triumph Over Depression

PATRICK DAY

Pyramid Publishers

Buffalo, Minnesota

Pyramid Publishers

Pyramid Publishers

1314 Grandview Circle

Buffalo, MN 55313

763-486-2867

pyramidpublishers.com

ISBN — 978-0-9851514-1-6

LCCN - 2010933648

Cover Design by Alan Pranke

Typeset by Melanie Shellito

Printed in the United States of America

INTRODUCTION

In the spring of 1972, when I was completing a Master's Degree in English Literature at the University of Minnesota, and desiring to be a writer of fiction, a strange thing happened in my study one afternoon. I can't remember exactly how it happened, but from someplace outside my consciousness, the name of a book, *Too Late in the Afternoon*, and the basic plot of it came into my mind in a matter of seconds. It couldn't have been my own thinking, because thinking for me takes time, not a flash like a lightning bolt.

I wrote down the title and plot, and there it lay for 36 years. It's not that I didn't look at it occasionally and think about putting pen to paper, but the journey of my life took a different turn.

Writing a novel is a dicey thing when you need to be bringing in money to support a family. I did write professionally, but it was as a technical writer and as an advertising copywriter. For that I was always paid. Eventually, I transitioned into an educational career of teaching and administration in a two-year college, while writing ads and brochures on the side.

Since I retired from Ridgewater College with a fixed income for my wife and me, there is now time to write without the pressure of being mercenary about it. And the deep desire to become a novelist returned to me. I have been pondering the book actively since 2003, and I have received input from friends regarding the plot, which has emerged as much more comprehensive than what I recorded in 1972. I finally started researching the physical settings of the book and writing a rough story line in the spring of 2008.

Too Late in the Afternoon begins in the Tangletown section of Southwest Minneapolis, where Mitch Jasper and David Logan grew up and prospered as fast friends over a 13-year period of time. There were two events that bonded them together closer than brothers during those childhood and adolescent years. One was at the Washburn Water Tower when they were still very young. Here they saw something right out of Norse mythology. The recognition of mythology was unfamiliar to them at the time, but had the power to mystify and fascinate them, and point them to the true north of kindred spirits. The other event was crawling over the arches of the Nicollet Avenue Bridge from one end to the other, a perilous adventure that took them across Minnehaha Creek and branded them as friends forever in a symbolic ceremony that took place on the far end of the bridge.

This "friends forever" took a lengthy detour when Mitch matriculated to Northwestern University and then into the advertising business in Chicago. He didn't see or talk to Dave for 40 years. His was a life of self-centeredness and blind ambition that ended in divorce and estrangement from his three children and his five grandchildren. When a doctor told him he needed to slow down after a serious heart attack or he wouldn't see his next birthday, Mitch sold his advertising agency and moved back to Minneapolis, Edina to be precise. Here he hoped to start another life, but his hope was soon shattered by a feeling of purposelessness, unfamiliarity, and nothing to do. This terrain of hopelessness transported him into the black dog of depression, a malady he finally triumphs over by a total healing regimen of body, soul, and spirit.

Dave, on the other hand, stayed in Minneapolis and went to college at the University of Minnesota. He was devoted to his wife, his three children, five grandchildren, and his parents. His was a life of forgetting about himself and paying close attention to the needs of those around him. Dave's path of life, in short, was almost a complete contrast to that of Mitch's.

They met again at the 40th class reunion of Washburn High School and picked up where they left off 40 years prior. Retirement was very good for Dave and very bad for Mitch. Through regular meetings at a local coffee house and a pattern of almost daily phone calls, Mitch allowed himself to be vulnerable enough to put himself into the hands of his friend Dave. It was a major awakening for Mitch when he finally took responsibility for all his mistakes. However, he felt he was in the afternoon of his life and for him it was "too late in the afternoon" to make major changes. And so the story takes a turn. Dave challenges that premise and serves as a mentor for Mitch to start making the changes in his life to pull him out of the depression he had fallen into, a pit of despondency that threatened to engulf him.

Dave represents much of what God wants Mitch to become. As such he is intrinsic to the story. Dave is more than outside Mitch. He represents the potential within Mitch. They belong together, closer than brothers, and Mitch will become whole only by weaving the stuff of Dave into his life.

Slowly, slowly, Mitch is transformed from a depressed semi-recluse to an outgoing man with friends and meaningful activities to one who finds a way to serve his fellow man and embrace a new purpose in life. In the movie *Second Hand Lions*, one of the main characters says he has outlived his usefulness. Mitch found a new usefulness that was radically different from his advertising career usefulness, and so much better.

A tragic car accident experienced by his youngest daughter becomes the catalyst for Mitch's new beginning with his family. It takes time for them to realize he is not the Dad who had abandoned them but the Dad who is interested in their lives in the same way Dave is interested in his family.

When Mitch moves to Minneapolis, he is an agnostic. Through the influence of Dave, a friend named Daniel, and an Anglican pastor, Mitch goes through a process of believing in God and eventually becomes a Christian.

The other settings in this story are Edina and Hopkins, Minnesota, Chicago, and Birmingham, Alabama. I selected these locales because I was familiar with them in the years I spent in Minneapolis and the many visits I have made to Chicago and Birmingham over the years.

Too Late in the Afternoon incorporates both real and imaginary places and events. Examples of real places are the Washburn Water

Tower, the streets of Minneapolis, Minnehaha Creek that empties into the Mississippi River, the Jemison Trail in Birmingham, and other public-domain settings. An example of a real event is a person I know who actually crawled over the arches of the Nicollet Avenue Bridge with his best friend. If you ever find yourself in that part of Minneapolis, stand down on the Minnehaha Parkway and try to imagine doing that.

Most of the private locations are fictional, except for the Metropolitan Ballroom and Clubroom in Minneapolis, the actual venue of Washburn High School's 40th class reunion. Although there are coffee shops on France Avenue, Coffee on France is imaginary, designed to have a meeting room where Mitch and Dave could have confidential discussions.

All characters and plot lines are fictional, though I have drawn from my own life experiences and personal knowledge of various people for aspects of characters' personalities, and for circumstances and situations that make up the lives of the players in the story. In short, what happens to my characters is accurate, believable, and happens in real life.

There were several questions I wanted answered in writing this novel:

1. Can a person turn a bad retirement into a good one?

2. Is massive change possible in two years, starting at the age of 58?

3. Is clinical depression permanent, or can one conquer it and put it in the past?

4. Can a neglected friendship be renewed even after 40 years?

I found the answers to these questions — and so will you by reading *Too Late in the Afternoon.*

DEDICATION AND ACKNOWLEDGMENTS

I wish to dedicate this book to a person with the most indomitable spirit I have ever witnessed — my brother Thomas J. Day, who passed away on February 28, 2010. Tom became a quadriplegic in a tragic car accident on July 21, 1977, and spent the rest of his life in a quest to stay out of a nursing home. He won that battle and lived at home for the last 33 years of his life. Tom triumphed over his disability and lived a more full life than many able-bodied men. He has been an inspiration to me and a model that anything can be accomplished if you have a positive attitude and never give up.

My other brother, William J. Day, holds a doctor's degree in psychology from Union Institute and University and is the model for Wally in *Too Late in the Afternoon*. He now calls himself Dr. Wally. I share a triple bond with Bill: he is my brother in blood, my brother in spirit, and my best friend. Bill edited my second manuscript and provided exceptional insight regarding Mitch Jasper's character. His critique of the book brought in the element of inner healing and other important threads that run throughout the book.

On March 24, 2008, I spent a day with Tom Balcom who lives in Southwest Minneapolis and is the historian of Tangletown. He was my source for the Tangletown setting of *Too Late in the Afternoon* and for a key episode in the book — climbing over the arches of the Nicollet Avenue Bridge. I knew that was possible to do because he once accomplished the feat with his best friend, when they were both in sixth grade.

Jack Harrold met with me 36 times to go through each chapter of the first manuscript and each chapter of the second manuscript. He encouraged me to press on when my commitment was faltering, and the questions he asked me caused me to rewrite more passages than I otherwise would have. This is a better book because of Jack.

I read every word of my first manuscript to my friend Marv Schaar, whom I visit at a care center every Saturday. He listened patiently and helped me listen to the spoken dialogue in the book. Marv suffers from muscular dystrophy and regales me every Saturday with his humor and joy of life.

Finally, I want to thank my wife, Diane, for her on-going acceptance of the hours I spent writing *Too Late in the Afternoon* — at home, in a coffee shop in Birmingham, Alabama, on vacation, on the phone with Bill, and all the meetings with Jack.

TABLE OF CONTENTS

CHAPTER 1
Class Reunion

Color me black... and color me white. Does that seem somewhat odd? It isn't, for my story starts in the darkness of hell and concludes in the brightness of heaven.

Today, August 1, 2007, is the first day of writing my narrative. The story begins June 25, 2005, and ends July 14, 2007 — a tale of two years.

When I look back over those two years, with a perspective I didn't have at the time, there is one word that explains how I changed from a miserable wretch to the person I am today. That word is grace.

From the time I was a senior in high school, at the suggestion of a business teacher, I started to journal, not every day, but the highlights of my life. It was extremely helpful when I was in advertising because I could pinpoint the day when something was promised or said that I could refer back to. It unnerved people when I said that such and such was said one year ago on March 24 at 3 p.m. It became difficult for anyone to say that he or she never said that.

I returned to Minnesota in May 2005, and began journaling every day, starting June 25, in a new journal I referred to as my "Struggle Journal." It gave me something to do, and it was invaluable in my writing now about the transformation that so dramatically changed my life. For I can write precisely about what happened to me and when, conversations that took place, even my innermost thoughts at the time, thoughts that seem strange to me now. But my life was what it was, and I need to be accurate about given times and what I was thinking, if my story is to be true and not fanciful.

To avoid confusing readers, when I write from my perspective of fall 2007, I use italics. When I write as my life was unfolding at the time, I use normal type.

***

I distinctly remember that day in June of 2005 as I stared out the front window of my fourth floor condominium in Edina, a suburb of Minneapolis. It was a beautiful day, one of those days in Minnesota that makes the winters worth enduring. The temperature was in the mid-70s, the humidity was low, and a few clouds were drifting lazily in the sky. I could see France Avenue below me and the movie theater just off France that played independent movies that didn't make it to the main theaters.

Most people in the Minneapolis-St. Paul metro area would think this was a perfect day. But not me. Shadows of darkness were permeating my inner being, and that was the filter with which I was viewing everything, including the weather.

***

There were a number of bad choices I had made the year before coming to Minnesota, when I was living in Chicago. A bad choice then was a choice I made not favorable to me. I didn't consider how my choices affected anyone else. That was a major character flaw that was beyond my inner vision as my outer vision took in the landscape of 50th and France. When circumstances were good, I felt good. When they were bad, I felt bad. I didn't have a lot of inner depth in my life.

***

Before coming back to my roots in Minneapolis, my recent Chicago past included a major heart attack that forced me to sell my ad agency, a divorce that included alienation from my three children, and a move from a familiar city of 40 years to retirement in a city that remembered me not. Thomas Wolfe wrote a novel called *You Can't Go Home Again,* and I was living out the title of that book. I couldn't stay in Chicago with all the bad memories; I was not welcomed back to Minneapolis.

It was confusing. I was damned if I stayed in Chicago and damned if I came back home.

***

Damned was an accurate word then because I was increasingly living in the vicinity of hell here on earth.

***

I thought it was a reasonable move to escape Chicago, and it was, for the first two or three weeks. I drove through my old Southwest Minneapolis neighborhood and visited the old haunts in Minneapolis and St. Paul. Some places were familiar; much had changed. Pearl Lake was no longer a swamp; it had been transformed into a large field. Washburn High School had a new addition to the west — a science building and computer labs.

Then I started going downhill. An uneasy sense of hopelessness pervaded my mind as I fast-forwarded to view days and days of bleakness until I died. I had no friends. Ads on TV exclaimed how wonderful retirement was, but for me the truth was that retirement was another word for nothing to do, nothing to look forward to, and no meaning or purpose in life. I didn't see any of this coming. I was blindsided.

I thought, "Oh, Mitch, Mitch, what have you done?" Hearing my name echoing in my mind reminded me of why I was named Mitch. My mother wanted to call me Mitchell after her grandfather. My father thought Mitchell was a name for a weakling. The compromise became Mitch. According to my father, Mitch Jasper was a strong name for the son he would raise

As I grew into manhood, Mitch was the right name for what I had become: a solid advertising executive with a solid physique. On my fifty-fifth birthday, I looked into a mirror and saw that solid had been replaced by flabby. I was carrying extra pounds and diminished muscles. Thinning hair and furrows in my face said what I didn't want to hear: "You're not in good health." This truth came crashing down on me two years later when I had a massive heart attack that brought me to the edge of death. It scared me so completely that I lost 25 pounds in less than half a year, to get down to my present weight of 215 pounds.

I recuperated at home for a couple of months; my routine was going to cardiac rehab three times a week. I was in a foul mood with so much time on my hands. Having my wife Kathleen underfoot all day every day made me especially grouchy. I spent more time with her than I ever had. And the more time I spent with her, the more I resented her. She was "put-her-religion-on-her-sleeve" churchy and told me God could bring me peace and healing. I didn't want to hear of it and became more and more hostile to her.

When I returned to work, I was limited to half days and felt like a cripple. I took my frustration out on Kathleen. Five months after returning to work, I decided to divorce Kathleen. I offered to move out of our condominium, but she said she couldn't stay there by herself. She moved in with a friend from Chicago, hoping I would come to my senses before the divorce was complete. The divorce went through within two months.

She entered a deep depression, which I was not sensitive to at the time. I could only relate to my own pain. Kathleen had migrated from a pleasant diversion to a burden and a scourge.

***

From the vantage point of more than two years later, I realize how cruel I was to her and how oblivious to her feelings. Back then I didn't think much about the feelings of anyone else. As we were signing the divorce papers in my lawyer's office, it put me back in my chair when she said to me, "Mitch, I forgive you for this and pray someday you will seek forgiveness yourself." Those were the only words she spoke.

***

I was in a fog at this time, so I didn't realize the repercussions of the divorce that came rumbling at me out of the darkness. My three children abandoned me when I divorced their mother.

***

It shouldn't have been a surprise, given the way I related to them. It was not a high priority for me to be a father to Suzie or Jane. I didn't understand them as they were growing up, mostly because I was too busy with my work to invest time with them. It was like they didn't have a father. With Michael it was a bit different. Michael was good in sports, and I went to as many of his sporting events as I could wrestle away from work. It seemed there was more common ground with my son because I thought I understood him better than the girls, but other than sports, I didn't invest time with him either. So Michael came to the same outlook as the girls — he didn't have a father.

***

Two of my children had married: Michael lived in Naperville and Suzie lived in Wheaton, both western suburbs of Chicago. When Jane graduated from college, she was single and living with a college roommate in downtown Chicago, near the bank where she worked. I felt my children were ungrateful. Hadn't I provided for them in every way? Whatever they wanted as they were growing up, I bought for them—a car when they were old enough to drive, designer clothes, and college degrees without any debt.

***

Now I realize I never gave them what they really wanted — my love and involvement in their lives. That was two city blocks from my consciousness in Chicago.

***

Still staring out the front window of my condominium, my thoughts entered a different path. There were no people who valued what I had to say any more. I stepped out of a picture of being somebody into a picture of being nobody. That thought darkened my consciousness. I was used to being the center of attention.

***

There is something I can say about myself now that was hidden from me then. I believed I was the main actor on the stage of life and everyone else played a supportive role. It was a self-centered viewpoint that made other people, including my wife and three children, seem to live in a different world. Those who didn't follow what I wanted them to be and do were troublesome and would bring me great joy if they just disappeared. In my mind I had a script of what should be, a script that was favorable to me, if not to anyone else.

***

I turned my attention from daydreaming in front of the window to a flyer that was forwarded to me from my Chicago address: "Washburn Reunion of the Class of 1965." How could it be 40 years? The July 9 date of the reunion was just two weeks away.

When I received the flyer last week, I sent in my reservation. Why not? I had an open calendar from here until eternity. Perhaps I'd connect with high school friends who still lived in the metro area, and my life would gain some life. I had second thoughts today because I was in the dumps mentally, but I decided I needed to go, dumps or no dumps. Maybe when I met old friends, I'd feel my old self again, the way I felt when I attended Washburn.

***

I was in the parking lot of the Metropolitan Ballroom and Clubroom in Minneapolis, looking at the front revolving door that led into the Washburn 40th Class Reunion. As I approached the front entrance, a woman, to whom time had been unkind, walked toward me. "Well if it isn't Mitch Jasper!" she blurted out. I stood dumbly looking at her. "You don't know who I am, do you?"

I didn't have a clue who she was and was embarrassed to say so. "You look familiar," I lied, "but 40 years is a long time. Give me a clue."

"Remember your old biology partner, Liz? After all the pranks you played on me, I thought I'd be one of the first you'd recognize."

Recognize? I hadn't entertained one thought about my old classmates since the summer of 1965. In the fall, I left for Evanston, Illinois, just north of Chicago, to attend Northwestern University. Four years later, I earned a B. S. Degree in Journalism, with a major in Advertising. Chicago was a city known for award-winning advertising agencies, and that was the career I had tracked since ninth grade. My parents were wealthy enough to send me to any of the best private schools in the nation. My father was pleased I chose Northwestern because he and his father, being good Methodists, graduated from there.

Once I entered the gates of Northwestern, I stayed in Chicago year round. I loved the city and worked summers at Carrington Smithson Advertising Agency. I went back to Minneapolis for Thanksgiving, Christmas, and Easter, and that was about it. I did my duty.

My old biology partner Liz! We used to call her Lizzie the Lizard. "Why Liz, you look so different than in high school. You've changed a lot. I mean we've all changed a lot. I mean...."

"You mean I look a lot older and frumpier now. Three marriages and seven children will do that. Plus working two jobs most of my life because of my worthless husbands. I didn't have trouble recognizing you though. I'll wager you're the same weight you were in high school, and you either color your hair or you have good genes."

"Thanks for the compliment. I don't color my hair, and you're off by 15 pounds on my weight. Now that you've refreshed my memory, you do look like the same old Lizzie," I said, trying to extricate my foot from my mouth.

"Do I really now? No one has made that comment in ages. As long as we're here, let's make a grand entrance together. That should set classmates buzzing. To put your mind at ease, my last husband is dead. He shot himself three years ago when his gambling debts climbed to over $100,000, and he couldn't cover them. He owed the money to Minneapolis mobsters, and they were terrifying him by telling all the awful things that would happen to him if he didn't come up with the money in a week."

"I'm sorry for that," I said in as compassionate a voice as I could muster.

"Don't be. He was next to worthless. He not only gambled a lot but also drank a lot. One of my children sent me a congratulations note when he found out Clarence shot himself. The others weren't so brazen, but they all told me I was better off without him."

The encounter with Liz was what I dreaded. I started having second thoughts about the reunion. What if I didn't know anybody? What if the evening was a series of Liz encounters? This was my first reunion; most other people had probably made all four.

What would I say to my classmates when they asked what I was doing?

"Well, I owned my own ad agency in Chicago and ran with a high-level pack—the Mayor of Chicago, the manager of the Cubs, the head of the Art Institute of Chicago, and the CEO of Wrigley Gum. After a significant heart attack, my doctor told me to sell my agency and develop a slower life style, or I wouldn't live to see my fifty-ninth birthday. So I sold the agency and moved back to Minnesota, where my life is so slow that dropping by the library is a significant outing. I thought returning to my roots would be gratifying, but after 40 years, the roots are still just roots. No tree has grown from them; the tree is back in Chicago. Minneapolis is no longer familiar, and I have no friends here."

That was the unvarnished truth, but I couldn't say that. I thought what I *could* say, and finally wrote in my mind ad copy that put a positive spin on my life.

"Are you going to stand out here all night lost in your thoughts?" said Liz with exasperation in her voice, "or are you coming into the reunion?"

"Let's do it. Have you been to the last three reunions?"

"I wouldn't have missed them!"

"Good, then perhaps you can point out some of our classmates to me so...."

"So you don't make the same mistake you made with me?"

"Right."

***

We walked through the revolving doors of the Metropolitan into a lobby where stood two registration tables set up in an L formation. On the first table was a sign that said: WELCOME CLASS OF 1965. A sign on the second table said: REGISTRATION HERE.

"That's Gloria Silversmith at the first table with the name tags and alumni booklets and Jane Hoffman at the second table for the registration," whispered Liz to me. "They should have their nametags on, but they don't."

"Thanks."

"Name please; I'm afraid I don't recognize you."

"It's Mitch Jasper, Jane. We were in a play together our junior year." Turning to my left, I remarked, "Gloria Silversmith, you look just like you did when we went to the senior prom together." I wouldn't have recognized either of them if it were not for Liz. I turned for more whispers from Liz. Unfortunately, she found a classmate just inside the ballroom and was busily talking to him. Perhaps that will be her fourth husband, I mused, as I put on my nametag.

Doubts returned. "I'll wander around in a fog all evening," I thought. "I should have stayed home and watched TV."

As I walked into a large space full of 200 people who were strangers, I took a visual picture of the ballroom. It was a stately venue for a reunion. The walls were dark-paneled wood with a rich tapestry of an Asian motif. A luxurious carpet was a multiple of colors and designs, with red being the predominant color. Across the ballroom at the back wall dwelt a crowd of people waiting to get drinks at a cash bar. In the ballroom itself were tables filled with hors d'oeuvres and a large number of gathering tables where people were eating. There was a small side room with regular-sized tables and chairs and not many people at them. The action was clearly in the ballroom.

The Castaways were setting up to play in a half hour. They had the hit "Liar, Liar," which was popular during my high school days. I felt that would be an appropriate song since most of my classmates would probably be lying about how successful they were or about their glorious retirement or what great jobs their children had. I, for one, was not going to play that game. My plan of not talking about myself was to ask so many questions of a classmate that he or she would not have time to ask me anything. One thing I learned in life is that most people like to talk about themselves, and given the chance they will monopolize a conversation. I was banking on that dynamic. If people asked about my life history, I'd simply say I owned an advertising agency in Chicago, sold it recently, and returned to Minneapolis to start the next chapter of my life. Then I'd pepper them with questions about themselves.

I walked past the first set of gathering tables. People were eating, talking, and glancing at nametags. I walked past the second set of gathering tables. More people glancing at nametags to see who they were talking to.

As I approached the third set of gathering tables, one person stood out like a beacon — my best friend from kindergarten to high school graduation. I recognized him immediately, though I hadn't seen him for 40 years. It was Dave Logan. Still six feet tall. Still with all his dark hair. Still the rock he was in high school. He was a walking advertisement for a health club—trim, muscular, and finely honed.

I walked up behind Dave and tapped him on the shoulder. Dave turned around and his eyes brightened. "Mitch! Is it really you? I sensed you would be here tonight. I prayed about it all day. And here you are."

Dave crushed me with a hug. We hadn't seen each other or talked for 40 years. Though that was totally my fault, Dave acted as if nothing had happened; he was overjoyed to see me. The look on his face reminded me of a well-known Bible story — the father's love for the prodigal son. I always remembered that story, though I spent little time reading the Bible after high school. With Dave's hug, I experienced a peace and happiness unknown to me for many years. I felt that 40 years had just been gapped in an instant.

"We have 40 years to talk about, Mitch, but you'd better load up on food first before it's all gone. I'll save you a spot."

I embarked to a food table, with an appetite that had been missing for two weeks. Seeing Dave Logan bathed me in a light that pierced the darkness within me. For now, everything was all right. The line at the hors d'oeuvres table was unmercifully long; it was ten minutes before I returned to Dave, my best friend whom I had ignored for 40 years. What turns would the conversation take? Anticipation and apprehension contended for control of my emotions.

While I waited in line, a movie of growing up with Dave played in my mind. My family home was in Tangletown, just east of Nicollet Avenue on West Minnehaha Parkway, overlooking Minnehaha Creek. It was one of the classic large houses built in the 1920s by people who had money and when sold was purchased by people who had money. It was fun to play in our neighborhood because of the wooded Minnehaha Creek pathway. There were bridges to walk over, trees to climb, and the creek itself which invited young boys to learn of its mysteries. The Logan family lived a few blocks north on the east side of Nicollet Avenue. Theirs was a more modest home built by people who were middle class and when sold was purchased by people of the middle class. Both of us went to Page Elementary from kindergarten to sixth grade, then to Ramsey Junior High, and finally to Washburn High School. We were best friends during those 13 years.

When I departed for Northwestern in the fall of 1965, our friendship came to an abrupt end. Dave went to the University of Minnesota, and, knowing him, would have wanted the friendship to continue. However, I established a new life in Chicago, a life that did not include Dave by phone calls or mail or even the three times a year when I returned for a home visit. I was hoping for a characteristic of Dave's I saw often when we were growing up — a forgiving spirit. The hearty hug he gave me ten minutes ago spoke of forgiveness.

***

"The hunter has returned," I said in a voice stronger and more enthusiastic than when with Liz. "The long wait was worth it. What I have on my plate is more a meal than hors d'oeuvres."

Dave had kept a spot open for me right beside himself, just as he said he would. I settled in and started eating, and noticed that Dave was focusing his attention on me as if there were no one else at the reunion. He introduced me to the other two people at the table who were talking to each other. They were familiar classmates who had been in the elite clique at Washburn. They acted as if they were still in that clique, hanging on to the popularity that meant something at the time but no longer did. Most of the elite clique moved on from what they were in high school to a maturity of career, family, and social life. When they came to Washburn reunions, they talked to everyone. Not so with Ned and Jack. Either they had never grown up since high school, or their careers and marriages were not enough to eclipse the days of old.

When my plate was clean, Dave suggested we walk around and visit with as many of the classmates we had been close to as time allowed. I was up for that. This could be a way for me to broaden my social network, which presently stood at zero.

In Chicago my social network numbered 100 people—business owners, executives, administrators, sports figures, political notables, and numerous couples Kathleen and I had befriended. I thought they all were great friends. After I divorced Kathleen and sold my advertising business, it was like I had the plague. That solid network of friends dropped me off their radar screens when I was no longer part of a couple and no longer an important advertising executive. And the prominent people I knew in Chicago extinguished their relationships with me once I retired. It was as if I had entered the world of the unknown.

***

That's what I wrote in my journal the day after the reunion. About one-and-a-half years later, I discovered my friends were not shallow. They didn't know what to say to me with all I had gone through. They were waiting for a call from me to unlock their comfort zones. While I was recuperating from my heart attack, I didn't have the energy to call. When I did contact them in 2007, they were all smiling faces and open hearts. I was welcomed back into the world of the known.

***

The evening seemed to fast-forward as we talked with old friends. We had been inseparable from K-12, and here we were traveling as a twosome again. Our classmates were amused when we entered their space. "Here come the Washburn twins again."

I exchanged phone numbers with a few of the classmates. They said, "Let's get together for lunch or coffee." Or "Let's play a round of golf together." The golf sounded good, a chance to breathe fresh air and engage in social networking. I was not overly optimistic, however, that anyone would actually call me, and I wasn't disappointed. How often people say, "Let's get together sometime," and it doesn't happen. It's more a way of ending a conversation. I could have called them of course, but I didn't have the confidence to do so. And then it was too late.

As the midnight bell tolled, Dave and I set a meeting time for next Tuesday to catch up on our lives since high school. "I have a lot to find

out about you," Dave said with a smile. "And you have a lot to find
out about me."

CHAPTER 2
Catching Up

Dave had suggested meeting at a coffee house near 50th and France, one of his favorite districts in Minneapolis (Edina to be precise), a short drive from his home in Hopkins. The 50th and France area is a charming business neighborhood that features nearly 200 retailers and professional services—apparel shops, jewelers, spas, salons, an art-house movie theater, gift boutiques, a gourmet grocery store, and 20 restaurants.

***

Dave arrived at Coffee on France a few minutes before I did. It was a two-block walk for me on a pleasant July day. My mind was whirling as I walked. I regretted ignoring Dave for 40 years. Would this be a re-start of our friendship or our last meeting? Dave had many friends in Minneapolis. He had an extended family. How would he ever have time for me? I started to feel sorry for myself, and that resulted in emotional darkness.

Dave had called ahead to get a conference room across from the coffee counter. As I stepped through the front door, Dave motioned for me to enter our private space. He dropped his notebook on the table, and we walked out to purchase our coffee. "I'll pick up the tab," I volunteered.

"Let's each pay for his own," countered Dave. "That way we don't have to remember who paid last time or compare what we order. I appreciate your offer, but I've found that paying for your own works best in the long run."

When I heard "paid last time…works best in the long run," I felt we'd be meeting again, which brightened my disposition.

It was fortunate we had a private place, for just as we entered the room, I noticed every table in the main area was filled. "This must be a popular place," I observed. "I wouldn't think a Tuesday morning at ten would be such a busy time."

"Every morning is a busy time," said Dave. "People come here to work on their laptops, have business meetings, or just take a break from work. The afternoons are less busy."

Dave closed the door of the conference room. We briefly discussed last Saturday's reunion, Dave's joy in seeing me there, and some observations about classmates we had and hadn't met. Dave, super-organized as usual, proposed an agenda for the morning: "Why don't you cover what has happened to you in the last 40 years, and I'll do the same for my years since high school. Then we can stroll down the street to a good Italian restaurant for lunch and see where we go from there."

I agreed to the agenda and my starting the 40-year review. I didn't think deeply about what I should cover or not cover. I just related what was natural for me at that time.

"When I left the familiarity of Minneapolis for a fresh start at Northwestern, it was like walking out of a book called *Growing up in Southwest Minneapolis* and stepping into another book called *A New Life in Chicago*. I thought it was important to put all of myself into the new book and close the first book. I thought about you that first year but never contacted you. I was too busy with my schoolwork, the fraternity I joined, and new friends. That first summer I was taken on by Carrington Smithson Advertising Agency in downtown Chicago, a prominent firm on West Wacker Drive. I felt I had arrived. I was doing well in college and doing well with my career-to-be.

"That first year I came home for Thanksgiving, Christmas, and Easter — a pattern that continued throughout college. I didn't call you during Christmas break because I brought my college friend Rick home with me. He became my best friend in Evanston."

I was thinking on the fly and trying to justify why I ended our friendship, but it sounded flimsy to me. What must it sound like to Dave?

I took a long drink of my latte and looked around the conference room. It was a cozy space 15-feet square, surrounded by brown and white textured walls, and a window with blinds facing the coffee counter. The blinds were half-closed so we were not distracted by the crowd in the shop. Dave took a sip of his coffee. When I mentioned Rick, Dave must have absorbed a blow to his midsection—Rick had replaced him as my best friend. Why did I bring up Rick? I felt turmoil within, but Dave looked calm.

I continued with my history. "I'm not proud of abandoning our friendship, but that's what I did. You must have been upset with me, and maybe still are. By my sophomore year, I thought too much time had passed to contact you, and then another year went by, and another year, and our friendship was gone. You must be bitter about my casting you off. I hope somehow I can make it up."

Was this Mitch admitting he had done something wrong? Yes it was. I would be bitter if someone abandoned me. I naturally assumed Dave would feel the same way.

"Let me stop you a minute," Dave challenged. "I tried to phone you several times at Northwestern that first fall, but you never returned my calls. I left word with your parents for you to call me that first Christmas, but you never did. I was taking a psychology course at the time that had a chapter on Helen Kubler Ross and her work with the five stages of grief. I went through all of them. At first I denied you had abandoned me. Then I became angry with you. That lasted until spring when I went into bargaining: 'This is a busy year for Mitch as it has been for me. When he comes back this summer, we'll be friends again.' When you didn't come back that summer and I didn't hear from you, I felt sorry for myself. In the five stages of grief, that's called depression. The last stage, acceptance, happened the fall of our sophomore year.

"I'm telling you all this to let you know I have no bitterness. Whatever happened in the past resides in the past, and I forgive you. You're here now, and we can be friends again. We can start all over. No one has to live a lifetime with failures, mistakes, or hurt feelings. You can always start over again at any time. That has become my philosophy of life. "

I hadn't gone through any stages of grief with losing Dave as a friend, yet he had struggled through five stages. How different we were.

***

At that time, I had difficulty understanding anyone's feelings other than my own. It's hard to believe now that I thought that way then, but it's all in my journal.

***

As Dave was talking, I realized I was going through the five stages of grief in a way with coming back to Minneapolis and realizing how cruel and empty retirement was. I had moved quickly into the depression stage and spent too much time thinking about how good the past had been and how bad the present was. If only…if only…if only was what I thought mostly about.

***

Depression was the word I used because it is the name of the fourth step in the five stages of grief. I had no idea I was slipping into actual depression. How could I?

Depression is defined by experience, not words. On that July day in 2005, I characterized my inner feelings as being "in a blue funk." I would understand the meaning of depression in the months ahead.

***

I felt a warmness in me I couldn't put into words when Dave forgave me. My best friend accepted me just as I was.

I continued, wondering if the room was getting warmer or I was getting uncomfortable with the disclosure process. "In my second year of college, I met a beautiful girl named Kathleen Hubbard. Her parents were big in iron ore and steel. She was an only child who stood to inherit a huge fortune.

"To my way of thinking, she had two positives—her beauty and eventual large inheritance—and one negative—her religion meant too much to her. The positives outweighed the negative, and I accompanied her to church until she thought religion was important to me too. My growing-up years included a heavy dose of religion: church on Sundays, Bible studies, confirmation, and youth activities. So I was able to talk the talk. I could convince people into believing I thought as they thought. I was an expert in linguistic imitation: using words and phrases other people used frequently to form a subconscious linkage with them. It served me well in procuring new clients for my advertising agency."

I saw Dave frown when I talked about religion and linguistic imitation. Not having time to reflect on his reaction, I detailed how I avoided Viet Nam by my father pulling strings to get me into the Army National Guard the day after I graduated from Northwestern, and that Carrington Smithson hired me full-time when I returned from training in November. Dave frowned again. What I considered merely matter of fact, Dave took as something distasteful.

I stopped to take a drink from my latte. I had talked almost non-stop for 35 minutes, and the last ten minutes had not gone well. I needed a break. We peeked out the window of the meeting room and saw the main area was still totally packed. I walked around the table in the meeting room. It was a large, square wooden table, probably maple, with ten wooden chairs around it of the same wood. There were other chairs along the wall in case more than ten people were in the room. Dave and I chatted about the weather before I sat down and began where I left off. I tried to stay with safe topics.

"I advanced quickly at Carrington Smithson from a copywriter to an account executive. I married Kathleen in June of 1971. My New Year's surprise the next year from Carrington Smithson was a promotion to Senior Account Executive, managing some of the larger accounts in Chicago, northern Illinois, Wisconsin, and Minnesota.

"With the promotion and boost in salary, we bought our first house, a two-story Tudor in Chicago's Lincoln Park, near Children's Memorial Hospital and less than two miles from Wrigley Field. It reminded me of my parents' home. Michael was born there in 1972, Susie arrived about five years later, and Jane became our last child in 1983. I distinctly remember when Jane was born because Kathleen's parents were killed in a car accident on the Eisenhower Expressway that same year. With a small portion of the 20 million dollars Kathleen inherited, I started Jasper Advertising on North Michigan Avenue.

"A prestigious ad agency called for a more prestigious home. I purchased a 5,000 square-foot condominium on North Lake Shore Drive in Chicago's Gold Coast. It was a great lifestyle. No more responsibility for arranging maintenance or repair. We were treated like royalty. Kathleen and the two older kids were unhappy leaving a house for a condominium, but I convinced them it would be better for my career and they'd learn to like it eventually."

Dave frowned once more and asked if my family ever learned to like the condominium. I was surprised at the question. I hadn't thought about it. I just assumed they did, and told Dave they liked the condominium.

***

As I reflect on it now, my mind's eye shows me they hated living there. Looking back, I see it in their faces and body language. They didn't say anything once the move was complete. I took their silence as acceptance of our new home, whereas it was really the resignation of a fait accompli.

***

"Jasper Advertising was successful beyond my wildest expectations. The agency grew to 30 employees—account executives, copywriters, art people, and those who didn't bring in money but were needed to run a business. Years rolled by smoothly and profitably until January 2004 when I was blasted by a massive heart attack. Two weeks in a hospital. Three months recuperating at home. One hundred eighty-five visits to a rehab center. When I returned to work, I tired easily and only worked half days.

"During the three months at home, it became evident Kathleen and I lived in different worlds, with different values and expectations. To relate all the details would take hours. I divorced Kathleen in the early fall. I lived in our condominium even though she received it in the divorce settlement. She stayed with her best friend in Chicago. Kathleen took the divorce like a hard punch and needed to get away where she had support. I started working full days again because the agency was facing critical issues.

"On April 2, 2005, the day of my fifty-eighth birthday, I had an appointment with my cardiologist. He thoroughly examined me and said the damage to my heart was more serious than he first thought, and if I kept working in high-level stress for ten hours a day, I wouldn't reach my fifty-ninth birthday. He strongly suggested, almost demanded, that I sell the agency and establish a lifestyle less stressful. Not wanting to be in the checkout line within a year, I sold the agency to a businesswoman from New York who wanted to live in Chicago to be closer to her extended family. She knew exactly what she wanted, and my agency fit her parameters. She moved quickly. The paperwork was done by the first part of May, and the agency was no longer mine on June 1.

"In mid-May, I flew to Minneapolis and bought the condominium on France Avenue where I now live. A moving van hauled everything I owned in Chicago and deposited it in my new home on May 25. Kathleen returned to the condominium in the Gold Coast three days later.

"Getting settled kept me busy for a while. After that I examined Southwest Minneapolis, our old stomping ground, and explored Minneapolis and St Paul. For two weeks I was content. Then the life of no stress that my cardiologist so highly recommended became a life of not much to do and not much to look forward to. Then came the reunion, and then came today. It's your turn."

I was smiling on the outside and hiding the gloom on the inside. I saw the life before me as hopeless: no focus, no purpose, no meaning, no hope. It was a bleak outlook. I was down in the dumps as never before in my life. But for the time being, all was well being with Dave, and I didn't want to venture into the dark side on our first meeting.

***

I little knew I was experiencing the birth of depression. The seeds were planted in Chicago, nourished in Minneapolis, and about to reach full bloom.

***

I looked at the clock on the wall in the meeting room. It was exactly 11 a.m. We had been coffeeing for one hour, and our coffee cups were empty. We stepped out for refills, and Dave started his 40-year history.

He started with his college years at the University of Minnesota. At the time, he wanted a career teaching in a high school, so he declared a social studies major and a psychology minor.

"Something happened my sophomore year that was more important than anything else I'll cover: I met the love of my life. Her name is similar to your ex-wife's—Catherine, Cathy for short. I married her the summer we both graduated from college—August 9, 1969. We'll have been married 36 years next month, and those have been the best 36 years of my life. My first son, Thomas, was born September 12, 1974. Almost four years later Peter was born on June 18. And we were blessed with a girl named Elizabeth on June 6, 1982. I say blessed because the doctor told us Cathy would not be able to have any children after Peter.

"I wanted you as best man for my wedding. I called your parents, they called you, and you said you couldn't make it. They said you hadn't been back to Minneapolis in over a year."

A dagger went through my heart.

"Are your parents still alive? You didn't mention them in your narrative."

I replied, "My father died of a heart attack about six years ago. He was clobbered like me 20 years before the second heart attack leveled him at 77. I remember his age because it's a benchmark of when I might expect a fatal heart attack, about 19 years from now. My mother died of cancer when she was around 80. That was two or three years ago."

Dave spoke with his face, not his vocal cords. His look said, "Why did you leave out that your parents had died?" I thought I'd get the jump on him before he asked about Sam.

"You remember my older brother Sam? He lives in Birmingham, Alabama, now. I haven't spoken to him for over 20 years. We both inherited several million dollars apiece. The rest went to Northwestern University and various charities my parents were interested in. With the sale of my ad agency and some good investments, I'm set for the rest of my life, especially if the end comes in 19 years."

Dave had been taking notes as I told my history, and I saw him write, "Hasn't talked to Sam for 20 years." He didn't notice I zeroed in on that sentence. I wish I hadn't told him about being estranged from Sam. I thought he'd immediately grill me, but he didn't. I was becoming more sensitive to the dark aspects of my story as I studied Dave's reactions to what I said.

Dave resumed his story. "The fall after we were married, I started teaching social studies at Hopkins High School. Cathy had an elementary degree and was hired to teach fourth grade in St. Louis Park. We lived in an apartment in St. Louis Park for a year and then bought a story-and-a-half home on Louisiana Avenue, just north of Minnetonka Boulevard. It was a good halfway point between our two schools.

"By the end of my second year at Hopkins, my interest in psychology was renewed. My passion fastened on guidance counseling. In the fall of 1971, I took a two-year leave of absence and started a specialist certificate program at the University of Minnesota. I completed a Master's Degree in Counseling and the required certificate credits beyond that in the spring of 1973. A guidance counselor at Hopkins High School retired at the close of the 1973 school year, and I was hired for his job. It was beyond coincidence."

"What do you mean by, 'It was beyond coincidence'?" I asked Dave.

"I mean that God had his hand in it," he replied.

***

I was skeptical about God interfering in anyone's life. I believed we advanced by our own efforts and resolve, and a lot of luck. I don't believe that any longer, since God engineered my transformation. My efforts and resolve to change were not enough. Luck was replaced by grace.

***

Dave went on. "Cathy's teaching job was enough income for us during the two years of my leave. We had Thomas in the fall of 1973, and it was Cathy's turn to take a two-year leave of absence to nurture our first child. When she returned to teaching, we found a woman who became our child-care angel for the next 12 years. Emily was a stay-at-home mom whose two sons had both left home to serve in the missions field overseas. Her husband was the pastor of our church. She took on our three children as if they were her own, in a big, old manse that was filled with mystery and intrigue. The huge back yard included a wooded area that became a childhood depository of fantasy and adventure.

"We started to look for a larger house because we planned to have more children. We found our home forever just east of Highway 169 and south of Excelsior Boulevard. It was a three-bedroom stucco rambler two blocks from Emily's home and is the house we live in today, with the addition of a fourth bedroom downstairs when Elizabeth was born."

Just then there was a knock on the door and it opened halfway. The manager of the coffee shop stuck his head in. "Remember, you guys have this room until noon. There's another group coming shortly after that for their weekly video series."

That explained the TV up high in the right-hand corner of the room. Right next to it was a wall-mounted whiteboard covered with two doors that would probably be opened for a discussion after the video. I nodded to Dave to continue with his biography.

"Our last two children were both born in June. Cathy and I felt so comfortable with Emily that Cathy didn't take a leave of absence for Pete or Liz. She nurtured them non-stop during the summer months and then entrusted the children to Emily in the fall, sort of their home away from home. Emily was like a grandparent."

The next portion of his account went into extensive detail about his three children. Tom was the all-around athlete of the family, and Dave spent hundreds of hours helping him develop his natural abilities. Tom received a full football scholarship at North Dakota State University, graduated with a degree in civil engineering, and was building bridges and roads in Hennepin County.

Pete's sport was golf. Dave taught him everything he knew, and then watched as his son played at a level his father could only dream of. He won the Minnesota State High School Championship his senior year at Hopkins. Like his dad, Pete had a passion for psychology and was a practicing psychologist in St. Paul. He and Dave had two shared interests—psychology and golf—that consumed many hours of friendly competition and lively discussions.

Liz, following the path of her mother, earned an elementary teaching degree and was teaching third grade in Burnsville. Her passion was in music and drama. Dave attended a lifetime of concerts and plays following the endeavors of his daughter. He was still a follower as her "other career" blossomed. Dave proudly suggested that Liz could earn a living acting if she wanted to.

"All three children are married now. Tom and Gail have three children. Pete and Rhonda have two. Liz and Bill just married last month. Our grandchildren keep us active; we spend as much time with them as we can. What a blessing to have our whole family in the Twin Cities area.

"I'd best wrap this up or you'll fall asleep. Cathy and I each reached the Rule of 90 in our educational careers last year—57 years old and 33 years of teaching. If we had taught and counseled three more years, we would have significantly increased our retirement income, but we wanted time with our children and grandchildren, so we took the first chance to retire. We'll live in the house we're in until we die. Our cars and other material possessions are not new, but we have enough to live on. When we qualify for social security in four years, we'll have more than enough money to see us through until God calls us home.

"My parents still live in Southwest Minneapolis, in the same house I grew up in. Their health is good, and their time is open. That's another reason we retired as early as we could. Sunday dinner at their home is a tradition we've had since we were married. Grandpa and grandma's home has been a special place for our three children and is now a special place for our grandchildren. Cathy's father died four years ago. Her mother resides in the family home in Roseville. We spend considerable time with her also; her love for the grandchildren and great grandchildren is as strong as that of my parents.

"Cathy and I volunteer at a local nursing home, visiting residents that don't have family or friends. We're both active in our church and dabble in community theater now and again. We are busier than we ever were when we were working. It's been a good life.

"I have an additional item I want to put on my list of quality things to do—being your friend again."

I was relieved to hear Dave's last statement. I was agonizing that he was so involved with family and volunteering that there would not be enough time left for me. The hope of renewing our friendship had become a life raft for me in unsettled waters. If Dave didn't have time for me, I would have sunk a fathom into the dark waters.

"It's time for lunch," said Dave. "There's a good Italian restaurant just down the street. How does that sound?"

***

We were quiet on our way to the restaurant, both lost in each other's story. Dave's biography was so different from mine. I talked mainly about myself. Dave talked mainly about his wife, his three children, and his parents. I reckoned grudgingly that Dave was a better person than I, whatever that meant.

***

The thought that Dave was a better person didn't come from my mind but from my heart, a region of my personality I infrequently visited.

Dave is possessed of a simple faith, great humility, and unwavering confidence—a powerful combination. During the latter stages of my transformation, I read a lot of and about C.S. Lewis. He had a remarkable transformation in his life. Owen Barfield said of C. S. Lewis that at some point in his life he ceased to take any interest in himself. The same could be said of Dave Logan. When I talked to him about it a year ago, he acknowledged that had developed within him. He related it didn't happened all at once. Over the years, slowly but steadily, he became more interested in other people than in himself.

***

After ordering mouth-watering pasta, Dave and I chatted about what was happening in the world. Dave was concerned about Afghanistan and Iraq. I talked about the economy and what a good time this was for the stock market.

"I've not been up-to-date in the stock market," said Dave. "We didn't have much money left to invest. We have tithed since we were first married, and we always considered that to be our main investment. Raising three children and helping them with college was another investment. Using our savings to help our two boys buy homes has been yet another investment, as will helping out Liz and Bill when they buy a home."

I had a hard time comprehending why Dave and Cathy put all their emphasis on their church and kids and nothing on themselves. Yet, somewhere deep within me, I realized the nobility of what they did.

As we finished our meal and were waiting for our checks, Dave suggested we meet sometime next week to explore the old neighborhood and the days of our youth.

"Let's call it a re-bonding of our friendship," Dave said enthusiastically. "We've caught up on the last 40 years. Now let's revisit kindergarten through high school. Does a week from today work for you? Tuesdays are usually good days for me."

I had an empty calendar for next week, so Tuesday worked fine for me.

CHAPTER 3
Re-bonding

From one Tuesday to the next was a week that seemed like a month. With little to think about besides myself, I spent most of the time thinking about myself. And that put me in a blue funk, a recently acquired emotion.

I had always thought downcast people had a character flaw. Kathleen dropped so low after our separation and divorce that she could barely function, but I had never experienced that depth or anything close to it. I was amazed how Kathleen had crumbled. There were so many crises and challenges in our married lives in which Kathleen was a rock. How could someone so strong become so weak? I didn't want to face that I may be weak. Somehow I had to pull myself out of my emotional dysfunction. It was mind over matter.

***

Mind over matter. What a ridiculous statement! I sounded like the agnostic I was. I had always been successful no matter the challenge. This was yet another challenge to overcome, and I'd walk out of the dark fog I found myself in. But the circumstances of my life were so different in Minneapolis than Chicago that I didn't know where to start.

During the week after our catching up at Coffee on France, a pattern emerged that has lasted two years. Dave could see I was struggling, even though I hadn't said much about it. He started calling me—cell phone to cell phone—almost every day. His opening line was usually, "How are things going, Mitch?"

After a few weeks, I started asking Dave, "How are things going for you?" Dave would answer by telling me something about Cathy and him, about his children and grandchildren, or snippets about his volunteer work. Cathy and Dave were involved in a community theater production scheduled for August, so that was included in the conversation for a season.

***

Dave's life was so much more active and purposeful than mine that I had to fight through a feeling of envy. In mind-over-matter analysis, I concluded that Dave was Dave and Mitch was Mitch, and there was no sense wasting time wishing it were different. I had to plow my own ground and plant a new life.

***

I thought in July 2005 that I could create a new life. Not so. I have since learned a new life comes from a new creation. The old Mitch would of a certainty carry his old baggage with him, making a new life impossible. It took a new Mitch, a transformed Mitch, to accept a new life given by Him who gives all life.

***

"Do you want me to pick you up?" asked Dave when he called on Monday. "You and I will be heading to an eating place near Tangletown. It will remain a surprise until we get there. Since I know the area better than you, it would be better if I drove."

"Fine," I said, wondering what the surprise would be.

***

Dave had chosen an old-fashioned hamburger and malt shop on 50th Street, just east of Lyndale Avenue, for our inaugural meal. I surveyed the scene and remarked, "It looks like some of the places we frequented when we were kids. This is a perfect place to start." The malts and burgers instilled in us a mood of years past, when we were fast friends.

While enjoying our meal, we talked over the places to visit that afternoon, and Dave wrote out a list of them. "Same old Dave," I observed laughing. "A list for everything and everything on a list. That's the way you were at Washburn."

Dave smiled.

The List:
1. Tangletown
2. Our two homes
3. Page School
4. Ramsey Junior High and Washburn High
5. Minnehaha Creek area
6. Nicollet Bridge where we crawled over the arches
7. Pearl Park
8. Washburn Water Tower
9. Anything else

Out the door we went, armed with the list and bolstered with enthusiasm.

***

We first drove through Tangletown, an area southeast of Lake Harriet and northwest of Diamond Lake, so called because of the serpentine tangle of streets that wander in curves, circles, jags, jogs, abruptly ending streets, and an abundance of Y and T intersections, unlike the straight north and south avenues and the straight east and west streets that make up the rest of Minneapolis.

"I didn't know how unique this area was when we were growing up," I said. "There is nothing quite like it in Chicago or any of the other large cities in the United States I frequented."

"Did you travel a lot?" asked Dave.

"Yes, a lot. I had accounts throughout the U.S. with Carrington Smithson and with my own agency. And Kathleen and I went on at least one major trip a year to Mexico, Europe, South America, or Asia. Ten years ago we traveled to Australia and New Zealand. That was an exciting trip, but London and Paris were our favorite destinations."

"Did the children go with you?"

"No. Kathleen wanted to take them along when they got older, but

I told her the big thing about getting away was getting away—from Chicago, from work, from family responsibilities, all of it. Her parents were happy to care for the kids, which made leaving them behind more palatable to Kathleen. After her parents were killed in the car accident, we hired a governess when we traveled. Kathleen was not keen about that, but the argument had been made, the pattern set, and we continued with 'get-away-from-it-all' vacations. I had jungles of stress at work and didn't need the weight of managing three children in foreign countries.

"How about you, Dave? Did you and Cathy travel?"

"Not like your traveling. We started annual vacations when the kids were older. The North Shore of Lake Superior was a favorite destination. We became back-of-the-hand familiar with Duluth, Gooseberry Falls, Grand Marais, and everything in-between. Our only destinations outside the United States were Thunder Bay and Winnipeg, and a vacation we took to Mazatlan one year when spring break was identical for the five of us. Some summers Cathy and I went on mission trips, and the kids stayed with their grandparents.

"A major benefit of working in education was having summers off. Although parents are proud of the quality time they spend with their children, I believe children really want quantity time. We had that in the summers as a perpetual fivesome."

Just then we turned onto Prospect Avenue. "Prospect Avenue!" I exclaimed. "The Washburn Water Tower! I stopped here two weeks ago but didn't exit my car. Being with you, Dave, brings back fond memories. We were seven years old the first time we ventured this far from home. It was a Saturday. We rode our bikes to Prospect Avenue, left them at the base of the hill, and walked up to the famous Washburn Water Tower, at least famous to little kids who lived in Tangletown. The eight 18-foot-tall Guardians of Health statues around the base of the tower made a deep impression on us."

"They certainly did," replied Dave. "We were awed with those sword-wielding statues. Your mother said they were Norse warriors. Although we didn't learn about Norse mythology until later, the song of something powerful played in our hearts. I understood then that we had a special bond between us—a kindred spirit that drew us together closer than brothers."

"I remember that," I replied. "We were little boys cemented in a deep friendship. I cracked the cement when I left for Chicago."

"But we're here now," said Dave with strong emotion. "And we can patch that crack. I've learned from experience that anyone can start over any day, any hour. This is the day. This is the hour we can become the friends we once were. That's my desire. What are your feelings?"

"That's what I want too."

I extended my hand to Dave, but he grabbed me in a bear hug. "This deserves more than a handshake. This deserves a hug to renew a bond of long ago."

From that first visit to the day we graduated from Washburn, we would often revisit the water tower. When we looked at the statues, we felt the sense of deep friendship. How could I have lost sight of a bond that bound us so together?

I was a history buff, so I researched the Washburn Water Tower. It was built in the early 1930s when there were water quality issues in Minneapolis, when typhoid and diphtheria were fearful concerns. It was named after the Washburn brothers—Cadwallader and William—who were also the namesakes of other areas and buildings, such as Washburn High School. In addition to the warriors at the base, there were eight eagles near the top of the tower. They too inspired us with a sense of awe.

***

The next stop was the house I grew up in—on the north side of Minnehaha Parkway, a few houses down from Nicollet Avenue. Some people referred to our house as a mansion. It was a two-story Tudor Revival-style building constructed of white masonry and decorative half timbering, with vines covering much of the front. The house looked as it did when I lived there. After my father died, my mother lived there three more years. For her last three months, it was a hospital staffed by nurses and managed by hospice. When she died, the estate sold the house for more than the asking price, two days after it went on the market.

Dave asked me, "Did you spend time with your mother in her last months?"

"Kathleen stayed with Mother a few days here and there and her final two weeks. My ad agency was in a crisis at the time and needed me there. A large ad agency in New York was courting some of our larger accounts, and I had to do extensive hand holding to keep those companies in our portfolio. We didn't lose even one account. I did fly to Minneapolis a few weekends."

I saw Dave looking fondly at the Jasper house. Finally, he said, "I can see myself walking up the steps and sidewalk to your front door and ringing the doorbell. The maid would answer the door or sometimes your mother. 'Is Mitch home?' I'd ask. And then you'd come running to the front door and off we'd go. What a house that was! I felt like I was visiting the governor's mansion. I really did."

"Let's walk to your house," I said. For some reason, I did not want to continue talking about my old house. Was it guilt? Maybe so.

As we headed to Dave's house, we stood before the wooden steps that climbed from Minnehaha Parkway to the top of the Nicollet Avenue Bridge, and gazed at the arch bridge we had climbed when we were in tenth grade.

"There's the sixth item on our list," said Dave. "Look at that bridge. Can you believe we climbed over those arches from one end to the other?"

"I can't believe we actually climbed across those arches," I responded.

***

A brief description of the 800-foot bridge will give an idea of how difficult our adventure was that late afternoon in September. The bridge is shown on the cover of this book. From Minnehaha Parkway, which is at the bottom of the bridge, to Nicollet Avenue, which is at the top, is about 40 feet. There are eight concrete arches on each side of Nicollet Avenue, sixteen in all, which support four large concrete beams on each arch. Those beams reach up from the arches to underneath the top slab of the bridge, extending perpendicular from one side of Nicollet Avenue to the other. The height from Minnehaha Creek to the top of each arch that spans the creek is about 30 feet.

It's absolutely amazing what we did. It would make most people's hands shaky and sweaty just looking at the bridge and contemplating such a feat. We climbed over each of the eight arches, having to slither with our feet along a two-inch ledge to maneuver around the four beams on each arch. It was especially harrowing and dangerous to circumvent the two beams nearest the top of the arches, with a creek and creek bed waiting below to catch bodies falling the 30 feet. Climbing over the arches can no longer be done because the city cemented the two-inch ledges at an angle to discourage anyone else from trying what we did. Apparently there were more brave and foolish teens who attempted the feat after us.

***

We walked on Minnehaha Parkway to the west side of the bridge where we could see the whole structure.

"If the ledges were still there, could you imagine climbing the arches now?" I queried.

"Not for a million dollars," answered Dave. "But there was a reason we climbed those arches then. Do you remember, Mitch?"

I asked Dave to recount the story because it was not complete in my mind.

This is the story according to Dave. "We took in an afternoon movie where two boys from Seattle, about our age, wanted to bind their friendship together in a dramatic way. Since Washington has many great mountain-climbing venues, they chose to climb 14,414-foot Mt. Rainier, 50 miles southeast of Seattle, a good challenge for them but not too dangerous. A camp at the base of Mt. Rainier provided two days of basic mountain-climbing skill training. The camp leader suggested they use a guide to shepherd them up the mountain, but they wanted to make the trek alone.

"Mt. Rainier was promoted as a beginner's climb. Its paths were moderately steep for a challenge and not abounding with treacherous terrain. Their mountain climbing equipment included a rope that tied them together. The symbolism of being tied together was powerful. Their route ascended the Ingraham Glacier, with a base camp one-day up.

"On the steepest climb, Alec lost his footing and was saved by Nick.

You see, I even remember their names. They made the summit and had a moving friendship ritual.

"Each used a sharp knife to cut into the palm of his right hand until blood flowed. Then they clasped their right hands together and promised, 'We'll be friends forever, no matter who else comes into our lives and no matter where we go.' When we exited the theater, we wondered what we could do to be friends forever? You're the one, Mitch, who suggested climbing over the arches underneath the Nicollet Avenue Bridge. Those arches were a compelling landscape each time we came out your front door and headed west. We never thought about climbing over them until that movie."

Dave continued. "We looked at each other and visually agreed that climbing over the arches would be our rendition of climbing Mt. Rainier. We weren't tied together with a rope, but we helped each other around those beams by bracing each other's arm onto the walls. I felt myself falling once, but you steadied me with your arm around my back, keeping me from completely losing my balance.

"It took us two hours to climb the length of the bridge, from the side of the wooden steps to the far south side. We were exhausted physically and mentally when we finished, and then performed the same ritual as Alec and Nick. You borrowed a razor blade from your dad's shaving drawer. We cut into our right palms until blood was flowing freely. Then we clasped hands and recited the words from the movie, 'We'll be friends forever, no matter who else comes into our lives and no matter where we go.' That was a bond even stronger than the bond at the Washburn Water Tower."

I said nothing when Dave finished the story. As he told why we climbed over the arches, it all came back to me. I felt a mountain of guilt. "Friends forever!" Both of us meant it then, and Dave still meant it now; but I had relegated that bonding adventure to the remote recesses of my mind. There were no friends forever for me when I left for Chicago. To me, friends helped me advance my career. When they ceased advancing me, they ceased being friends. I had buried the depth of the friendship between Dave and me until we reached the Washburn Water Tower and relived the arches adventure. What a poor friend I had been. I didn't want to discuss my feelings with Dave until

I processed them. "Keep your emotions to yourself," was a maxim I lived by in my advertising career. "Don't let emotions interfere in a good business decision." But this was different. I needed time alone for reflection.

***

Dave and I climbed the steps from Minnehaha Parkway to Nicollet Avenue and walked the three blocks to Dave's parents' house, a bungalow on the east side of the avenue. If Dave's parents had lived on the west side of Nicollet Avenue, we wouldn't have both attended Page Elementary and wouldn't have become friends forever.

"Do you want to go in and see my parents?" asked Dave.

Mrs. Logan answered the door and invited us in. Mr. Logan was sitting in his favorite chair in the living room. I recognized the distinctive shape of the chair through a new fabric. We sat down and talked non-stop for 25 minutes.

"I'm glad to see you again Mr. and Mrs. Logan," I said.

"It's been a long time," responded Mr. Logan. "I know the two of you became reacquainted at your 40th class reunion, so it must be 40 years since we last saw you. You look enough like you did in high school that I would have recognized you if you had come to the door unannounced and by yourself."

"Dave said you've renewed your friendship," said Mrs. Logan. "Al and I are so pleased you've returned to Minneapolis and are spending time with Dave. He is so enthusiastic when he talks about you, his long-lost friend."

Nancy Logan hadn't meant that last statement to be hurtful; she would never hurt anyone intentionally. But it hurt me nevertheless. I was the one responsible for the "long-lost friend." I was the one who ended the "friends forever" pact.

As I was standing there, I saw a vision in my mind's eye. I had been Dave's friend in the morning of my life, and now it was the afternoon. "Long lost" was the middle of the day, 40 years to be exact. That vision enveloped me in darkness, and I wanted to escape the Logan house.

We exchanged a few more pleasantries as I planned an exit strategy. "It was enjoyable talking with you Mr. and Mrs. Logan. I'd like to visit with you longer sometime, but Dave and I have a list to accomplish this afternoon. You know Dave and his lists. If he doesn't complete the list, he pouts." Everyone laughed and off we went.

***

We returned to Dave's car and toured the Minnehaha Creek area where we had explored creeks, woods, paths, and footbridges so extensively when we were boys. We knew every inch of the creek area one-half mile either side of my boyhood home. From Minnehaha Creek we visited where Page Elementary once was—east of 35W and north of Diamond Lake Road. When we started kindergarten, it was a wooden building with six classrooms. Eventually a new school was built, and we were the first graduating class from it in 1959. Those seven years were idyllic ones, with problems that were insignificant and adventures that were life-giving. The school was torn down and a development of condominiums built up. In the vicinity of Page was a recreational area called Pearl Park. When we were growing up, it was a swamp begging young boys to explore it. The swamp is now filled in and inhabited by sports fields and athletic buildings.

***

Our final stop was Ramsey Junior High and Washburn Senior High. We ran up the steps to the first floor of Washburn and stood outside reminiscing. "I feel it's 1965 all over again," I said, with emotion in my voice. Where did the emotion come from?

***

The bonds of being kindred spirits at the Washburn Water Tower and friends forever at the Nicollet Avenue Bridge were beginning to seep into that small part of my heart that was flesh instead of stone.

***

As I looked to the football field that lay between the two schools, I recollected practicing and playing games there over a period of six years. I was struck by a bolt of realization. How different was the Mitch then to the Mitch who went to Chicago. I recaptured a glimpse of my youth and felt the deep friendship Dave and I had from kindergarten to high school graduation.

"Dave, do you remember the 1963 football season when you were left halfback and I was right halfback, and we won the City Conference title at Parade Stadium? You were the best blocker on the team. I can still see some of the key blocks you made in the secondary to spring me for long gains."

"I remember those blocks," said Dave. "I gained my share of yardage in 1963, but the greatest joy I had was helping my friend become the best runner on the team. When I was lying on the ground seeing you racing by for a touchdown, I was pleased with myself and happy for you."

How different I was from my best friend Dave! He himself could have been the best runner on the team, but he didn't have me to block for him the way he blocked for me. My conscience started to come to life. My glittering pride as the best runner on that championship team became tarnished.

"Let's see if we can look around inside," advanced Dave.

We entered the side door facing east. As we climbed a short flight of stairs, we observed two policemen and a staff member checking in and out every student that entered or left the school. What a different Washburn than the one we attended! A number of recent nationwide school shootings and the rampant crime in Southwest Minneapolis changed Washburn forever.

We explained to the policemen that we were alumni from 1965 and wanted to look around the school. Just then, a secretary from the administrative offices walked by and heard the conversation. She also was from the class of 1965 and told the policemen she would take responsibility for the two of us.

It was fortunate Jill was willing to give us a tour because some of the areas we wanted to look at were locked, and she had the key. Washburn was built in 1926, and by 1965 it was bursting at the seams with students, and a little tattered around the edges. The graduating class of 1965 was the largest one to that date, some 700 students.

"Could we see the two gyms?" I asked.

They were in tough shape in the mid-60s. The floorboards had dead spots, so we practiced in different schools when we could and played our games at the Minneapolis Auditorium. Jill opened the doors to each gym—one for boys and one for girls. The gyms had been renovated except for one throwback—the backboards were still the old half-circle metal ones. It was obvious by the smell that the do-over had been recent.

Jill, who had been a basketball cheerleader, drew from her memory. "You two were fun to watch playing basketball, and it was obvious you were best of friends. You came to practices and games together; you left together. When you were on the floor, you seemed to know exactly where the other would be. There were passes between you two that seemed to be guided by mental telepathy. A recurring cry from the crowd punctuated each game: 'I can't believe that pass.'"

I was thinking the same thing. "There is one game that sticks in my mind, Jill. Dave had two men on him about fifteen feet from the basket. He was facing to the sidelines but somehow he knew I was under the basket and not guarded. With his back to me, he bounced a pass with his left hand around one of the defenders that hit me chest high for an easy lay-up."

Dave concurred with the story I had just told. "That *was* an amazing pass. I could hear you not with my ears but in my mind saying, 'Throw it under the basket, Dave; I'm wide open.' I thought at the time it was a kindred spirit pass."

The rest of the tour included the auditorium that had over 1,000 seats and the cafeteria, which was in a different location. What really brought back fond memories were the stairwells between floors that served as social networking venues between classes and over the noon hour.

***

When Dave dropped me off at my condominium, we both agreed it had been a memorable day. Our friendship was not as deep now as from K-12, but was deeper than the day before.

What good friends we had been was starting to seep back into my mind and emotions. I had both a warm feeling about our friendship and a guilty feeling about how I ended that friendship. But wasn't our friendship returning? Wasn't it a new day?

I entered my condo feeling different from when I left. But the joy of re-bonding turned into darkness the next day.

***

When I read in my journal what I wrote about that next-day darkness two years ago, I was shaken: "What am I to do now? It's hopeless. I feel like I'm falling into a deep hole without a bottom. Dave said nothing about getting together again. Is this the end of our friendship?"

I didn't realize how paranoid I was becoming. Dave later told me he felt I should initiate the next getting together. He didn't want to pressure me. I respected Dave's busyness and waited for a call from him. Neither one of us communicated our standpoints, so we had a self-imposed formula for not getting together for a while.

CHAPTER 4
Confession

Three days had passed since Dave and I explored Tangletown. That day had been a bright spot in an otherwise dreary emotional landscape. However, the darkness of my condition soon blotted out the light. I ruminated too much those past three days. I thought and thought about my life in Chicago. I began to see that life as filled with many searing mistakes that were the cause of my darkness. I began to see Dave's life as a benchmark for a fulfilled life, of which I fell miserably short.

When I pictured the future, I saw a life of uselessness and despair. Even my condo looked bleak. My bedroom had a king-sized bed. My bathroom a huge walk-in closet and marble counter with two sinks. My living room a leather couch, two matching reclining chairs, two end tables, an ornate coffee table, colorful landscape portraits on the wall, and a window from floor to ceiling overlooking France Avenue. The dining room a heavy mahogany table with six chairs. The kitchen designed for a gourmet chef. And the den lined with dark bookcases and a huge roll-top desk with a window beside it facing 50th Street. All this for one person! It was a testimony of my aloneness.

A heaviness and darkness pervaded my being. When I viewed my world, it was as if there were a dark-blue translucent sheet before my eyes. I had never felt like this before. I was not normal. What was happening to me?

For 40 years, my life formula was that choices were only bad if they were bad for me. The thought of my making mistakes was outside the door of my consciousness. The last three days erased that formula, and there was nothing to replace it. My head was swimming in dark water, my stomach a knot of anxiety. I could not submerge the mistakes haunting my mind. They kept bubbling up over and over and over.

I was all by myself and of no comfort to myself. How was I to pull myself out of the dark waters? I remembered Dave outlining the five stages of grief at Coffee on France but had forgotten what they were, so I sat down at my computer and opened up a search engine. I entered "five stages of grief," and the first entry was Helen Kubler Ross. When I clicked on that link, there they were: denial, anger, bargaining, depression, and acceptance. Wasn't this the path I was on? I could identify with denial and anger. I must have skipped bargaining, which would put me at depression. Depression was a word that frightened me. I didn't wish to put that label on myself. I had some of the symptoms of depression, but certainly not depression itself. I clicked again to find the symptoms of depression. Here's what popped up:

1. A feeling of hopelessness most of the day, nearly every day
2. Lack of interest or pleasure in activities
3. Change in weight or appetite
4. Sleeping more or trouble sleeping
5. Agitation
6. Loss of energy
7. Feeling worthless or guilty for no reason
8. Difficulty concentrating
9. Thoughts of death or suicide

Wow! Those were the very symptoms I had been experiencing the last month. When I was with Dave, they were greatly lessened. The one symptom I didn't have was thoughts of death or suicide. I would pull myself out of this before life got that desperate. It was mind over matter.

***

My confidence was not well placed because it was placed only in myself. My depression would eventually descend into thoughts of death and suicide. That time was just around the corner.

***

I seriously needed to talk to Dave and punched in his cell phone number. He answered on the third ring.

"Hello, Mitch. I was about to call you. It's been three days since Tangletown. How are you doing?"

"Not very well. I've been struggling the last three days. I think I may be in depression. I match most of the symptoms. I need help, Dave."

"I didn't want to confront you, Mitch, but I witnessed your depression at the class reunion—the way you carried your body, the sound of your voice, the look in your eyes. When I was a guidance counselor at Hopkins High School, I worked with hundreds of kids who were depressed. My interest in depression advanced me into the role of resident expert. All kids with depression were sent to me."

"I thought as much. Can you help me, Dave? I'd like to get your professional opinion. Do you have time to talk now, or could we schedule a phone conversation for later?"

"This kind of conversation doesn't work well by phone," said Dave. "It's about 9 a.m. right now. I have a few small items that are important for me to complete. How about we meet at the coffee shop on France about 10 o'clock? I'll call ahead to see if we can get the conference room. Does that work for you?"

"It does," I replied. "That will give me time to prepare for you. Right now my thoughts are fragmented."

***

I opened the door to Coffee on France as Dave's car pulled up to a parking spot right in front, a rare occurrence. France Avenue in that area usually had no available parking spots; you parked on side streets. I waited for Dave and we walked in together, purchased our coffee, and claimed chairs in the conference room.

I pulled a sheet of paper from a folder. "You may find this amusing, Dave, but I've written out a list like you do. I've pondered how deep I want to delve into what I've discovered about myself. You're the only friend I have right now, and I don't want to lose that friendship by revealing what I'm not proud of and what you may be offended by.

It's said that confession cleanses the soul, and my soul badly needs cleansing."

Dave listened intently and nodded his head. He waited about 15 seconds before answering, which made me uncomfortable.

"Mitch, what I'm about to say, I want to say clearly and with absolute sincerity. If you revealed to me that you murdered someone ten years ago, you'd still be my friend. There isn't anything from your past that could change that. What we vowed after climbing over the arches of the Nicollet Avenue Bridge is etched into my brain forever. 'We'll be friends forever, no matter who else comes into our lives and no matter where we go.' I could add, 'or no matter what we do.' My friend, I desire to share in your life. I want to understand you so I can help you. That's what friends are for—to help each other. I'm not offering to be a psychiatrist or a psychologist. I'm offering to be a friend you can confide in, someone you know will always be there for you."

I was moved by what Dave said and how he said it, and decided to proceed ahead with baring my soul to him. This was a major departure from how I had lived my life to this point. I never analyzed why I did anything. I simply did what I felt was right, and everything worked out fine—for me. But things were not fine now, and that led me to search my soul for the last three days, amidst a sea of dark thoughts.

"Dave, I have three categories of confession on this sheet. But first I want to share with you a strange occurrence.

"For the last three days, I've stayed in my condo like a recluse and have spent hours in a recliner looking back at my life. What I saw was depressing. At one point, I heard a voice within me say, 'Your greatest sin is your self-centeredness.' It was not an audible voice. It was a voice that entered my mind from inside me. Instantly, I recognized it as a truth I never would have articulated. Then I started reflecting how that truth had affected my whole life."

Dave interrupted. "That voice could have been God speaking to you or the evil one trying to push you into a deeper depression. Satan means 'the accuser.' Was there anything else you heard within you?"

I replied, "Yes, there was something else I had forgotten until now because the first statement was so dramatic. 'Start here. This is for your salvation and for your healing, not for your destruction.'"

"Satan would never have said that," replied Dave. "I needed to check the origin of the voice. Continue on."

I stared at Dave for a brief moment and put my head down. I knew I must reveal my sordid past for my own good. I was convicted and needed a confessor—Dave.

"When I analyze my life, Dave, from the time I left Minneapolis for Chicago, everything I did was for my own benefit. I didn't consider how my plans or actions would affect anyone else.

"My first confession is hardest because it has to do with you. We were close friends from kindergarten through high school. We established ourselves as kindred spirits at the Washburn Water Tower when we were kids. We pledged to be friends forever climbing over the Nicollet Avenue Bridge arches. We were known in high school as the Washburn twins. All that was significant to me then. Your friendship was the most important item in my life.

"Then something happened when I left for Northwestern that I still don't understand. Whatever crept into my being, my self-centeredness blossomed. Not that I wasn't self-centered in Minneapolis, like most of us, but I went over the top in Chicago. Maybe it was my new life in a prestigious university. Maybe it was the classmates I hung around— rich and full of self-importance. You and I were apart, and you couldn't benefit me. My friends at Northwestern could. I had wanted an advertising career since early in high school, so I put my efforts into networking and making friends who could help me attain that goal. I didn't make a conscious decision to write you off as a friend, but that's exactly what I did.

"When we toured Tangletown four days ago, I was confronted with what I had done. I abandoned the very person I could have shared my life with forever. So for 40 years you ceased to exist. I rarely thought about you. I am ashamed of my behavior. Can you forgive me, Dave?"

I was spent. I sipped my coffee, looked out the conference room window to see the busyness of the main section, and settled back in my chair. Dave was thinking again; this time I knew he was crafting what he wanted to say.

"Do you remember our first meeting at this coffee shop when I told you I forgave you?" I nodded my head.

"Today is different," Dave continued. "You didn't ask for forgiveness before. You didn't think you had done anything wrong. I could see it in your face. So my forgiveness of your writing me off was one-sided. Today, you have confessed that what you did was wrong and have *asked* for forgiveness. My forever friend, I forgive you with all my heart and soul. I forgive you for every year of the 40 years we have been apart. I will never bring it up to you. I have forgotten it as far as the east is from the west."

I met Dave's eyes with tears running down my cheeks. "How can I thank you enough for your graciousness? I can't adequately explain the relief I feel. It's like an iceberg has been lifted off me. For the past three days I have pictured in my mind over and over how self-centered I was and how proud to chart my destination without giving you a second thought. I was uncertain you'd be able to forgive me once I uncovered what a monster I was."

Dave said, "Don't go over it in your mind any longer. You're torturing yourself. When we said we were friends forever, it was true then and is true now. We just didn't know there would be a 40-year gap in that friendship."

I wiped tears of happiness from my eyes. "I say this to you, Dave, with all the allegiance I have within me: we are friends for life, and I will never again walk away from that. I only hope one day to be in a position to help you."

"Don't worry about that," Dave replied. "Friends help each other naturally; they don't look for a return benefit. Some day I'll want your help, not because you owe me something but because I'm a friend of yours. Does that make sense?"

"It does," I said. "I have much to learn about being a real friend."

I had switched from sipping to gulping my coffee and needed a refill, as did Dave. We walked out of the quiet conference room into a din of people talking, coffee machines running, and coffee beans grinding. It was a noisy world. We were fortunate to reclaim the quiet world of the conference room.

I was more at ease and sipping my coffee slowly.

"It's time for my second confession, Dave." I breathed deeply. "From the days of Northwestern to the time I left Chicago, I had a perverted expectation of a friend. I believed I was a person that anyone would want to befriend. To restate what I said earlier this morning, I accepted friends based on what they could do for me and not what I could do for them.

"At Northwestern, in my job at Carrington Smithson, with my own agency, and in my Chicago social life—such as being friends with the Mayor of Chicago, the manager of the Cubs, and the head of the Art Institute of Chicago—it was always how people benefited me. There was prestige in being friends with notable people. That's how I thought the world worked. I concluded people were my friends because I was the magnet that attracted them.

"After I divorced Kathleen and sold my ad agency, I didn't hear from those friends. That's a major reason I left Chicago and returned to Minneapolis. I blamed them: what shallow people they were. Now I see myself in a mirror clearly. I was the shallow one."

"Mitch, you have made an enormous leap to recognize yourself plainly. Many people never see themselves as they really are. You should thank your depression for showing you the truth. Now you need to reach beyond yourself into God's reality. You may think you are one of a select few who have shallow friendships, but don't beat yourself up too severely. More than a few of the people in this world share the same credentials. Anything else?"

"Yes," I answered. I continued to use the term confession because that meant I had done something wrong, something to feel guilty about. I had considered using the term "sins," but that seemed too harsh, though I knew intellectually what one confesses *are* sins.

"My third confession haunts me grievously. Kathleen was one of the prettiest and most popular young women on the Northwestern campus. There were scores of guys who wanted to date her, but she was attracted to me. And why not I thought? I was the guy all the girls wanted to date. Looking back now, understanding how filled with myself I was and how unselfish she was, I can't imagine what she found of value in me and why she married me. I do know what I saw in her at the time, though I'm ashamed to admit it. She had the intelligence and looks to be an asset to me in my advertising career. Stepping into the future, I could see heads turning when she arrived at a social function, when she visited where I worked, or when we walked down the street. She was a woman I could proudly call my wife. The second thing I valued was that her parents were prominent in Chicago and very wealthy. They liked me because my upbringing and financial well-being were similar to their daughter's. They thought we'd be a perfect match.

"Kathleen informed me on our third date that she was a virgin and intended to stay so until the day she married. I wasn't thrilled with that announcement, but she said it with such conviction that I knew if I tried to convince her otherwise she would end our relationship. There were plenty of women in Chicago not devoted to virginity. I was careful not to seek out anyone on campus for fear it would get back to Kathleen. My net was cast into the businesses I worked with for Carrington Smithson. There were two women in that setting willing to have sex with no commitment. So I cheated on my wife-to-be with no qualms of conscience. I thought it was my entitlement.

"Kathleen and I were married in June of 1971, and I ended the two affairs. I see now how despicable those affairs were. I saw women as commodities and that carried over into our marriage." Dave started to make a comment, but I informed him there was more to the Kathleen confession.

***

As I'm reading my journal to write this story, with thunderclouds and a storm raging outside, I'm reminded of God's loving-kindness. I've been forgiven for my sins by the amazing grace of God. As I was making my confession to Dave, I did not have that sense of forgiveness.

***

"Throughout our marriage, I always demanded my own way to any final outcome. Kathleen would occasionally oppose me, but she always gave in at the end. I can give you two examples of that pattern, which I can see now but didn't then.

"The first is when we moved from Lincoln Park to the Gold Coast. We had a beautiful house in Lincoln Park; Kathleen and the kids loved it. I wanted to climb higher in social status and pushed for moving to the Gold Coast and into a condominium. Almost all residences in the Gold Coast were condominiums, especially on North Lake Shore Drive where I wanted to be, overlooking Lake Michigan.

"Leaving the neighborhood where Kathleen and the two oldest kids had made friends was bad; moving into a big condominium was worse. There were a number of ugly scenes with the kids and Kathleen. Finally, I proclaimed that I was the provider for this family and knew best what was good for us. My rationale was that I was starting my own ad agency and living in the Gold Coast was more prestigious than living in Lincoln Park, and I needed prestige for the agency to be successful. I shouted that we weren't going to talk about it any more, and we didn't.

"I have analyzed that scenario over the last three days and have come to recognize there was a feeling of deep-seated resentment from my two oldest children. The youngest was too young to form her own opinion. I have also come to recognize I hurt Kathleen with the move, but hers was a life of following the lead of her husband, and she made the best of it. She tried to help the children emotionally by painting as rosy a picture of moving into a condominium in the Gold Coast as she could. Michael and Suzie soundly rejected her painting."

I was feeling up to my neck in mud and didn't know if I could continue. Beads of sweat drenched my forehead. I looked up and saw Dave smiling at me and nodding his head in encouragement.

"The second example is something I knew at the time pained Kathleen profoundly, but I didn't care. Do you remember, when we were touring Tangletown, you asked if I did a lot of traveling? I factually told you Kathleen went with me on some business trips, and we fit in at least one major vacation each year. We never took any of the children with us because I felt it was good for us to get away unencumbered. In my soul searching the past three days, I realize it was for my convenience that we left the kids behind. I didn't want to change my agenda for what they may want to do. I wanted to do what I wanted to do. I realize now how selfish that was. Kathleen pleaded to include our children. She said they needed to see the world too. Eventually she gave up and went along without protest, like a good wife.

"How I hate those words now—'like a good wife.' I was incredibly inconsiderate and insensitive. My selfishness reached a crescendo the day I divorced Kathleen, when I felt my life would be better without her. I never considered what was best for her; I looked at our relationship only from my perspective. When she desperately asked me to see a counselor with her, I told her she could see a counselor by herself. In truth, I needed a counselor ten times more than she did."

There was silence for what seemed like an hour, though it was a minute at most. I looked out the window of the meeting room and saw people coming into the coffee shop with umbrellas. The rumbling of a July storm was so loud I could hear cracks of thunder with the meeting-room door closed.

Finally, Dave looked me straight in the eyes. "This is heavy stuff, Mitch. I'm proud of you for recognizing the mistakes in your life and taking responsibility for them. Most people never get to that point. It's fascinating how the darkness of your depression lit up the interior of your life to show you things about yourself you've never before recognized."

I bent my head down and put my hands around the back of my neck. "There are two more confessions to make before I say I'm through.

"My career and ad agency were so important and time consuming that I didn't take time to be involved in my children's lives. There were three deprived young people living in my condo who were strangers to me and I to them. Kathleen was their only source of comfort, nurture, and guidance. What you did with and for your children, Dave, I never did. When you informed me about the closeness of your family, I felt uncomfortable but didn't know why. My discomfort turned into guilt these past three days as I pictured how I ignored my kids. Little wonder they don't have anything to do with me. I thought I was being a good father because I provided for all their needs. Whatever they wanted, I gave them—toys, cars, clothes, whatever. I gave them everything except love and time, which they needed most. I doubt they ever will forgive me."

I lifted my head and looked at Dave. His face showed compassion, not horror. He was accepting me as I was. What a friend!

"A similar blunder was how I treated my parents. I was not unlike my father, but I carried his negative traits to an extreme. He spent *some* time with me, even though his work came first. He wanted to vacation alone with mother, but she convinced him it was best if Sam and I were included. My mother was as nurturing and loving as Kathleen. What did I give back to them for all they did for me? I came home Thanksgiving, Christmas, and Easter while attending Northwestern. After I started my agency, I trudged home maybe once a year. They were welcome in Chicago, but when they were there, I was busy at work. Kathleen became closer to them and I more distant."

The most agonizing part was to come. My head almost rested on the table. "I'm ashamed to tell you I did not grieve when they died, any more than when Kathleen's parents died. There was a substantial inheritance, and the inconvenience of their living died with them. No more birthday cards or presents. No more Christmas guilt. No more celebrating Mother's Day or Father's Day. No more interference with my work. I was free of any obligations…what an appalling testimony!"

I told Dave that concluded my confession. I took one last gulp of my coffee, then waited for Dave to respond.

He had a question I hadn't anticipated. "What about your brother Sam? You haven't talked to him for 20 years."

I answered, "That's a book in itself—some of it's my fault; some of it's Sam's fault. Let's deal with that another time. What's your response, Dave? You must feel like a priest in a confessional."

"Mitch, I told you earlier how proud I am of you. You have looked inside yourself and have seen the unvarnished Mitch. That's an important start.

"So what do I think of you now? I don't see you as an intentionally evil person or as a villain. You were a victim of faulty thinking that caused you to make many bad choices. We'll probably never know for sure why your thinking and values changed after high school. But they did. It wasn't your goal to hurt people. Your thinking was so distorted you didn't even suspect you were hurting them. Your focus was entirely on yourself, and you've come to understand that. You're still my friend as much as before your confession."

"You mentioned an important start. What comes next?" I asked.

"The next step is to make radical changes to restore your *real* life. Changes in your heart, changes in your thinking, changes in the way you relate to people, changes in how you view the world, changes in how you view yourself."

I was not ready for radical changes. I had just revealed the dark side of myself and felt a mountain of guilt had been lifted off me. Now it looked like a new mountain was to be dumped on me—a mountain of radical changes.

"Dave, I'm in the afternoon of my life. I'm too set in my ways to make radical changes. Isn't confession enough? How does one make major changes in his life when he's 58 years old? I'm afraid it's too late in the afternoon."

"Confession isn't enough. Repentance and renewal are required. No exceptions. And it's never too late to make changes," said Dave with strong conviction in his voice. "Not while a person has breath in his lungs, a mind that is clear, and a willingness to do what is best for himself and others. It's never too late!"

We had been in the coffee shop for two hours. Dave told me when we arrived that he had a luncheon engagement in Hopkins at noon, for which he would be late. We had lost track of time.

"I really need to be going, Mitch, but we're not finished. Can I call you later this afternoon after you've had a chance to digest some of what I just dropped on you?"

"My schedule is open," I said, with an attempt at dry humor. "I'll wait for your call. Thanks for listening. Now you can never say, 'Oh, you're not all that bad, Mitch.'"

CHAPTER 5
Too Late in the Afternoon

The clock lingered on three in the afternoon. Why hadn't Dave called? The luncheon he was scheduled for must be over by now. I paced from one room to the next, occasionally looking out over France Avenue, trying to take my mind off time. In Chicago, time galloped, and I wanted to slow it down. Now, time trotted, and I wanted to speed it up. The phone rang. It was Dave.

"I'm sorry it took so long for me to call," said Dave. "The luncheon engagement lasted until two. When I reached home, I felt a need to think out what I wanted to say to you."

I responded, "That's OK, Dave, I figured something must have held you up. When you promise to do something, you do it." I felt better talking with Dave and didn't want to reveal to him that I was anxiously awaiting his call.

"Mitch, this morning you covered all the bad things you have discovered about yourself. I want to balance those negatives with positives about you. Rehashing the negatives over and over feeds your depression. Changing the negatives and acknowledging the positives define the road to wholeness.

"From the time we met in kindergarten to the time we graduated from high school, you were the best friend anyone could have. You were committed to our friendship. I can remember many instances where you sought what was best for me, even if it was not best for you. We all have much selfishness in our flesh, waiting to jump up and overpower our better instincts. During those 13 years, your self-centeredness was way below average.

"When you moved to Chicago that changed for reasons we may never fully understand. You're most likely well steeped in symbols through your advertising career. I encountered symbols in many psychology courses. In my work with depression in teenagers, I often found symbols to be the best way to explain their depression to them. For you, I see Chicago as a symbol of the sickness of your soul that you confessed to me this morning."

I interrupted, "You're right, Dave. Everything I told you this morning had to do with Chicago."

Dave continued. "I'm not saying Chicago is a bad city. I've been there with Cathy and the kids a few times, and we all felt it's a wonderful city, kind of like a big Minneapolis. Chicago itself is not a representation of all that is bad, but it's a symbol of what went bad with you. Your faulty behavior could just as well have happened in New York, Los Angeles, or Pittsburgh."

I interrupted again. "If Chicago is a symbol of what is bad in me, then perhaps Minneapolis is a symbol of what is good."

"I was about to bring that up," said Dave. "You have hit the mark exactly. Minneapolis can be a symbol of the healing that will restore you to the goodness that was in you when you graduated from high school. I can already see that happening since you've been back. You're not the same person I met at the 40th reunion. You have become more reflective. You have become more sensitive and less self-centered. You are starting to become the friend again I knew 40 years ago. Those are all positive things."

A beep-beep-beep came into my cell phone. I looked and it was the library, probably telling me the book on depression I requested had arrived. My attention immediately turned back to Dave.

"To be honest about the balance between good and bad, you weren't all bad in Chicago. You did enough right things in your marriage to keep it together for 34 years. You were faithful to Kathleen once you were married. You took her to social and business events and on vacations. You accepted her right to have spiritual values so different from yours. You shared money with her to spend as she wished and did not deny her whenever her giving nature was focused on your children and grandchildren. In short, you were very generous to Kathleen and your children. You did not hoard money or use it all on yourself.

"Your motives and ways were misguided in nurturing your children, but you cared for their needs as best you knew how. You provided them with food, shelter, and clothing. You provided them with transportation, college educations, and encouragement to start a career. You were proud to introduce them to your friends and colleagues. As they grew older, you took them to events the mayor invited you to and to Cub ball games with tickets the manager gave you. You didn't totally ignore them."

I later noted in my journal that Dave was a good questioner and listener. He put together specific positive behaviors gleaned from our many phone conversations and face-to-face meetings. Why hadn't I thought of positives when I was castigating myself for past mistakes? I saw only the negatives. Dave forged ahead with more positive characteristics.

"From what you've told me about your advertising agency, I can visualize a pattern of benevolence on your part: you operated the business well, you sought the best interests of your clients, you treated your employees with respect. You did well with what was provided you. You were not a tyrant, nor did you micromanage the people who worked for you. You were a commendable boss. People chose to work for your firm because you dealt with them fairly.

"You were an admirable friend to your friends. You disclosed that you made friends with those who advanced your career and agency or who gifted you with their prominence. That's a motive. However, if you had been shallow with them, they would have deserted you. Obviously, you delivered substance in return because they were friends for a long time. I would venture to assert that the qualities of friendship you showed to me through high school were so ingrained that they evolved within your friendships in Chicago."

Dave paused long enough for me to ask kiddingly, "Are you done with my positive qualities?"

"I *thought* I did a rather thorough job," answered Dave with a smile. "I might be able to come up with a couple more if you want."

"No," I chuckled, "You've made me feel better about myself than I have for the past three days. I never thought about those 13 years of my life with you. The depression steered me away from any positive memories. The negatives far outweighed the positives in Chicago, but you've opened my mind to see I had at least *some* redeeming qualities."

***

When a person is enveloped by darkness, everything looks dark. The fog of depression dominates a landscape—no light can penetrate, no joy appear, no momentary enjoyment exist. The heaviness of depression is suffocating. My chest was tight, my breathing shallow, my stomach nauseous, my mind in turmoil.

I experienced only that fog for those three days. My spinning mind thrashed against it looking for an escape. On my own, no escape was on the horizon, no light visible, no hope forthcoming. Only someone from outside me could pierce the darkness. Only Dave.

***

I heard another beep-beep-beep. This time it was in my mind, not my cell phone. Dave's life was what I wanted for my life. I thought of Dave's life as a benchmark that I fell miserably below. I had perceived it darkly, as in a clouded mirror. The mirror was suddenly clear, and I viewed Dave as a real person in a real world living a real life. I wanted that life for myself. I had a deep desire for an existence that counted for something beyond myself.

"Dave, I wish I had a life like yours, a life of integrity and honesty. A life of goodness. A life that didn't need the massive changes I doubt I'm capable of making at my age."

"Well," replied Dave, "that's a perfect segue into our second topic. When you completed your confession to me this morning and felt you may not be able to change, I knew it was time for me to confess a hidden part of myself. I've made mistakes in my life; my motives have not always been pure. I needed time to think after the luncheon before talking to you."

Dave was hesitating and had a very serious, nervous tone to his voice. I had not experienced Dave anything but confident and joyful before. Something dramatic was coming.

"When Cathy and I were first married, I afforded more consideration to my sports buddies than to her. I had played with the same softball team for years. After each game, we'd celebrate our win or loss with hamburgers and beer. I'd have a couple of beers, three at most, and go home. Cathy had no problem with my playing softball and spending time with the guys afterwards. So I kept the same softball routine after we were married. However, these guys didn't go home after two or three beers like I did. They stayed until the bar closed. When I followed the same pattern of leaving before they did, they kidded me about being married and henpecked and not able to lead my own life like they did with their wives. It was relentless.

"Eventually I weakened under the storm of being called a wimp, so I stayed a little later each night until I was still there at midnight. And I was no longer having two or three beers. We'd drink pitchers of beer, the equivalent of a dozen beers apiece, after each game. Sometimes there were two games a week. I never drank that much before, even in college. I developed a nasty trait of becoming belligerent when I got drunk. By the end of the evening, I picked fights with whomever I thought deserved a thrashing. When the team we played came to the same bar, a fight was a certainty.

"The softball season lasted from May to September. Cathy became upset with my coming home late, especially when Hopkins High School was in session. She had become friends with two women who taught at Hopkins. These two were genuinely concerned about me but felt they could no longer confront me with the gravity of my behavior because I was so defensive. They reluctantly went the route they wanted to avoid—letting my wife know the danger I was in. Hopkins High teachers were gossiping about my coming to school looking like a boxer who had lost a fight and my being detached from my work. When the principal got wind of it, I was close to being fired. I would have been defenseless."

I was stunned by Dave's confession. A fighting drunk? How could it be? He might have heard a muffled gasp from me, but he continued as if on a mission.

"The arguments between Cathy and me were becoming ugly. Cathy demanded I return to a pattern of two or three beers, home early, and no fights. I accused her of attempting to run my life. I insisted a man needed time with other men, and once or twice a week was not unreasonable. I refused to acknowledge I had a problem. I truly believed she had the problem.

"Then one Saturday morning in early September—I'll never forget the day or the conversation—Cathy told me I either had to quit my excessive drinking and fighting or she would leave me. It was a punch in the face harder than anything I had experienced in a bar fight. I gazed intently at the only woman I had ever loved, my best friend, the woman I wanted to raise a family with, the person I wanted to grow old with. You talk about the difficulty of making changes. I had no difficulty making a dramatic change in a nanosecond.

"There was a greater 'yes' in my love for Cathy than the 'yes' of spending time with my softball buddies. I told her from that day forward I would play softball, go out for hamburgers only, and not drink any beer. Not even one glass. And I'd come home when I finished eating. She said it wouldn't hurt to have a beer or two. But I didn't want the temptation of getting caught up with drinking or fighting ever again. My marriage was too important. From that day on I never had another alcoholic drink, not because there is anything wrong with drinking in moderation, but I didn't know I could trust myself to stop when I should. I didn't want to ever take that chance."

Dave was not done. I heard him take a deep breath, pause, and then start speaking again. I had a sense the next confession was going to be something worse than the first one.

"There's more. Five years later, when young Thomas was a year old, another counselor at Hopkins High School took an interest in me—as more than a co-worker. She was an attractive woman who had recently been divorced. I was flattered by her attention. We had lunch together almost every day, found time to visit each other's office several times a day, and communicated by e-mail. She wanted to have dinner with me one night, but I drew the line there. A little flirting at work was one thing; if I went out on a date, that would be unfaithfulness to Cathy. Once again, I blocked out that I was doing anything wrong. If men can have men as friends, why can't they have women as friends? I didn't find it hurt the relationship with Cathy, until one night when I was making love to Cathy I thought about Marilyn. That was my wake-up call.

"I went to school the next morning and asked Marilyn if she would come to my office about 10 a.m. She said she could change a scheduled meeting with a student to later in the afternoon. When she entered my office, I told her our frequent meetings and interchanges were not appropriate for a man who was married. Funny thing, she argued the same 'friends of opposite sex' that I had used to justify my behavior. I told her we had gone several pages past being just friends, and I wanted to stop that relationship right now. We could be friends, but only on a professional basis. I doubt she understood my perspective, but she respected me and we became professional friends. If she felt a grudge about my setting things straight, she never let on."

Once again, I was flabbergasted. I was never drawn into a relationship with any woman once Kathleen and I were married, and I had plenty of chances. I also had no personal experience with heavy drinking or fighting; my profession would not allow it. I had to be on top of my game all the time. Dave was not finished with the Marilyn story.

"Then came the hard part. I knew I must talk to Cathy. My conscience demanded it. My Christian faith demanded it. I confessed that I had wronged her and repented of it, and I had closed the chapter with Marilyn that morning. Cathy was gracious. She said I was an attractive man and could see why Marilyn was taken with me. Besides, the relationship had never advanced to an affair or adultery. Because I told her before someone else did, she knew she could trust me in the future. I asked for her forgiveness, and she forgave me with a hug and a kiss. I promised I would never let a relationship with a female get to that point again."

I stated to Dave that these were changes made in the summer of his life, when change is easier. He did not buy that argument. There was strong emotion in his voice when he declared that change is difficult at any time of life.

I glanced outside my window at France Avenue and caught sight of a steady stream of cars hustling for an early start home on a rainy afternoon. Within an hour, the street would be a snarl of rush-hour traffic. Dave cleared his throat. Another confession was on the doorstep.

"There's one last incident I want to disclose to you, one closer to the afternoon of *my* life. Six years ago, I was elected an elder in the church Cathy and I were attending. I felt proud and important. I had never been selected as a church leader before. I had no experience being a leader and yet was expected to see our church through good times and bad.

"The bad times commenced three years ago. Pastor Jim had become a good friend. He was an exceptional preacher and teacher, but his administrative skills were not well developed. The preaching and teaching were why we called him; church administration was less important and could be assumed by others on staff.

"A group of about 30 members felt otherwise. They contacted the denomination headquarters, which sent out a person to survey the congregation regarding Pastor Jim. Although the survey was 85 percent positive, the elder board focused on the 15 percent negative comments. The pastor was asked to leave within a year. I cast the one dissenting vote. He left in six months, and that troubled me greatly. The elders and the opposing 15 percent knew I strongly opposed the dismissal of Pastor Jim, and I became persona non grata.

"'How dare they do this to me?' I thought. Why did they reject reason? I thought only about myself, not Pastor Jim or the 85 percent of the congregation that supported him. I was so personally hurt I resigned. Pride had found its way into my heart, the same pride that caused Adam and Eve to sin. I didn't see it that way at the time, of course.

"Cathy was an effective counselor. She didn't confront my pride, for she could see how defensive I had become. She called Pastor Jim, who had accepted a call to a church in Boston, and summarized the whole story for him. I have to tell you, Mitch, I was a miserable, miserable guy. Pastor Jim called and gave me a personal sermon I'll never forget.

"In a deliberate voice, Pastor Jim said, 'Dave, I was deeply hurt when the elder board mandated that I leave within a year. I felt pride crouching beside me, waiting to claim my soul. I knew if I took this personally it would make me bitter and an awful ambassador for God. I prayed and fasted and waited to have truth revealed to me. And it was.

"'God closed one door and opened a better door. My church here has an administrator that manages all the things I'm not good at. I've learned from him what was needed of me back at our church in Edina. The congregation loves and supports my family and me. This will be our church for a long time. God put me where I fit best.

"'I appreciated your friendship greatly and your support for the three years you were an elder. But think about it. If you had your way, I'd still be in a church where I was struggling. I was frustrated daily with my inability to be the administrator the elder board wanted. What you thought was good for me would have kept me from experiencing what was best. The good is always the enemy of the best. What I'm going to confront you with now is not meant to hurt you but to convict you.

"'The pride that was crouching at my side is crouching by yours. However, you haven't brought it to the Lord. You have allowed it to control you. I should have spoken to you as your pastor. When you were on the elder board, I could see you were becoming more and more filled with your own self-importance. You meant well, but your motives of self-centeredness and pride missed the mark.

"'Our friendship kept me from confronting you. A few times when we played golf, I tried to subtly bring the pride issue to your conscience, but you were beyond subtlety. You needed a direct hit, and I didn't give it to you then. Now I am.'

"Mitch, that conversation hit me like a tsunami. My first reaction was denial. Then I recalled that one of Pastor Jim's greatest gifts was discernment. If he said I was full of self-centeredness and pride, it must be true. I descended to the den in the lower level of our home, the place where I spent time in prayer and meditation. I pondered what Pastor Jim said. I had taken notes as he spoke and reviewed them. I could see the truth.

"I had listened to lies that assailed my mind. I was prideful and full of myself. It was a deception that crept into my life when I was elected an elder and had become a stronghold of sin in just three years.

"So at the age of fifty-five, in the afternoon of *my* life, I committed to a major life change—to stop thinking I was so important and let God have control of my life. I asked Him to take the pride out of me, and He did.

"I asked our pastor if I could speak to the congregation, and he agreed once I told him what I was planning. I climbed into the pulpit, with my knees knocking and sweating like I was in a sauna, and confessed my pride and self-centeredness. The congregation looked at me in bewilderment. They hadn't heard a confession from the pulpit before, especially from an elder.

"I explained why I had resigned from being an elder and that it was best for the congregation and for me that I did so. Instead of seeing my confession as a mark of strength, they saw it as weakness. The church body no longer accepted us in a loving way. Cathy and I were not comfortable staying in that church after that and switched to the Anglican Church in Hopkins, where I'm content to be just another parishioner and occasional Sunday school teacher.

"You see, Mitch, it *is* possible to make changes in the afternoon of your life, and that's the last topic I want to discuss with you. First, though, what's your response to my confession?"

Now it was my turn to wait several seconds before answering. I removed the phone from my ear. My perception of Dave was altered for sure. I looked out the window to collect my thoughts, breathing in deeply before responding.

"Dave, my first reaction is shock. This is not the Dave I know. I thought you were Mister Perfect. My second reaction is gratefulness that you were willing to reveal your shortcomings to me. My third reaction is more of an observation. You had a reason for making changes beyond anything I have experienced—your overwhelming love for Cathy. I don't have that compelling a reason for change. Besides, I've enough baggage in my life to fill the hold of an airplane. It's too late in the afternoon for me. You only had to make course corrections. I need to reverse course 180 degrees. It's too overwhelming."

It seemed Dave was waiting for my last comment and jumped on it like a tiger.

"It's *never* too late to make changes in your life. That's Satan's lie. Don't believe it. As long as you have breath in your lungs and a willingness to become a better person, you can make changes.

"At any season of your life, at any moment in time, you can start all over again. You can draw a line in the sand and say, 'All that is in my past is in my past. I'm going to start a new life right now. It won't be easy, but I can do it.' You've heard the old cliché so overused that people have tuned it out. But it's true. 'Today is the first day of the rest of your life.'"

I listened to Dave intently. But instead of absorbing his words into my heart, I was thinking how to poke holes in his philosophy.

I said, "You made three major changes in your life, but look at the time frames. The drinking and fighting occurred over less than half a year. The fling with your co-worker lasted a few months. Your being filled with pride happened over three years. My bad habits have become ingrained in me over a period of 40 years. With that length of time, personalities become defined in concrete. Thought patterns become deeply etched fissures in the brain. The traces in the soul become darker and darker, until they are a permanent dye."

Dave pounced on me again. "It's *never* too late, *never* too late. Think about Scrooge in *A Christmas Carol* who underwent a profound experience of redemption over the course of one night. Scrooge was a financier who had devoted his entire life to the accumulation of wealth for himself, more than 40 years by the way. He held anything other than money in contempt, including friendships, love, and the Christmas season."

I was familiar with the story. "I'll grant you that one," I said, "although it's not a story based on a real character."

"Stories don't appear out of thin air," responded Dave. "I expect Charles Dickens was familiar with a real person who had made such a change at an advanced age.

"If you want a real person, take my Grandfather Alex. Do you remember him when you came over to our house when he was visiting? He was a crotchety old man and had been tight fisted and a hoarder of money for 37 years of his life. He was greatly affected by The Great Depression, and his personality and thinking were cemented from that time on. My grandmother told my mother Grandfather Alex was the sweetest and most generous man in the first 15 years of their marriage. When he was 40 years old in 1935, he lost his job, his house, and all his savings. He had to start all over again. He became very successful in real estate but always thought another Great Depression was around the corner. That thinking robbed him of most pleasures in life. He had a constant anxiety that life would throw him back to where he was when he was 40.

"In 1965, when we graduated from high school, he was 70 years old. When he was 77, with 37 years of being a miserable old man who was heading to the poorhouse, he got a wake-up call. He was diagnosed with inoperable brain cancer. He underwent chemotherapy and was in remission the last ten years of his life. Six months after the diagnosis, we started to see a remarkable change in him. He became a new person. He was joyous, generous, a very kind person, and someone you wanted to be around all the time. It can be done. You had a major heart attack a year ago. You're living on borrowed time. You could just as well be dead. You can become a new person just like Grandfather Alex—today."

I had no argument for Grandfather Alex. I remembered him as Dave described him. He was friendly to me, but he wasn't a very interesting person. I knew Grandfather Alex was wealthy from what Dave told me. I wouldn't have ascertained that myself from the car he drove, the clothes he wore, or what he talked about.

I had to concede to Dave. "If your Grandfather Alex could make such a massive change at 77, I suppose anything is possible."

Dave leaped at my concession. "So you believe change is possible in the afternoon of your life. I don't mean to claim it's a smooth transition. It rarely happens that you can change your life through reasoning alone. The old self you want to change does not want to be changed. Your mind is not where the battle is won. No matter how fully you agree to what is revealed by reason, you will continue to stuggle along the old habitual paths of your life. Until, finally, one day you realize that your life is so empty, frustrating, and without meaning that the old life you have lived for 40 years is no longer viable."

"How do I make the change then?" I sighed. I was confused. I always thought change was a result of your thinking—mind over matter.

"You'll make it in your heart," said Dave. "There is a prophet in the Bible named Ezekiel. In the 36th chapter of his prophecy, he says the Lord will give you a new heart. You said a while ago that the traces in your soul have become so dark they can't be removed. What is in your soul is influenced directly by your heart. Your heart is the core of your being, the place where your true values and beliefs lie. Your soul is your mind, will, and emotions. The heart may become so hard that it is without life, and the soul has no foundation for change. But God promises He will give you a new heart and a new spirit. You can hold Him to that promise."

I had been only on the fringes of religion for some time. Dave was a continent ahead of me. But I could fathom the truth of what he just told me.

"I do see the possibilities, Dave, but change won't be easy, living by myself in Edina, with only you as a friend, without outside encounters. Will you help me?"

"I will," answered Dave. "Here's an important point to keep in mind: don't be frustrated with your inability to be consistent. If you work on change and then backslide, don't beat yourself up. Recognize you went backwards and start over again. For example, when I'm playing golf poorly, I convince myself that any moment in the round is a time to start over again. I forget all the bad shots and concentrate on how to correct my swing. It works for me. It can work for you.

"I suggest you read *The Autobiography of Benjamin Franklin*. He worked on 13 virtues he felt would bring him to moral perfection. It was more difficult than he thought when he started. He never reached perfection, but he was very persistent and became a much better person as a result of this experiment. You'll realize by reading Franklin not to attempt all changes at once. Pick one and work on it until you have made significant progress. Then start on another. Eventually you'll be a new person. It's definitely not too late in the afternoon."

Dave paused and changed the subject. "Cathy and I are taking our annual getaway to the North Shore of Lake Superior one week from today. We'll be there for a week—hiking, reading, relaxing, and renewing our marriage. We're staying at a unique place called the Naniboujou Lodge, 15 miles north of Grand Marais. There are no TVs in the rooms or telephones, and the food is fantastic. I'll build cell phone conversations with you into my schedule. This next week will be a busy one for me. The kids are coming to our house this weekend. Monday is my father's birthday. Tuesday and Wednesday are the last two days of the community theater play we're in. Thursday we'll be packing for the North Shore, and Friday we take off. Don't let that put you off, though. If you need to talk to me, call my cell, and I'll get back to you when I can."

I thanked Dave again for calling me. "This conversation has given me a different perspective on my world and a different perspective on your world. I'll be OK next week and look forward to talking to you in Grand Marais."

As I closed my phone, I felt a twinge of anxiety in my stomach. I would not call Dave next week, respecting his busyness. It would be a week on my own. Was I up to that? I'd soon find out.

CHAPTER 6
The Deepening Shadow of Depression

I thought I could hang on through the next week until I talked to Dave again. Our two conversations yesterday gave me hope. After the afternoon conversation, I felt strong emotionally. I went to bed that night and slept the best I had in a long time.

However, Saturday morning arrived with a thump. Yesterday's hope was sapped from me by the deepening shadow of depression. The thought of not talking to Dave for a week smothered me. He encouraged me to call if needed, but a seed of consideration for others growing in me asserted, "Don't call." He had a full agenda next week and didn't need another item, so I promised myself I wouldn't call unless I was heading to the emergency room.

*****

As I'm writing this story, some two years since that difficult week, I have a perspective I didn't have at the time. It was too early in my transformation to understand what was happening. I was naïve when it came to depression. I no longer am. I used the term, "the deepening shadow of depression," based on what I felt, not on what I understood.

I had experienced heavy-duty stressors in the year and a half prior to this point in the story: a heart attack, divorce, selling my ad agency, retiring, and moving from a city I had lived in for 40 years to a city that was no longer familiar to me. I had suffered situational depression ever since moving to Edina about a month and a half before this fateful week. I was able to fight through that depression somewhat in my mind and somewhat as a result of my meetings with Dave. If a carpenter's level were used to measure emotional stability, with a bubble between the lines being normal, I was operating at about a half-bubble off level. That is, I was emotionally below what was normal for me but still able to function with other people and with myself. I felt best when with Dave or talking to him on the phone. But with Dave not available for a week, I became much worse. I found myself a bubble off level and barely able to function. I had entered a new stage of depression that became clearer to me within the next two weeks. Let's return to the journal entries of two years ago and allow what I wrote then to explain the new stage of depression.

***

I had enjoyed reading the Minneapolis StarTribune before this day, going for walks around Lake Calhoun—which I did almost every day that was nice—and watching some TV. I started following the Twins again, which was a staple of every sports-minded Minnesotan after the Twins came to Minneapolis in 1961.

Starting Saturday, I stopped reading the newspaper or doing most anything else. It was difficult for me to concentrate on TV, unless there was a sporting event on. The one thing I forced myself to do was continue walking around Lake Calhoun, ending up on the west side of the lake where there was a softball field and a couple of benches, one on the first-base side and one on the third-base side. I always sat on the first-base side.

I read an article on the Internet that depression affects about ten percent of the people in the United States. I was part of that statistic. A common symptom is a feeling of sadness; and my crying without reason because I hurt so badly emotionally fit another symptom. I was also hit by other symptoms. I didn't have an appetite and started to lose weight on an average of one pound a day. I had been sleeping until 8 a.m. since I moved to Minneapolis, a far cry from getting up at 6 a.m. when I was working. Now I was experiencing trouble getting to sleep and was wide-awake at 4 a.m., unable to return to sleep. I still didn't climb out of bed until eight, and that left early morning hours for dark thoughts of hopelessness and worthlessness that became so etched in my mind that they set the tone for the day.

After breakfast I slumped into one of my reclining chairs and my mind started spinning—"Why did you retire…why did you leave Chicago…there's nothing for you in Minneapolis…why would Dave want to be your friend…your whole life has been a mistake…Kathleen and your three children hate you…you're a sorry excuse for a human being." On and on and on I was bombarded with negative thoughts and dark fantasies. My past haunted me like a terrifying dream. I was beset with guilt. I analyzed it all—over and over. The darkness of my being enveloped me. I hated when it was time to eat. I did not feel like preparing a meal, and had to force food down. It was a triumph when I finished my evening meal.

I was a recluse. I rarely left the condo, except to grocery shop and go for walks around Lake Calhoun. I lay for hours in a reclining chair, feeling sorry for myself and revisiting over and over the dark thoughts from the morning. I tried to pray, but I couldn't. I just kept ruminating on mistakes, dark thoughts, and the hopelessness of the future. What would become of me? I couldn't go on like this for the rest of my life. That thought made me feel even worse.

I didn't dwell on suicide, for whatever religion I possessed said "No." I did have dark thoughts of death, though—the final escape. I imagined over and over having a final heart attack. I would be taken to an emergency room, and a doctor would tell me I would not survive this attack. I would shake his hand and thank him. This fantasy would take up an hour or more at a time, with variations of how the attack came and what happened in the emergency room. I had all the words down. I could have made a movie out of it: *Mitch's Final Days*. It gave me a perverse sense of joy. What was the sense of living? The idea of living out the rest of my days as I now was made me wish I had never been born.

I looked out the window at people walking by, wondering what it was like to be normal. I thought if there were a hell, this is what it would be like—alone and in unrelenting depression for eternity. That thought terrified me and made me more depressed. I didn't feel heaven was within my reach. I played computer games to keep my mind off depression and watched as much TV as I could handle. Even though

I had a hard time concentrating, it was better than thinking about my problems. After short tries at these two endeavors, I would end up back in a reclining chair.

On Tuesday afternoon, four days into the full-bubble-off-level depression, I felt a strong nudging to get out of the condo and walk around Lake Calhoun. I drove my car to the west side of the lake and parked it by the softball field.

****

It was three miles around Lake Calhoun, about one hour to think my way out of this excruciating depression. I started walking slowly counter-clockwise around the lake. I was determined. I was hopeful that when I finished the walk and spent time sitting on the first-base side of the softball field, my depression would be dissipated. I willed it to be so. That's how I solved other problems in the past, and I would solve this problem as well. I felt better just thinking I would pull myself out of the shadows.

A crowd of people were walking and running around the lake. A solid line of bikers, interspersed by a few roller bladers, was riding on a second path built around Lake Calhoun. It was a beautiful day for July, not too hot, not too humid.

"OK, Mitch, what is this depression all about?" I said to myself. "I've been on the fringes of depression ever since moving back to Minneapolis. Now it's deepened. Other than not being able to contact Dave for a week, nothing is different. How do I bring myself back to at least how things were before Saturday?"

I approached two women pushing baby strollers who were talking together and having a good time. How I envied them because…because they had joy in life and enjoyed what they were doing. I surmised they both had good marriages and led meaningful lives, lives with a purpose. That's exactly what I didn't have—a meaningful life and a purpose for living. It had all been lost. How would I get it back?

The more I thought about meaning and purpose, the more depressed I became. It was hard to concentrate on anything for any length of time. The runners, the walkers, the bikers, and the roller bladers all distracted me.

I encountered an elderly couple walking together and holding hands. They were in their 80s. I saw a guy on roller blades who had tattoos on both arms and both legs. He looked like he was the leading attraction in a freak show; yet the look on his face was one of satisfaction and happiness. Why was everyone happy but me?

I had purpose in my life throughout my entire advertising career. I moved up in Carrington Smithson, bought my own agency, and kept increasing its size. It was up to me to craft the agency into one of the finest in Chicago. It was up to me to maintain the creative edge and find large companies throughout the United States as clients. I had a purpose, a very important purpose. The agency staff listened to me. They depended on me. My optimism wore off on them. My creativity was absorbed by them. My leadership gave them jobs and bountiful raises. What a fun time that was. I wish those days had never ended.

Yes, I had meaning in my life back then. My social life outside the agency included rubbing up against some of the most prominent people in Chicago. They were interested in what I had to say. I was a celebrity because I was so successful. "Tell us about your latest advertising campaign," was a constant request. "What would you do to promote Chicago?" asked the mayor. I was on the board of one of the largest churches in Chicago for six years. The board members turned to me when it was time to solve problems or promote the church. I was the voice they listened to. I was the one who had the experience to know what should be done in almost every circumstance, in almost every situation.

My thoughts turned to the present. "No one cares what I think now. No one seeks what I have to say. No one even asks about my past career. I have no purpose or meaning left. I'm adrift in a no-man's land. Dave says I can find meaning and purpose in my life again, but it will be different from what it was. I think it's too late in the afternoon for me to make major changes. My past was vibrant and full. The present is suffocating, the future hopeless. Change to what? It's a blur. How does one turn around and head in a different direction? All I can think about is my smothering depression. I am in its grasp."

I had walked halfway around Lake Calhoun, and my mind was spinning out of control. I was thinking only about myself and how bad

I felt. I was having a pity party, and it was a very successful party. Just when I was feeling totally hopeless and helpless, I came upon a man in a wheelchair. His right wheel had slipped off the tar path and was stuck in mud. He was unable to move forward or backward. I thought, "That's kind of where I am; stuck on the side of the road and not able to move in any direction."

"Say, friend, can you help me back on the path?" he asked. "My mind was in Baltimore, and I wasn't paying attention to what I was doing."

"Sure," I said. "I can help you."

"My name is Daniel. Why don't you wheel me over by that bench? I can rest from my battle with the mud, you can sit down, and we can talk. What is your name, if I may ask."

"I'm Mitch Jasper." I was not eager to talk to anyone. My single purpose that day was to think myself out of depression. But Daniel said something that piqued my curiosity.

"Do you think it was an accident you came by after I went off the path? I don't believe in accidents. I was there for a reason; you were there for a reason. Let's see if we can figure out what the reason is."

Daniel looked at me with a gaze that went right through me. "I can see you are troubled. You have the eyes of a very sad person who has maybe one friend in the world."

"You're right," I said in wonderment. "I have exactly one friend in the world, a very good friend, but he's not available this week. So I *am* feeling sad."

I'm not one to share my life with strangers. However, there was something about Daniel that gave me hope he would be able to understand and help me. I don't know exactly what it was. It came from within me, a strong recommendation that I should trust him.

"I know that look," replied Daniel, "because I saw it in the mirror too often during the first year of my affliction. I was a baseball player for the Baltimore Orioles, in the fourth year of batting over .300. I was a hero. I was making a ton of money. I had friends and fans that catapulted me to top of the world. I had an oceanfront house and a fiancé who was beautiful and intelligent. I had it all.

"Then one night I was returning home from a party at a teammate's house. It was two o'clock in the morning, a time when drunks make up a larger part of the driving mix than any other time of the day. I had no alcohol in my system because I was taking pain medicine for a hamstring injury. I crossed an intersection on a green light, and a drunk sped through a red light and hit my side of the car. The impact broke my back at the twelfth thoracic vertebrae, a displaced fracture that caused spinal cord injury and paralysis. The doctors told me right from the beginning that I would never walk again. There would be no recovery. I would be in a wheelchair the rest of my life. I was angry for the three months I was in the hospital and receiving therapy for a life without legs. Then I dropped into a deep depression.

"The Orioles paid for a counselor I saw three times a week. A psychiatrist prescribed antidepressant medication that helped take the edge off the mental pain of my condition. One day the wife of a good friend of mine—she was a counselor—came to visit. Her name was Ann. She sat on the edge of my bed and whispered in my ear, 'Can you see yourself playing baseball again?'

"I nodded yes.

"'Can you see yourself playing golf and tennis?'

"Again, I nodded.

"'Can you see yourself walking around and doing all the things you've always done?'

"I couldn't comprehend where she was going, and I was becoming agitated. She was bringing up exactly what I had been thinking. This time I loudly said, 'Yes!'

"'Can you see yourself being married and having a normal relationship with a woman?'

"With my lips pursed, I gave her an emphatic yes.

"'Can you see yourself being an active person with two good legs?'

"This question really sunk me. It was the summation of all the other questions. Softly I whispered, 'Yes, yes, yes, that's what's causing me to be so depressed.'

"Then she did something that will dwell in my mind forever.

"She screamed in my ear so loudly it startled me, 'Stop! You'll never do those things again. You're starting a new life and need to focus on what you can do, not what you can't do. Every time you think about any of those things you used to be able to do, I want you to yell

Stop! Shout it aloud or in your mind. Shout it every time you start feeling sorry for yourself. Do you understand?'

"I still had *Stop*! ringing in my ears, so I said I absolutely understood.

"She said, 'Fine,' and left to meet with one of her paying clients.

"You may think I was instantly changed, but that wasn't the case. I received another blow when my fiancé told me she didn't want to marry a cripple. That was a hard word. I kept seeing my counselor and told him about my encounter with Ann. He laughed and said, 'Perfect. We'll make that a foundation of your counseling with me.'

"And so for the next year, I discovered what I *could* do. Whenever I felt sorry for myself and thought about what I used to be able to do, I shouted, 'Stop!' in my mind. There were days I shouted 'Stop!' every five minutes. Gradually, I said 'Stop!' less often. I had accepted I was a different person with two legs that didn't work.

"Now, when I awake in the morning, I don't think about what I can't do. I think about what I can do. And I've found I can do quite a bit. I can drive a car again with special adaptations. I have a part-time business selling health products. I paint landscapes. I've competed in the Special Olympics. I even do marathons in my wheel chair.

"The book of my being a major league baseball player is closed. I'm living in a new book and am as active as I want to be. I'm living a full life. I sold my house on the ocean and moved back to Minneapolis where I grew up. I live in a condo just across from Lake Calhoun. That's why I'm here wheeling around the lake most days spring to fall. In the winter, I go to a health club that has a running and walking track."

Daniel's story was inspiring. His circumstances were substantially more dire than mine. "Thank you for revealing your struggles. But I'm curious. Why did you choose me as a listener?"

Daniel answered, "I find I'm in stronger mental shape than most people I meet in the course of my day. I've taken from others in arriving where I now am. It's time to be a giver. I am fulfilled when I'm able to help someone else, whether it's a friend or a non-accidental meeting with someone like you. It takes time to give, but that time returns a purposeful and active life for me.

"I perceive you have abundant time on your hands that feeds your depression. I'd be depressed too if I just sat around all day. But look at today. I've wheeled myself around Lake Calhoun and enjoyed being around people. That takes two hours. Then I ran into you, which happens more often than you may think, and there's another hour. When I get back home, I've had a really meaningful half day."

"How did you know I have abundant time on my hands and am depressed?" I ventured. "You've never met me before."

Daniel replied, "I have the gift of discernment—a still, small voice within that reveals, 'Here is a snapshot of this person.'

"I had additional clues with you. You're walking around the lake by yourself, and the way you walk and the look on your face say, 'I am depressed.' You admittedly have only one close friend. You were not reluctant to sit down and talk to me, which tells me you are not on a tight agenda. Let me discern further. You are recently retired, don't have many acquaintances, and you don't have any hobbies or outlets to keep you busy. Am I right?"

Daniel was able to read me with minimal information. If that's what the gift of discernment was, he had it. "You are exactly right," I answered. "I don't have to say anything, and you know the condition I'm living in."

Daniel and I talked for an hour more. I explained to him the shortcomings of my life that I had confessed to Dave. I could hardly believe I was that open with him. What was it about Daniel?

He responded by encouraging me. "You have another purpose waiting for you. You haven't found it yet, but you will. Realize this meeting with me is a step in recovering your mental health. I'm not going to propose we meet again by appointment. However, you walk around Lake Calhoun and I wheel around it; when you need to talk to me again, we'll run into each other."

"And not by accident," I said.

"Indeed, not by accident," Daniel answered.

I had half the lake left to walk around, and my thoughts were suddenly more focused. I reflected on Daniel having such a full life and my having such an empty life. If he could pull himself out of depression, there must be hope for me.

I examined in my mind everything Daniel had said. If only I had something to write on. I'd need to enter the discussion with Daniel in my "Struggle Journal" when I got home. By this time I reached the food building on the northeast side of the lake and realized it was past noon. I was hungry, and I had not experienced hunger since the depression hit last Saturday. Daniel was the difference.

I had a hot dog, chips, and a fountain soda. I actually enjoyed sitting on a park bench, feeling the sun's warmth on my face, and watching people walk by. Light from Daniel had penetrated my darkness. This was the best I had felt since last Friday.

From the food building, I walked the rest of the way around the lake until I reached my car by the softball field. I sat on a players' bench alongside the first base line, which afforded me a good view of a group of young people playing lacrosse in center and left field. I knew they were playing lacrosse from the equipment they were using, but I didn't know anything about the game.

As I watched them having fun and enjoying the camaraderie of a team game, I compared myself to them, my lifestyle versus theirs. An unwelcome thought came crashing into my mind. I had outlived my meaningfulness. The way of life these young men and women were enjoying was never to be mine again.

I instantly forgot everything Daniel had explained to me; my depression was as deep as it was when I started my walk around the lake. The more I watched the lacrosse game, the more I compared myself to the young players. After the game, they'd probably go somewhere for a beer and hamburgers. Then some would go home and prepare for their evening plans. Others would start the evening agenda without going home first.

Oh, joyful youth, you embrace all the richness of life and dream longingly of all that is before you. When I dreamed of what was before me, I felt the pangs of depression. When I meditated on the life of meaning and purpose that I had lived, knowing that it was all in my past, I sank into darkness. And why shouldn't I? My life as I knew it was over, and there was nothing to replace it. I sat on the bench for about an hour, thinking dark thoughts as I continued to watch the game.

***

As I'm in the Minneapolis library, typing this story on my laptop, I cringe at how destructive comparing myself to others was at this point in my life. I had felt so marvelous talking to Daniel, so filled with light and hope. And then it was gone in a flash. A person who has never been depressed might wonder how someone can go from great hope to great despair so quickly. A person who has suffered from depression is all too familiar with hope that is strong one moment and dashed the next. It is a fragile life—that of being depressed.

The spirit of depression could overwhelm me at any time, like a riptide grabs a swimmer and drags him out to sea. I didn't know it then, but a new stage of depression was living within me and could take over at any time, whatever the circumstances, whatever the situation. My situational depression put such stress on my whole body that a chemical imbalance developed in my brain, which dropped me into a pit at unlikely times and places, like sitting on that bench watching lacrosse players. It was a cycle of up and down, mostly down, that defined how I saw the world. For moments I could escape it, but it was always there by my side, waiting to take over.

***

The lacrosse players finished their game and left the field quickly to embark on their next adventure. How I envied them. They had something to do. When they disappeared, I was the only one left. My mind went back to Daniel's message; yet, at the same time, I was thinking about the lacrosse players.

"Stop!" I yelled in my mind. "Stop thinking about comparing yourself to those who are young. That season of your life is over." I said "Stop" loud enough to surprise myself. "Stop! Stop! Stop! Stop comparing yourself to others."

If I wanted to compare myself to anyone, it should be to Daniel. Daniel couldn't play lacrosse. Daniel couldn't do many things. Yet Daniel was happy and fulfilled.

That thought brought me peace. I relaxed on the bench and took in the beauty of the softball field and the lake beyond. Ah, yes, softball and baseball. Games of rules and predictability. It always made me glad to watch a good baseball game. Even a bad one. And the Cubs had plenty of bad games. I thought I'd ask Daniel when I saw him again what it was like to play major league baseball. He said it wasn't an accident we met; it wouldn't be an accident when we met again.

Wednesday was hard. It was a dreary day, with rain and fog, and a temperature more like October than July. I cloistered myself in the condo all day, and the weather mirrored my mood—dreary and depressing. I forced myself to eat breakfast and retreated to my reclining chair for three hours. My mind was whirling with the comparison of what my life had been and what it now was. How foolish to spend so much time at my business and so little time at home. How foolish not to be involved in my children's lives. Little wonder they didn't want to have anything to do with me. What a blunder to divorce Kathleen, the only person I loved. I was doomed to depression. I deserved it.

***

I dropped my head on the library desk as I wrote these words. Yes, I loved Kathleen early in our marriage. But after a few years, the only person I cared about was myself. I buried that fact deep in my subconscious because I couldn't face a man devoid of love. My self-love and coldness to others was shielded from confronting me directly, but not shielded from poisoning my mind in many subtle ways. I could think outside my self-centeredness for short periods of time, but eventually it came back to what was best for me. This was my undoing and kept me in an unreal world for 40 years.

If only I could scream "Stop!" to all my ruminations, to all my comparisons, to all my looking backward instead of forward. But I was so depressed that my mind, soul, spirit, and bodily energy were shut down.

***

I stumbled about the condo, tried to read the paper with the concentration of a four-year-old, and stood before the living-room window overlooking France Avenue, gazing out but seeing nothing. I dreaded the arrival of lunchtime. I forced myself to eat a sandwich of deli meat and some fruit. I finished eating and choked almost to the point of throwing up. I went quickly from the kitchen to my recliner and flopped into it for another four hours. As I lay prone with my hands folded on my chest like a corpse in a casket, I considered the same dark thoughts in my mind over and over and over again.

Those thoughts went from dark to darker to darkest. I imagined I had another massive heart attack and died in the chair I was lying in. It's tough to fathom that thought could consume two hours, but it did.

I experienced in my mind a jolt of pain in my chest, the pain spreading out to my arms, a mixture of panic and relief, a quick last gasp of breath, and then growing cold as I left the emotional pain of this earth.

From life to death covered what would be less than a minute in real time but more than 30 minutes in imagination time. It was a panorama that I replayed repeatedly in my mind.

How long would I lie dead before someone found me? Dave said he'd call next week. He'd eventually call the condo office to check up on me after only voice greetings. I've never failed to return a call to Dave within the day he called.

What a stench there would be after my being dead six days. Who'd arrange for my funeral? Where would I be buried? What would Kathleen and the children think? What would the people in Chicago think when they read the obituary? Would there be anyone sorry I died besides Dave? All these thoughts worked through my mind repeatedly, with my imagining various scenarios to the questions.

Would Daniel come to the funeral? I expected my wife and children would attend because it would be expected of them. What would they think as they looked into the casket? Would they forgive all my mistakes and love me again. Or would they be as cold to me as I was to them. Both scenes went through my mind, with different words spoken each time and different looks on their faces—sometimes sadness, sometimes a blank look, sometimes warmth. My thoughts grew darker and darker until I yelled in desperation, "Stop!" It didn't work. I kept revisiting the heart attack and the funeral because it was the only thing that brought me some hope of peace. I grasped at any means to end the mental pain. Oblivion would suit me just fine.

The fatal heart attack was my favorite fantasy, followed closely by car crashes, cancer diagnoses, and criminals with handguns. When I played an interior movie of a doctor informing me I had pancreatic cancer, I shook his hand and thanked him.

Suppertime was the third dreadful time of day. I didn't have an appetite or desire to fix myself a meal. It had stopped raining, so I walked to the grocery store with a deli where I could buy a full meal. I ordered lasagna, garlic bread sticks, and a glass of milk. I chose to eat it there to escape the recliner for a short time. I ate slowly, trying not to choke on the food, and experienced a perverse sense of joy when I was finished. This was the last meal I'd have to endure that day.

The remainder of the evening I watched the Minnesota Twins on television. The closer I approached going to bed, the better I felt. I went to sleep within an hour, and had restful sleep until four in the morning, at which time I laid in bed for another four hours, sometimes dozing off but mainly awake. I didn't want to get up at four. The day was long enough as it was. Yesterday seemed like 80 hours.

Thursday was a carbon copy of Wednesday. It was raining again, and the dreariness of the day fueled the depression in my soul. Amidst the thoughts I had Thursday, most of which were like Wednesday, came this new one: How can I keep going on like this? How can I survive one more day? Is this what the rest of my life is going to be like? Constant depression until the day I die? I can't live this way. I can't go on. I was filled with despair.

I wanted to call Dave. Oh, how I wanted to call Dave! But I promised myself I wouldn't. In the afternoon, I forced myself to attend a movie showing at the theater below my condo. It was a comedy. Others in the theater were laughing heartily, but I wasn't. My goal was to stop being a recluse without reprieve, and in that I was successful.

Friday the sun shone warmly again, and I drove to Lake Calhoun for a walk. Seeing and feeling the sun bolstered my emotions, so I was not in depression as deeply as the last two days. Besides, I hoped I'd encounter Daniel again. I needed to talk to him.

***

Halfway around the lake, there was Daniel heading at me in his wheelchair. "Want to talk?" asked Daniel.

I leaped at the invitation. "I sure do. I suppose this is one of those non-accidents."

"I suppose that is true," responded Daniel.

***

A few months later, I found out from Daniel that our first meeting wasn't as coincidental as it seemed. Tuesday wasn't the first day he had seen me walking around the lake. He told me he usually traveled the way I went, counterclockwise, and I would pass him along the way without noticing him. I was predictable with the time I went walking— usually starting around nine in the morning. On the Tuesday we first met, Daniel proceeded clockwise around the lake because he sensed I needed help. He could tell by the way I walked that I was carrying a suitcase packed with trouble.

***

We found a bench nearby. I sat down, and Daniel faced me in his wheelchair. "What's on your mind today?" asked Daniel.

"Let's talk baseball," I said.

"My favorite subject," said Daniel with obvious excitement in his voice. "Where do you want to start?"

"What was it like to play major league baseball?" I ventured.

His face lit up. "It was a dream come true. Ever since I was a little kid watching Mickey Mantle and Hank Aaron, I knew I wanted to play ball in the major leagues. I practiced as if I were already a professional player. That was my secret. My dad pitched to me in the park down the street until it became so dark I couldn't see the ball. He paid for a batting coach when I was ten years old. That's when I learned a swing that was so simple and effective that I never went into a slump. I only played two years in the minors before I was brought up to the big show. My first year I batted just under .300. The next four years I batted over .300 and was in contention for most valuable player in the American League my last year, the year of the accident."

"That's what I wanted to discuss with you, Daniel," I said. "How could you dedicate yourself to being a major league baseball player, live out your dream, and then never play again? How could you just forget about all that and live a totally different life in a wheelchair?"

"Do you remember what I told you last Tuesday?" said Daniel. "It wasn't easy at first. I felt like I had been dropped into a deep hole and could see nothing but blackness. Through a year of counseling and antidepressant medication, I finally came to a point where I saw my life up to the accident as a book that was closed, and I was living in a different book. I was healed emotionally. I could look back into the first book and enjoy talking about baseball and my life in it without dropping even into a shallow hole, because that book is not the one I am living in any longer. My present book portrays me as a paraplegic and my life is one of helping other people. I keep myself in good shape and have a group of friends I can relate to just as I am.

"Everyone has a handicap or two, Mitch. Mine shows. Yours doesn't, but it's a worse handicap than I have. I'd rather have two legs that don't work than be in depression. In my opinion, with the experience of having been there, nothing is worse than the hidden handicap of mental anguish, and that's where you are. You probably dread getting up every day. I look forward to waking up every morning. My days are full. I'd never change places with you, not the way you are right now. But you'll change, as I did. There's hope for you. Meeting with me these two times is part of your healing process. You need to see all 40 of your Chicago years as a book that's closed. Start living in a new book without depression and feeling sorry for yourself. You can't change books in the snap of a finger, but you can put transformation as a goal before you."

We talked at least an hour more, and I listened most of the time. I realized Daniel had real-life insight for me because of his experience with depression, and I needed to hear it. Waving good-bye, I continued around the lake one way and Daniel the other.

I could hardly wait to reach the softball field to think about my life being separated into different books. I picked up the pace. The concept excited me when Daniel presented it, not in my head this time where most ideas landed, but in my heart.

***

I sat on the first-base-side bench again, a metal bench that was dirty from the rain of the past two days and years of rough usage. I pulled a newspaper out of a nearby trashcan and brushed off the dirt and dampness. I was ready to consider the books of my life.

Daniel had two books that encompassed his life. After much thought, I came up with three books for mine. The first book was *Young Mitch*, which covered the cherished years of my youth up to graduating from high school. The second book was *Chicago*, which covered 40 sordid years I wish were different. The third book was *Back in Minnesota*, which was yet to be written.

As I thought about the three books, I contemplated closing the *Chicago* book and living in the *Back in Minnesota* book.

Daniel had to forge his way into his second book by extensive counseling, medication, and the "Stop!" technique. The first part of that second book was a terrible struggle. But as the book progressed there gradually evolved the new and improved Daniel, handicapped but living a life of fulfillment and meaning. My hope was to follow the same progression in my final book—a struggle at the beginning but meaningful and fulfilling at the end. Daniel told me my new book would eventually contain no depression. Oh, how I wished that would soon be true.

Daniel was living with a handicap that would follow him his whole life. I was dealing with a hidden handicap—depression—that hopefully would not follow me my whole life. My final book didn't seem to parallel Daniel's final book. It was confusing. Darkness of doubt snuffed out my light.

***

Saturday and Sunday were two more hard days. I kept thinking about my mental affliction and what a mess I'd made of my life. The dark fantasy of a second heart attack returned, as well as other ways I could escape my misery—the armed thief, a truck crossing the center line, pancreatic cancer, and other such morbid events that happen to someone someplace almost every day.

I didn't want to bother Dave the first two days of his vacation. Dave said he'd call me. It would be tomorrow. It had to be tomorrow. I couldn't cope with my depression one more day.

CHAPTER 7
From the North Shore of Lake Superior

I have come to a point in my story that was critical for my emotional healing, but I wasn't writing in my struggle journal then. I was barely able to record my thoughts and activities the last week of July that were in the previous chapter. During the first week of August, I didn't have the energy to pick up a pen.

A few weeks after Dave returned from his North Shore trip, he mentioned that he journaled all travels since the kids left home, and the North Shore trip was more detailed than usual because of his interactions with me.

In the first week of August 2007, exactly two years since the North Shore trip, I asked Dave if he would write this chapter using all his notes and recall. He hesitated because of some personal comments about me and discussions with his wife about me—none of which he had shared with me.

Unhesitatingly, I said that was exactly what I wanted. I doubted anything in his journal would offend me. I was in pitiful shape during the last week of July and the first week of August 20005, and it was necessary to receive someone else's perspective on that time. Dave agreed to tell all.

***

On July 29, 2005, Cathy and I left for Duluth, known as the gateway to the North Shore of Lake Superior. We came to Interstate 35 above the Minneapolis-St. Paul loop and stayed on that road all the way. It took a little over four hours because we had to stop at our favorite restaurant in Hinckley for a late breakfast and some mouth-watering bakery goods to accompany us up north.

***

As we reached the crest of Interstate 35, the freeway started descending into Duluth. Cathy said, "Oh, Dave, this has always been a favorite view; it's so beautiful."

She was right. Looking over the entire city of Duluth, Duluth Harbor, and the city of Superior to the east is a sight that brings a gasp to most people when they first see it.

"I remember the first time we saw this," I remarked—"our honeymoon in August of 1969. Now 36 years later, it brings the same sense of joy it did then."

Looking at Cathy, I said, "It's like our marriage. I love you as much now as I did 36 years ago. No, that's not true. I love you more."

"And I love you more," responded Cathy. "Seeing how involved you were in raising our three children, how much you have loved your parents and mine, how concerned you have been for other people, including your friend Mitch, make me glow inside. How blessed we were to find each other."

"Speaking of Mitch, I wonder how he's doing," I thought out loud. "I told him I'd call him once we reached the Nanibijou Lodge on Monday."

***

Cathy and I spent Friday afternoon in the Waterfront District of Duluth. We observed a large ore boat enter the harbor from Lake Superior and pass through the canal and the Aerial Lift Bridge. This was another sight we never tired of. We bought snacks from a kiosk on the street and headed for a hike on the Lakewalk, which runs alongside the shore of Lake Superior. This gave us an uninterrupted chance to talk.

"How do you think Mitch is faring?" questioned Cathy.

Although Cathy had not yet met Mitch, she obviously knew I was spending considerable time with him, in person and on the phone. She also knew life presently was exceedingly hard for him.

"You know there are details I can't reveal to you," I answered. "Eventually, you'll get to know him personally and find out some of those details. In the meantime..."

"In the meantime," Cathy said smiling, "you are the counselor and he is the counselee. I know that's not really the case. He's a good friend that you're helping adjust to life after retirement. You still have the life blood of a counselor running through you, and I'm proud of you for sticking to the code of conduct you committed to when you first started counseling."

I thanked Cathy for trusting me in what I could and couldn't tell her. "Mitch has some terribly troublesome issues he needs to work through, and I'm acutely worried about him. He's teetering on the edge of getting better or getting much worse. From the first time I saw him at our 40th class reunion, I have reckoned he's in a depression that, on a scale of 1-5, with 1 being terrifyingly depressed and 5 being normal, is about a 4 and sometimes a 3. A 4 is moderate depression at the low half and mild depression at the top half, and a 3 is severe depression. He's a strong 4 when he's with me, but when he's in his condo he quickly slips back into the low 4s and sometimes the 3s. I can hear it in his voice.

"I'm worried that without contact with me, he may have slipped into the 2s, and that's major depression where a person can't function. He hasn't talked to me for just over a week. I'm hoping he has worked through some things we talked about, but my experience with depression tells me he's close to needing intervention to survive.

"I'm planning to call him Monday when we're settled into Nanibijou. It may sound cruel, but I feel a need to see how bad things get for him after two weekends and the week in-between on his own. Often, a person has to hit bottom before he's willing to do what it takes to get better."

Cathy and I spent the rest of our hike on the Lakewalk talking about our kids and parents and some of the activities we were involved in together and separately. It was a bonding time for us. When we finished walking, we had a great meal at Grandma's restaurant in Canal Park and went to our hotel for a good night's sleep.

Mitch was never far from my mind. Was I doing the right thing in not calling him until Monday? How desperate was he? Should I call him now? I prayed on it and sensed in my spirit that waiting for Monday was the right thing to do. With that, my mind eased and I slept peacefully.

***

The next morning we had breakfast at our motel and headed out on Interstate 35 until we got to Highway 2 and Spirit Mountain. This was a tradition of ours—to take the Skyline Parkway, which stretches 25 miles from Spirit Mountain, overlooking the port city of Duluth and offering incredibly beautiful views of the harbor and the endless shoreline of Lake Superior. We took advantage of a hiking trail to obtain some exercise and see the beauty of God's nature that surrounds Duluth. From Hawk Ridge, we drove on an extension of the Parkway via the Seven Bridges Road and returned to Duluth proper at Lester Park. From there we dropped down to East Superior Street, had lunch, and drove to Gooseberry Falls.

***

We took old Highway 61 instead of the interstate, a scenic alternative that closely follows the North Shore. We had an hour to talk.

"Something's bothering you," said Cathy. "You've been withdrawn all morning."

"I can't help thinking about Mitch," I responded. "I have a feeling he's not doing well. I wish he'd call me. I don't want to be an alarmist and call him."

"Maybe you should call him right now," suggested Cathy. "You could talk to him about our trip and then casually ask how he's doing."

I waited a long time before answering. Cathy was used to my "thinking time." If I thought Mitch was a threat to himself, I'd follow Cathy's advice. But I was committed to following God's leading, and that was to call Monday morning.

"I would love to call Mitch right now. I wanted to call him yesterday just as badly.

"I don't know if I can explain this well, but as a counselor I developed an interior compass related to timing. Early in my career, when I felt I needed to take action, I did it right away, only to realize later I should have waited. Gradually, I was able to discern not only what action to take with a particular student but when to take it. My success rate with students climbed when I combined the right action with the right timing.

"It's like Jesus waiting two days before traveling to raise Lazarus from the dead instead of healing him when he was still alive. If I intervened now, I might not be bringing about what's best for Mitch in the long run. I sense he needs to hit bottom before he's willing to do what needs to be done for healing to take place. I have a strong insight that I shouldn't call him before Monday morning."

My decision to wait was reinforced when I found out from Mitch later that he was hitting bottom that weekend. His depression had moved from a low 3 down to a 2. At a 2, a person is on the road to a mental hospital if that intensity of depression continues. He never descended into a 1, which is a terrifying and surreal territory where suicide becomes an acceptable option. Even a 2 that goes on too long can produce thoughts of suicide. A 2 is a level of depression needing intervention quickly before it sets too deeply into the brain and relegates healing into a difficult and often long-term process.

***

Coming up quickly was the Gooseberry River Bridge. We were fortunate to find a space in a parking lot a short walk to the visitor center at the base of the falls. There was a crowd of people in the visitor center. Outside the center, Gooseberry Falls was packed with people romping around in the rocks and taking pictures from every conceivable angle that a picture of the falls could be taken. Some people climbed up a bank on the north side of the Upper Falls to get their picture taken from below. It was dangerous if they went too far up.

We spent three hours at Gooseberry Falls State Park and then it was on to Tofte, where we stayed the night at one of the storied resorts along the North Shore. We spent the rest of Saturday afternoon and early evening lounging on a deck overlooking Lake Superior. After that was a late supper, some reading time, and an early bedtime.

***

Sunday morning Cathy and I went to church in Tofte and found a small restaurant for breakfast. It was about an hour's drive to Naniboujou, but we made a few stops along the way. At Lutsen, we drove a mile up Highway 61 to The Caribou Trail. We walked up to the Superior Hiking Trail and hiked one hour through the forest. During that time, we forgot the troubles of the world, Mitch's difficulties, and our own challenges. We observed the beauty of nature and experienced the quietness of being alone. It was a God-moment, and better than the sermon we heard that morning.

"It's so peaceful here," said Cathy. "It makes you want to stay here a long, long time, alone with your thoughts and nature. It gives me a sense of insignificance that is refreshing and joyful. We don't require all the striving we engage in. If we just relaxed, most things would get done in God's timing." I nodded my head to Cathy's observations and had nothing to add.

***

After Duluth, Grand Marais was our favorite city along the North Shore. Grand Marais is a city where the past meets the modern world and both live in respect of each other. After our recent hike, we were hungry for lunch. There are some unique cafes in Grand Marais, and we found one of them. On the table to one side of us, two bearded and grizzly men were talking about buying traps and provisions to resume their trapping. On the table to the other side sat three artists discussing Vincent Van Gogh's ingenious device that he used to put objects in perspective, establish vanishing points, and make his drawings look as realistic as a photograph. Van Gogh's instrument was a rarity, so each one of them explained the technique they used for capturing Lake Superior and the boats in the harbor with an accuracy that could only be equaled by a camera.

One artist went over to the two trappers and asked if she could sketch them. They were flattered and agreed to pose for her after lunch.

From the café, Cathy and I walked over to Broadway Avenue to visit our favorite place in Grand Marais — a large, rustic general store made out of logs. This store sells whatever you can think of and several things you've never thought of. From the general store, we walked down to the lake along the east pier to a rocky bar that extends east of the harbor out to Artist's Point.

All the while in Grand Marais, Mitch occupied my mind. My experience with depression told me Mitch was suffering greatly at this very moment. He had more issues to deal with than any one person should have, and I expect he was overwhelmed with all he had confessed to me. It was a dangerous time for Mitch. I've seen people recover fully from depression after hitting a bottom point. And I've seen people that never recover, and only survive by relieving their symptoms with medication for the rest of their lives.

I was not about to let Mitch lose his battle with depression. He needed medication to stabilize before he could start putting his life together. He needed to work with a psychologist to discover the root causes of the depression and the real issues, whatever they may be. The third leg of the stool necessitated dealing with his spiritual being. That was my responsibility. It had to be a comprehensive approach—body, soul, and spirit. Mitch was not going to go under on my watch. Tomorrow I would call Mitch. I was praying all the pieces would fall into place in God's timing. I was anxious to make that call.

***

Leaving Grand Marais, we reached Naniboujou Lodge in 15 minutes. What a beautiful sight—a lodge that has remained the same since 1929 and is on the National Register of Historic Places. The original cypress siding still covered the exterior. We entered the dining room and were awed by its striking appearance. The walls and ceiling were painted in a Cree Indian style. A massive fireplace on one wall was built of two hundred tons of native rock that came from the beach. It was as impressive a restaurant as you'd ever want to see, and the food was as delicious as the atmosphere was beautiful.

The Naniboujou Lodge is unlike any place we've ever stayed. There are no TVs in the rooms and no telephones. The only land phone is in the front-desk area. Cell phones have made the outside world more accessible than in the past, but many people turn off their phones and enjoy the peace and quiet the lodge was built to offer. There are no two rooms exactly the same. We had a room on the West Wing with a queen bed and no fireplace.

***

The next morning, Cathy and I went down to the restaurant. I had a Naniboujou omelet and Cathy had an orange pecan waffle. When we finished eating, Cathy went outside to sit in one of the Adirondack chairs by the lake, and I went to the upper deck to make a phone call to Mitch.

***

I took a deep breath, prayed a short prayer, and dialed Mitch's cell phone. He answered almost immediately. That was a sign he was waiting for my call.

I started the conversation. "How are you doing Mitch? How has the last week and two days been?"

"Not well," stammered Mitch. "It's like I was hit by a bus the Saturday morning after we last talked, and dragged along until last Friday. This Saturday I woke up even more depressed. Sunday and this morning were frightful. Dave, I'm at the end of my rope. I can't go on one more day. I'm ready to come apart."

Mitch was talking fast and the strain of emotional pain was in his voice. Not being able to go on one more day was a desperate cry for help. I had to arrange major intervention quickly. He was at a 2.

"Are you thinking about committing suicide?" I asked.

Mitch replied, "I can understand why people in depression commit suicide, but there's something in me that resists that siren call. However, I think about death much of the day and how pleasant it would be to have a massive heart attack and be done with it."

I followed up: "How is your ability to function? Can you eat and sleep and buy groceries and things like that?"

"Dave, I've spent most of my time sitting in my recliner going over and over in my mind the mistakes I've made, comparing myself to people who are happy and not depressed, and wondering if this is how I'll finish out the remainder of my days. I force myself to eat and dragged myself to the grocery store on Sunday to get a prepared lunch and supper because I didn't feel like making anything. I'm sleeping five hours a night at best. I'm a mess, Dave. I'm just a mess."

"I'm sorry I can't be there for you in person, Mitch. But you're in no condition to wait until I return. You need relief now. What do you think about taking medication to diminish your symptoms?"

"I've not been one for taking medication," replied Mitch. "I thought about seeing a doctor for depression medication this Saturday, but I buried that thought. I'm afraid if I start taking medication I'll never get off it. But if you feel I should take something, I trust you're looking out for what's best for me."

If Mitch had not hit bottom, he would have resisted medication.

"Good," I said. "I'm glad you trust me. If you were to try to see a psychiatrist, which is what I recommend, it would take three or four weeks for an appointment. You don't have that kind of time in your condition. Could you drive a few miles to Minneapolis to see a psychiatrist friend of mine? I could call him now and get back to you."

I made the phone call to my friend Zeke. His parents had named him Ezekiel, but they were the only ones who knew his real name. From the time he started first grade, the name he used as his given name was Zeke. As it ended up, Zeke had a meeting coming up at 11 a.m. that he said he could cancel to see Mitch.

"Things have worked out for you, my friend," I said enthusiastically when I called Mitch back. " Zeke can see you at 11 a.m., which is one hour from now. His clinic is 20 minutes from your condo. I'll give you directions."

***

Mitch called me shortly after his session with Zeke, while I was having lunch with Cathy in the lodge dining room. He told me he had called my friend Dr. Hartman out of proper respect, but Zeke said to call him Zeke.

"I spent one hour with Zeke in his office, giving him my health history and the litany of events leading up to my depression.

"Zeke told me I had some heavy things I'd gone through, and he wanted to start me on a common antidepressant—a Serotonin-Norepinephrine Reuptake Inhibitor, SNRI for short, to take the edge off my pain and move me back into a functioning mode. "

"He said, 'I want to be honest with you. Different people react differently to different medications. The SNRI I'm prescribing will make you feel better, won't make any difference, or will make you feel worse. The medication may take up to four weeks to reach its full effect, but you'll know in two or three days if it's making you worse. If it does, I want you to call me right away, and we'll jump to Plan B.

"'I also want you to keep track of the depth of your depression on a scale of 1-5 so we can both determine where you are at any given period of time. A 5 is normal. A 4 is feeling uncomfortable but still able to function; an upper 4 is mild depression and a lower 4 is moderate depression. A 3 is severe depression in which you have significant problems with thinking, eating, sleeping, and socializing; it is where hopelessness sets in and you just want to cry. A 2 is major depression that is not sustainable without some sort of relief. Thoughts of death arrive at this stage as a means of escaping the extreme anguish of the psyche. A 1 is a depression so dreadful and deep that, without intervention, a person considers suicide, and either embraces it or lives a life more horrific than anything the worst physical suffering can bring.'"

The reader will remember I explained that same rating system to Cathy as I was describing the stages Mitch was experiencing. If my system seems similar to Zeke's, it's because Zeke taught it to me years ago. A refresher from Mitch was helpful because I was missing some of the explanations for the various numbers. I told Mitch that Zeke had shared that rating system with me, and Mitch could use the same numbers with me.

I looked outside, and it was sunny and filled with hope, like Mitch's voice after meeting with Zeke. That hope alone was enough to lift him out of the worst depths of his depression. I prayed that Zeke had prescribed the right medication. Not that I questioned Zeke, but I knew from experience that selecting the right depression medication is like playing roulette. The doctor chooses what he or she thinks is the best medication and hopes for a good outcome. It's not an exact science by any means.

***

Tuesday morning we set out on a long hike into the Judge C.R. Magney State Park and up the Brule River to the Devil's Kettle. Devil's Kettle is a very mysterious place on the Upper Falls in which half the Brule River goes over the falls and half disappears into a churning cauldron that has eluded all attempts to discover where the water empties. We were planning to spend most of the day in the park area.

On one of the side trails, I found a bench and asked Cathy if she could head down the path while I called Mitch. She knew I needed privacy and proceeded to a rest area a quarter mile away. I watched as she went and was overwhelmed with love for her. Lord, how did I deserve someone as wonderful as Cathy?

***

"Mitch, is the medication helping?"

"I feel better because I have hope that I won't have to be like I was yesterday morning for the rest of my life. I believe this is the right medicine. I've moved from a 2 to a 3, a high 3 I'd say."

I also wanted this to be the right medicine for Mitch, but I knew there was often a sense of euphoria that came from taking anything when one is in Mitch's condition, even a placebo.

"Fortunately, Mitch, depression is treatable. Once you find what is effective for you, the goal of treatment is relief from your symptoms until you are healed and whole again."

I did not want to complicate matters by telling Mitch he also needed to deal with his mind, will, and emotions (soul) with a psychologist, and work with a spiritual director for his spiritual state. Medicine is a stabilizer of chemical imbalance, but it doesn't deal with the source of depression. A comprehensive approach is needed for full recovery. However, with some people, a chemical imbalance *is* the source of depression, especially for those who are bipolar. Even in these situations, a comprehensive approach is beneficial to cope with the depression.

The rest of the phone conversation was Mitch's wanting to know about our trip so far, which reinforced he was feeling better. Yesterday, Mitch could only think of himself. I told Mitch I'd call him tomorrow morning to see how he was doing.

***

Wednesday morning Cathy and I went back to Grand Marais. We found a coffee shop not far from Lake Superior and discussed our plans for the day. Grand Marais has an active community theater, and there was a production showing that night at 7 p.m. We decided to relax at Naniboujou that afternoon, have an early supper, and return to Grand Marais for the play. When we both had enough coffee, Cathy said, "Dave, why don't you call Mitch from the bench outside the general store, and I'll go visit Artist's Point to see what's happening with the art crowd."

I thanked her for her thoughtfulness for Mitch. "Yes, I am anxious to find out how Mitch is doing today."

***

"How's the battle today, Mitch?"

I noticed a quiver in his voice. "Dave, I'm not doing as

well as yesterday. It's probably the medication starting its work. I've slipped down to a low 3."

Mitch was trying to speak with hope, but his voice told me the medication might not be working. The euphoria of yesterday was replaced by the edges of fear.

"Dave, I'm using a technique that Daniel taught me."

"Tell me about Daniel," I responded, for it was the first time I heard that name.

"I'll tell you about him later. Briefly, he's a man in a wheelchair who used to play major league baseball until he was crippled in a car accident. I learned a bookful from him in two chance meetings around lake Calhoun.

"He showed me how to say 'Stop' to negative thoughts. I've been saying 'Stop' over and over this morning.

"Dave, I'm afraid. I feel there are major changes to make in my life to be healed of depression. And I keep thinking it's too late in the afternoon to make those changes."

"We've been over that before," I answered as kindly as I could. "It's never too late to make changes. Each moment in your life is a chance to totally turn around and start all over again. I'll give you an example. A few weeks ago I was playing golf with a couple of friends. I shot a 46 on the front side. I told myself I could shoot a 34 on the back side for an even 80. I didn't shoot that 34, but I did score a 37, and that was nine strokes better than the front side. You see, on a practical basis, I changed my golf game around. I started all over again. You can do the same with your life. It's not going to happen in a day like my golf round. It will be a process, and I'll be there to see you through."

I was not hard on Mitch for being stuck on "too late in the afternoon." It was yet another indicator he had fallen back into a deeper depression than yesterday. Some people become frustrated with loved ones who are depressed. They tell them something one day, and the next day they feel they weren't heard the day before, but that's not the case at all. The depressed person's fears overwhelm the truth. A person in depression needs to hear the truth over and over and over again.

Mitch responded to me with a quiet and humble voice. "Yes we've been over that before, but I keep going back to the negative. Thanks for reminding me that it's not too late in the afternoon. I feel hope when I talk to you. I don't know what I'd do without you."

The rest of the conversation focused on Mitch's explaining his fears and my reassuring him they would not be realized. I suggested he go for a walk around Lake Calhoun and take in a movie to get his mind off himself. Mitch agreed to those two suggestions.

***

Mitch called me at ten Thursday morning. I was in an Adirondack chair down by the lake. "How are you doing today, Mitch?"

"This will be a conversation you were not expecting," answered Mitch. "I thought I was going to die this morning. I plummeted down into the 2s and may even have entered into the 1s. I feel like I'm losing my mind."

There was an urgency and fear in Mitch's voice I had not heard before. He didn't think I was anticipating such a call, but I was not as surprised as he thought.

"What happened this morning?" I questioned.

Mitch's speech was slurred and racing, as if he didn't have control of himself. "I woke up this morning at four in a panic. I took the third dose of my SNRI, and the panic became worse. I've never been close to anything like this in my whole life. First I was afraid I would die. Then I was afraid I wouldn't die. I was desperate. I couldn't sit still, so I left my condo and walked down 50th Street for two miles, turned around, and walked back home. I collapsed in my recliner, still in awful panic. When I looked at my watch, it was 7 a.m., and I was paralyzed with fear and anxiety.

"I thought if there were a hell, this would be it. All by

myself in total panic for eternity. That made me more afraid. I wanted to call you, Dave, but I couldn't even pick up the phone. I was terrified."

I had seen this too many times before. Mitch's depression had descended to a scale of 1. One was a state of unrelenting, horrific depression that struck terror into one's soul. It's where suicide seems the only way out. It's where reality and reason disappear.

Mitch continued. "I had dark thoughts of suicide that frightened me. Suicide seemed so reasonable, but I couldn't go through with it…. I didn't know what to do. It was like a surrealistic dream I was living in. When I went into the bathroom and looked in the mirror, I didn't recognize myself. This went on for three hours, and then the panic lifted. I immediately called you."

I was quite sure Mitch was experiencing a chemical reaction to the medication he was on, and he'd be in and out of panic all day without intervention. The roulette wheel had landed on the wrong medication.

"Mitch, listen closely to me. I'm going to call Zeke because you wouldn't be able to get through to him, and I'm going to ask him to call you. Can you stay put for the next hour or so?"

Mitch said he could.

I was able to reach Zeke within minutes and covered with him the state Mitch was floundering in. Zeke agreed it was most likely a chemical reaction to the medication. He said he'd call Mitch immediately.

Mitch called me an hour later.

"Dave, this will be a much different conversation than the last one we had. The panic was again creeping into me—I was back to a 2—when the phone rang. It was Zeke. He listened to what had happened this morning and said, 'I want you to stop taking the SNRI. We need to do something immediately or the panic attacks will continue. What pharmacy do you use?'

"I told him the pharmacy on 50th street that was nearest

my condo.

"'I'll call in a prescription for a benzodiazepine I want you to take three times a day. That will stop your panic attacks and will also help with your depression. You'll feel relatively normal from the first pill. Then I want to see you after four days, when the SNRI prescription is out of your system, and we can try something else you won't react to so violently.'

"I waited ten minutes, Dave, and called the pharmacy. Zeke's new prescription was there. I almost ran back to my condo to take the first pill. He was right. Within an hour not only was the panic gone but also the depression. I felt better than I had since I came to Minnesota. I felt like my old self. I went from a 2 to a 5 in a flash."

Mitch called me again that evening. He had taken the other two pills as the day wore on, and the feeling of well-being continued.

"It's like a miracle, Dave, a miracle. This morning I was ready to die and this evening I feel like a million dollars. Thank you for being involved in my life. Thank you for helping me. I feel like a new person. Maybe this is the medication for me. Maybe I don't need to try something else."

I breathed a sigh of relief for the transformation of his body. Mitch thought this was the final destination, but it was only the first step of the journey. He had a long road ahead to be cured of his depression and anxiety.

"I'm ecstatic to hear you're feeling so great, Mitch. I have to tell you something important, though. The benzodiazepine you're taking is not a long-term solution. It's a temporary buffer drug that deals with anxiety."

"Dave, how do you pronounce benzapeen? I've never heard that word before."

"It's called ben/zo/di/az/a/peen. People familiar with that family of drugs call it a benzo. Why don't we use that term?

"You need another antidepressant you can take for six

months to a year until the chemical balance in your brain is restored. You wouldn't take a benzo that long. It's a drug like a tranquilizer that is highly addictive, the more so the longer you take it. Zeke will probably have you continue taking it until the next antidepressant he prescribes takes hold. It's not uncommon that the first antidepressant doesn't work. It's uncommon though to suffer as dramatic a reaction to it as you just did. Usually, it just won't work. Your experience will give Zeke some insight into a safer medication in four days."

"Dave, I'm fortunate to have you for a friend who can explain all this to me. I like Zeke, but I don't always understand him."

I was slowly walking the grounds of Naniboujou and watching the sun set over the hills above Lake Superior. Cathy was back in our room reading a book.

Mitch asked me if we were enjoying our trip to the North Shore and how my children and grandchildren were doing. That's when I knew for sure Mitch was temporarily out of his depression and his thinking was actually changing.

"Mitch, two days ago you thought it was too late in the afternoon to make changes, but you *have* started making significant changes in your life. Your asking me about our vacation and about my family is something very different for you. I've seen this change coming for the last couple of weeks, before you dropped into deep depression. Now that you feel normal again, you are demonstrating that, whether you think you have changed or not, you have. And I'm very pleased to see the change."

"Thank you, Dave. I guess I really have changed my thinking. It's *not* too late in the afternoon. With your help, I know I can continue making changes."

***

It was Friday morning and time for us to leave the Naniboujou Lodge and head back to Hopkins. I was ready long before Cathy, so I went to the upper deck for a last call to Mitch. "How are things this morning, Mitch?"

"Dave, they couldn't be better. I'm able to sleep again. I went to bed at ten last night and slept soundly until eight this morning. I'm back among the living. I called one of our classmates to play golf tomorrow, and he invited me over for supper after that. I'm going to a church nearby on Sunday—I'll bet that's a surprise—and I'm taking a walk around Lake Calhoun in the afternoon. I see Zeke Monday morning, and in the afternoon I'm going for another walk around Calhoun and do some meditating on the old softball bench."

"Mitch, that's great. You're starting to reach out. That's a definite sign you're better. It's been a couple of weeks since I've seen my old friend. How would you like to visit one of my favorite places in the Twin Cities on Tuesday—Minnehaha Falls? We used to bike there sometimes when we were kids. How does that sound to you?"

"Perfect," said Mitch. "Call over the weekend or Monday to set a time."

And so, during the week Cathy and I were on vacation at the North Shore of Lake Superior, Mitch was on a roller coaster ride back in Minneapolis. This was the last entry in my journaling of the August 2005 North Shore trip. I was too busy in thought about Mitch to write anything of our adventures on the way back.

CHAPTER 8
At Minnehaha Falls

The time of the Minnehaha Falls adventure was here—Tuesday, August 9, 10 a.m. After the depths of depression I had recently endured, I was feeling downright lighthearted, thanks to Dave, Zeke, and the medication. I returned to recording in my "Struggle Journal."

We parked our car in front of the park area leading to the falls and walked 50 yards to a mighty oak tree. In his best thespian voice, Dave quoted from *The Song of Hiawatha* by Henry Wadsworth Longfellow:

> By the shores of Gitche Gumee,
> By the shining Big-Sea-Water,
> Stood the wigwam of Nokomis,
> Daughter of the Moon, Nokomis.
> Dark behind it rose the forest,
> Rose the black and gloomy pine-trees,
> Rose the firs with cones upon them;
> Bright before it beat the water,
> Beat the clear and sunny water,
> Beat the shining Big-Sea-Water.

Dave surprised me with his recitation until I remembered he had memorized portions of the *Song of Hiawatha*, which he presented at an assembly in eighth grade.

As if reading my mind, Dave stated enthusiastically, "There was something in that epic poem that brought joy to me when I was a teen-ager and still makes me joyful today. Let's walk to the statue just west of the falls, the one of Hiawatha carrying Minnehaha in his arms."

And so we walked to the statue through the park that was populated by large oak trees.

We both gazed at the splendor of the statue, and Dave taught a history lesson on Hiawatha and Minnehaha.

"Just think of the contribution these two Native Americans have made to Minneapolis in names—Hiawatha Avenue, Hiawatha Golf Course, train routes in the past with the Hiawatha name, the new Hiawatha Light Rail train system, and various businesses named Hiawatha this and Hiawatha that; Minnehaha Creek, Minnehaha Parkway, Minnehaha Park, Minnehaha Academy, Minnehaha Falls, and Minnehaha Avenue, as well as many businesses with the name Minnehaha in them. Minnehaha's 'laughing waters' flow beneath the Hiawatha Avenue Bridge on a course destined for the Mississippi River and the long journey to the sea."

"Tell me more about Hiawatha and Minnehaha," I pleaded. "Were they real people? What happened to them?" Two benches were situated in front of the statue. Dave and I sat on one of them as he answered my questions.

"History indicates the Hiawatha of Longfellow's poem was really a Native American who lived much earlier than Longfellow's setting, around the 15th century, before Columbus undertook his voyage. He was a solitary warrior who brought together the Five Nations of the Iroquois of New England. An Ojibway scholar named Henry Rowe Schoolcraft made an erroneous connection between two Native American gods, and Longfellow followed the false trail Schoolcraft presented in his book on Indian legends. The fictional Hiawatha was the result. Despite being historically inaccurate, the poem inspired a love for the natural beauty of the Minnesota Forest. Remember the Grand Rounds Scenic Byway—the 53-mile bike path we used to ride on through Minneapolis, around lakes and creeks, into historic neighborhoods, and by large parks, including a loop into the Minnehaha Falls area? The path covers both the fact and fiction of the *Song of Hiawatha*. It was our goal to bike all 53 miles at once, but we never accomplished that.

"So, yes, Hiawatha was a real person, but not the one in Longfellow's poem. Minnehaha is also a fictional Native American woman whom Hiawatha courts and eventually marries.

"I'll finish my lesson with the poem itself: the *Song of Hiawatha*. There is an introduction by Longfellow, followed by 22 sections of the epic, with each section being 200 lines or more. Hiawatha was born to the daughter of Nokomis. His mother died in childbirth and Nokomis, his grandmother, took care of him. On a trip back home from meeting with his father, he came across the Dakotas, where lived the beautiful Minnehaha, the one called Laughing Water. Disregarding the warning of his grandmother that the Ojibways and the Dakotas disliked each other, Hiawatha traveled back to the Falls of Minnehaha to court the woman he loved. He took Minnehaha back to his tribe and to Nokomis, who graciously accepted her grandson's choice. Their marriage sealed a new friendship between the Ojibways and the Dakotas, for Hiawatha was a great peacemaker. When Minnehaha died of famine and fever during a cold and cruel winter, Hiawatha was devastated. Some time later, after missionaries came to his tribe, he stepped into a birch canoe and went westward to the Land of the Hereafter where he would see Minnehaha again.

"Any questions?" asked Dave.

"No," I answered. "You have presented a good background of Hiawatha and Minnehaha and what the statue in front of us is all about."

Dave put his head down for a second and then looked directly into my eyes. "How are things going for you, Mitch? How are things really going?"

I knew Dave was looking for something other than things were fine.

"I saw Zeke yesterday, and he put me on another antidepressant that also helps with anxiety. It's called a Selective Serotonin Reuptake Inhibitor. I wrote that down in Zeke's office. He says to just call it an SSRI; it has different characteristics than the SNRI that put me in a deadly tailspin. And, just like you said, he is keeping me on the benzo while the new medication takes full effect in my system. So I'm feeling fine emotionally… Dave, I'm afraid."

"Afraid of what, Mitch?"

"I'm afraid I don't have any control over my life anymore. I asked Zeke why I was mildly depressed in June and able to do things, and less than two months later I was hit with a depression so horrific that I was paralyzed emotionally. He explained the initial depression was situational to the major stressors in my life that had recently occurred: a major heart attack, divorce, retirement, and moving away from a city of 40-year familiarity. If I could have changed those situations, I wouldn't have been depressed. He gave me an example of a person who loses his job and feels worthless and depressed. Then he gets another job and the worthlessness and depression go away. But I'm still living with a damaged heart, still divorced, still retired, and still living away from a city that had become so familiar to me.

"Zeke informed me that my major stressors took a toll on my brain, like the trauma of an accident to the head, but in a different way. The stressors succeeded in altering the chemical balance of my brain, and the situational depression itself was another stressor that contributed to the trauma. The end result that happened two weeks ago was a culmination of all that stress catapulting me from situational depression into clinical depression, which needs medication to heal, not just changes in situations. Zeke explained that now, if all my stressful situations were resolved in some way, I would still be depressed. I need to be on medication until the chemical balance is restored and I'm able to resolve the stressors of my depression. Only then can I be healed. Dave, I'm afraid the resolution may not be possible, may never take place, and I'll be depressed forever, taking medication forever."

***

I remember this discussion with Dave so well. There I was mouthing the words of Zeke and had no idea what I was talking about. Depression is best understood in retrospect, when one is finally able to grasp the big picture.

Situational depression is caused by stressful situations or circumstances that have recently occurred or are hiding in your subconscious or conscious mind from the past, perhaps many years back, perhaps from early childhood.

Clinical depression is an alteration of your brain chemistry caused by the risk factors of genetics, psychological states, physical chemistry, or environment. The more risk factors you have, the greater the chance of suffering from clinical depression.

Often there is a link between the two types of depression in the areas of psychological states and environment, as there were with me.

***

I started slipping into darkness talking to Dave, and the cloudy sky, which seemed just above our heads, didn't help my mood. It was not a threatening sky, but it was gloomy.

"So now I have another illness, like my heart condition, that I don't have control over. And I don't have control over the divorce, retirement, and moving from Chicago. I keep coming back to the same thing—it's too late in the afternoon for me."

"And I keep coming back to the same thing," Dave replied, in a voice that matched my frustration. "It's not too late in the afternoon for you. I sent you to Zeke because I know he is not a psychiatrist that will medicate you for the rest of your life. He wants to get you off medication as soon as he can. But you need to heal your brain, and you need to heal your soul and spirit.

"Let's take a walk from Minnehaha Falls down to the Mississippi River. It's cloudy and gray, but the forecast doesn't predict rain. When we come back, there is something I want to talk to you about. It will take us about an hour or so to hike to the big river and back. If we were intent on speed, it could be done in half an hour. We'll go slowly and talk along the way. Before we start, let's grab something to eat at the food court back there."

We walked from the statue to the café within the park, and I noticed the vast majority of trees in the park area were large oaks. We both ordered crab cakes, the specialty of the house, and ate them at one of the green, round metal picnic tables that surrounded the café. We were fueled for our adventure.

***

Funny how some things remain so vivid in your memory. I can see Dave and I descending five flights of stairs—125 steps on the north side of Minnehaha Creek—and standing just below the falls, then crossing a bridge to the south side of the creek and starting the journey to the Mississippi River. The path was interesting, really four different trails that made up the one. It started out with gravel and rock, gentle, wide, and wending lazily through woods. The second part was a wood boardwalk three bridges down from the falls. First-time walkers would think, "What an easy route to the river." They'd be surprised when the boardwalk ended in less than five minutes and the road turned treacherous, narrow, rugged, sometimes steep, sometimes over tree branches, sometimes over ragged steps of shale, sometimes at an angle threatening to throw you into the creek. The fourth segment became smooth again near the river, with limestone and sandstone cliffs guarding the way to the Mississippi. It's still a clear motion picture in my mind.

***

Dave proposed, "Let's stand here a minute before starting down the path. This morning in my prayer and meditation time, a vision of the symbolism of the entire journey we're about to take passed through my mind. I'll unveil some of the symbolism now and some as we proceed.

"We are beholding Minnehaha Falls behind us. The Nicollet Avenue Bridge is four miles west of here. The symbolism shown me this morning is that the four miles represent the 40 years that passed since we graduated from high school. We were kindred spirits as seven-year-olds looking up at the Norse figures on the Washburn Water Tower. In tenth grade we were friends forever after climbing over the arches of the Nicollet Avenue Bridge, and those bonds lasted through high school.

"Now you're back from Chicago, and Minnehaha Falls represents our coming together again. These falls drop over 50 feet into a gorge that's larger than a football field and then the creek wanders on until it becomes part of the Mississippi River… don't you see, Mitch, we can start over again. You can start over again. The falls is the dividing line. The journey to the Mississippi River is the path of our lives together again—kindred spirits and friends forever. Let's head for the big river."

I had listened intently, and the symbolism Dave revealed resonated within me. "When you said before that it was not too late in the afternoon, that I could start all over at any moment, what you said made sense in a shallow kind of way. With the symbolism you have just revealed, I can understand what starting over again means. It's in the form of a real-life story and not a self-help book. I finally understand what you've been telling me. I see it clearly through the symbolism. Let's start taking the trip of the rest of our lives."

***

Dave and I placed our feet on the path to the Mississippi River. By mutual agreement we didn't speak until we reached the boardwalk. I thought about the symbolism of the falls.

"This is interesting," I thought. "I'm seeing new terrain unlike that which I've seen the last two months. Perhaps this landscape is preparing me for a newness in my life. Look at the trail wandering through dense foliage and the steep banks rising up on both sides of the creek. Dave is right. I don't have to continue the same life-path. I can choose to walk another avenue with new experiences and new meaning."

I was feeling excitement I had not felt for years. Dave was a trustworthy guide. Though I had been walking in darkness, Dave was a light unto my path. Dave arranged for me to see Zeke when all was hopelessness and despair and I couldn't even function as a human being. I saw him confidently walking before me, leading the way.

***

A love for Dave fell over me at that moment, what C.S. Lewis called the love of friendship, a coming together of two individuals to be friends in such a way that they are drawn apart from the rest of the crowd. It was the love that Alfred Lord Tennyson had for Arthur Henry Hallam when he wrote "In Memoriam." It was a manly love that two close brothers could have.

***

When we reached the boardwalk, Dave said, "This is the part of our lives that is smooth and easy to walk. However, smoothness like this doesn't continue forever. That's a pattern of life."

Across the creek from us was a woman engaged in meditation on a level rock above the creek. She had two dogs running loose on the north bank of the creek; they never strayed too far from her.

We continued on the boardwalk. For a half block, we walked by a beautiful patch of prairie grass and prairie flowers. Then the landscape changed, and there was foliage on either side of the boardwalk. Soon the boardwalk ended, and Dave explained what was coming next.

"There is rough terrain ahead of us. It's unlike the smooth path we started on or the boardwalk we have just walked off. This too portrays our lives. We will both encounter rough times and be tested. We must persevere and overcome, or give up. For you, Mitch, I sense there will be challenging times arriving for you. What they will be I don't know, but they will appear as surely as the sun rises in the morning. It is critical you continue to heal both physically and mentally to withstand the stress. You can record in your ledger that I'll be there with you in the rocky times approaching. I will not forsake you. I promise you that. You will make it through."

In one way, the idea of a rocky life of challenges frightened me. But deep down I sensed tough times fostered inner strength. I remember reading T.S. Eliot in college: "And the way up is the way down, the way forward is the way back." That left an impact on me. And didn't my kindred spirit and friend forever say he would be there to help me through?

"I'll lead," said Dave. "I'm familiar with this way. Sometimes the road goes in two directions. One is rugged but passable and the other next to impossible."

***

I have been writing for hours and am tired. When I just wrote what Dave said that day about a road going in two directions, I suddenly became wide-awake. Isn't that a great truth of life? We approach a fork in the road, take one path or another, and that makes all the difference in the playing out of our lives.

An accomplishment possible in tenth grade is impossible at 58, like climbing over the arches of the Nicollet Avenue Bridge. But that is replaced by an accomplishment at 58 or older not possible in tenth grade, like writing this book.

One of the most important truths given me in my transformation was the realization that one can't compare or try to recapture the past with the present or future. As one enters a new stage in life, the role played is different than the role played in previous stages. We are always developing into new creations. It is never too late in the afternoon because the adventure of a changing life continues on until we die, and beyond.

***

We hadn't traveled far when we encountered two couples looking up into trees on the south side of the path. "What are you seeing up there?" Dave asked.

One of the men, who seemed to know wildlife, answered, "There are two wild turkeys up there."

"How do you know they're wild turkeys?" asked Dave.

"Because I hunt wild turkeys in southern Minnesota," answered the man. "By the way, my name is Carl and my girl friend's name is Kris. And that's Jack and his wife Monica. This is our first time here. What can you tell us about Minnehaha and Hiawatha? We saw the statue before we came down here."

Dave introduced himself and me to the four and then proceeded to recite the part of the *Song of Hiawatha* that he had quoted when we first arrived:

> By the shores of Gitche Gumee,
> By the shining Big-Sea-Water,
> Stood the wigwam of Nokomis,
> Daughter of the Moon, Nokomis.

Carl laughed before Dave recited more. "That's exactly what Monica quoted when we were looking at the statue, but she doesn't know any more than those four lines she learned in grade school. What more can you tell us about this area?"

Dave proceeded to cover with them what he had told me on the bench facing the statue. And then he told them, "Mitch and I grew up on the banks of Minnehaha Creek four miles west of here. This trip is part of returning to our roots. Mitch has been in Chicago for the last 40 years."

Dave didn't mention that we had not talked to each other during all that time. The two couples stayed behind to see where the wild turkeys were going, and Dave and I continued down the trail.

I had been especially quiet and somber when Dave recounted how we grew up together and then my being in Chicago. "I know you have forgiven me for not contacting you those 40 years, but as you were telling them the story, I thought what a huge mistake it was for me to have ignored my kindred spirit. How twisted my priorities were! I know I'm changing, Dave, because I've never felt so much remorse about those 40 years as I do right now. I was so focused on myself, so incredibly self-centered. You are the most important person in my life, and I abandoned you for 40 years."

Dave was quiet for a minute, which seemed like an hour. "Mitch, don't beat yourself up for those 40 years. You weren't the same person you were when we were kids and young men, and now you aren't the same person you were for the past 40 years. I can tell in your voice you've changed since our class reunion. Now you can continue from here. We've recovered our friendship. That's what's important. And if we can do that, perhaps you can be reconciled with your children and maybe even Kathleen."

"Do you think so, Dave? Do you really think so. In my mind, I see my family in a room I'm not allowed to enter. I'd at least like to be in the same space they are."

Dave answered, "Yes, I think that could happen. You'll need to become more your new self before taking on that challenge. That can be a discussion when this hike is over."

We continued on the rugged path to the Mississippi River. At one point, we were walking across a sloped shale rock that was still wet from an early morning rain. Dave heard me stumble behind him and turned quickly to catch me before I fell into the creek.

"Thanks for catching me, Dave. Even I can see the symbolism here. I'll be slipping, stumbling, and falling as I'm becoming a new person, and you will be there to help me."

Dave stopped and looked directly into my eyes.

"That's exactly how I see it, Mitch. There may also be times when I stumble and fall, and you will be there to help me. That's where the friends forever comes to life. It wasn't just chance we came together again. It was in God's plan that we become friends once more. Part of the plan we already know. There is much of this story yet to be written."

"What really amazes me," I said, "is that you have an extended family and a network of friends that fill your days to the brim. Then I come back, and you have time for me as if I were in your inner circle."

"That's where you have greatly missed the mark, Mitch. When we said we were friends forever, the forever was woven into the fabric of my life. Though we did not communicate for 40 years, you were still my friend forever. It was always the case. In my inner spirit, I knew you would come back, and we would be friends again. And so I kept a place for you, not within my network of friends but as a friend closer than a brother. When you returned from a long sojourn in Chicago and we met at our 40th reunion, the place I had waiting for you in my heart was filled. Does that make sense, Mitch?"

"It does. But I didn't keep a place in my heart for you, Dave, and I'm ashamed of it. You are closer to me than a brother, closer to me than any other friends I have ever had. If only I could erase those 40 years and be where we were before we graduated from high school. I didn't realize it in Chicago, but those were the happiest days of my life."

"You can't go back in time and relive your life, Mitch. We don't have that option. But you can take back your past in the present and the future. You can recapture pieces of your life you thought were gone forever. I'm talking about your family."

"Oh, if only that could happen, but I've burned so many bridges with my wife and children that I don't know if there is any way to reach them."

Dave did not respond to my statement but turned and proceeded down the path. There were no more mishaps on the way to the great river. As we reached the final stretch of the journey, limestone and sandstone cliffs and a smooth path guided us to the mouth of Minnehaha Creek.

***

And then there we were, where Minnehaha Creek flows into the mighty Mississippi River. A rough beach made up of sand and rocks was on the north side of the last bridge. A man was fishing right where the creek enters the river. He did not acknowledge that we were anywhere around. We looked north and saw Lock and Dam No. 1, which is one of 29 locks and dams on the Mississippi River that provide a stairway for cargo ships between Minneapolis and St. Louis. We looked south and saw the Mississippi winding endlessly to the Gulf of Mexico. An eagle was flying high above the river on the west bank.

"This is where it all ends, Mitch."

That was not what I expected to hear. "Where what all ends?" I questioned.

"Mitch, this is where our lives end and flow into eternity. Picture this: our lives here on earth are represented by Minnehaha Creek. This is the creek we lived by through high school. It was a part of our lives then, and it symbolizes our lives now. This is the creek we crossed crawling over the arches of the Nicollet Avenue Bridge. Minnehaha Falls represents where we have come together again after 40 years. From the falls to the river is the rest of our lives on earth. The path we have just traveled represents the path of our lives that we will walk together. Imagine, Mitch, that our journey today is the third bond in our lives, the bond that cements our friendship until the day we die. Are you willing to make that a bond between us?"

I had tears in my eyes by this time. "Yes, Dave, I am willing to commit to that bond right here, right now."

I extended my hand to shake on the bond, but Dave grabbed me in a bear hug. "We're beyond shaking hands, Mitch. This bond is too important."

There we stood, looking south down the Mississippi River, thinking our own thoughts about what had just transpired.

This third bond was an epiphany for me. I couldn't explain it in words, but I felt a moving in me that I had never felt before. Three bonds. The number stuck with me because of the force of this third bond with Dave.

***

What was the significance of three bonds? I remember calling Dave the next day to ask him, once the exhilaration of the day before had turned into a peaceful, meaningful joy. I carried the answer he gave me in my heart and drew on it two more times in this story.

Because I did not take detailed notes, I asked Dave to give his answer again here.

***

When I was 32 years old, I attended a Bible study on Ephesians at our church. I turned 33 half way through the study, a significant age because it was Jesus' age when He gave up his life for His creation.

During that study, we took a side trip on broken relationships. A person named Heddy brought it up because she had just lost a friendship that had been vibrant since childhood. It made me think of Mitch and our broken friendship. I wondered what I could have done differently.

The next week, the Holy Spirit hit me over the head with the third verse of Chapter 4: "Make every effort to keep the unity of the Spirit through the bond of peace." In our discussion of broken relationships, I brought up that verse and we discussed bonds. If we keep a bond of peace with God, shouldn't we also keep a bond of peace with each other? In our discussion of that verse, we agreed there might be multiple bonds between those close to us. We listed three of them — the bond of peace, the bond of friendship, and the bond of love. We could have listed more, but that evening's study came to an end. Somehow, the number three stuck in my mind. I'm not saying friends aren't friends without one bond or three bonds or seven bonds. I'm saying three bonds became important to me, and eventually to Mitch.

Mitch and I didn't use the word *bond* when we were growing up, but I observed in retrospect that what we referred to as being *special friends* was brought about by two bonds—standing in front of the Washburn Water Tower when we were seven years old and climbing over the arches of the Nicollet Avenue Bridge when we were in tenth grade. Those two bonds obviously did not solidify our friendship, for we had no contact over a span of 40 years. And then it happened—as we stood looking at the Mississippi River after completing our walk from Minnehaha Falls. In my mind, this was the bond that cemented our friendship for the rest of our lives here on earth and into eternity.

I told Mitch that for me, next to God, the relationship between two people gives meaning and purpose to life.

Bonds of friendship are not ritualistic or magical. They are not moments created or events manipulated by people into something significant. For me they are significant experiences of what God puts into the life of two people. If you look for bonds of friendship in a good relationship, you will find them. I have. They are rooted in an event or circumstance. They happen without effort on your part. Grab onto them and share the discovery with your friend. In my life, by circumstance and not design, bonds have come in threes. There have been three bonds with my wife, my three children, and with Mitch. Should all lasting friendships consist of three bonds as a formula for success? Absolutely not, but for me they were.

Mitch was struck with this pattern as well, probably because there ended up to be three bonds between us. Maybe there will be more bonds between us in future years, or maybe not. In any event, Mitch found three bonds engineered by God in his relationships with me, with his brother Sam, and with his wife Kathleen.

***

The return trip to the falls was uneventful and mostly quiet. I was the quiet one, meditating on the symbolism of the trip to the river, and Dave respected my quiet time. When we were back in the park area, I said to Dave, "You said there was something you wanted to talk to me about when we got back here."

"There is, Mitch, but it's 4 p.m., and I need to head home. Our kids and families will be with us for supper tonight, and I'm the grill chef. How about we take a walk around Lake Calhoun this Friday, and I'll cover with you what I wanted to talk to you about today? Besides, I think we each have enough to think about for now, and I don't want to introduce a new topic."

I trusted Dave that if there were something immediate he had to discuss with me, he'd take the time.

"How about nine in the morning before it gets too hot?" I asked.

"That's fine with me," answered Dave. "I'll pick you up at a quarter to nine."

Friday was only three days away.

CHAPTER 9
A Walk Around Lake Calhoun

The following morning, I reflected on yesterday's trip to Minnehaha Creek. It had been exactly one month from the class reunion. As I stared out the window overlooking France Avenue, I thought out loud. "I've come a long way; I've a long way to go. If it weren't for Dave, I shudder to think where I'd be. He encouraged me constantly. His pushing me to see Zeke was a lifesaver. I would never have seen a psychiatrist on my own."

I was mentally under attack about it being too late in the afternoon. I'd win one skirmish only to find myself in another battle ten minutes later. I needed to move beyond endless introspection. My fingers and a computer keyboard were my instruments of action. I typed "late bloomers" into a search engine, and the results made a stunning list: Ray Kroc, who started a worldwide network of McDonald restaurants when he was 52, with major health problems and a life of neither fame nor fortune up to that point; Colonel Sanders; Grandma Moses, who started painting when she was 78; Nelson Mandela, who came out of prison to be President of South Africa on his 89th birthday; Charles Perrault, who published Cinderella and Tom Thumb when he was 69; Francis Chichester, who sailed around the world solo in 1967, when he was 65; Peg Phillips, who started acting professionally in her late 60s after retiring from a career as an accountant. And many others.

The person in my search who had the most influence on me was Norman Maclean. I had read the book *Young Men and Fire* ten years earlier because I was interested in the Mann Gulch Fire in Montana in 1949. The book moved me, and I was not easily moved then. After reading the excerpt about Maclean on the Internet, I went to my bookcase, pulled down *Young Men and Fire,* and reread all 301 pages of it on Wednesday and Thursday. There is much biographical information in his book, and I expanded on that by a thorough computer research exercise.

Norman Maclean retired from teaching at the University of Chicago when he was 71. Thereafter, he espoused a non-shuffleboard and non-geese feeding philosophy of old age. He published *A River Runs Through It* when he was 74. After that, he immediately started writing *Young Men and Fire* and was doing research in the heat of Montana late in his 70s and writing the book in his 80s, up to three years before his death. His wife died when he was 66, and he lived in both Montana and Chicago after that, going back and forth in his research of *Young Men and Fire*, focusing on Montana in the summer and Chicago in the winter. His friends and children lived in Chicago. He died in 1990 at the age of 87.

My impression of Maclean was that he was a riveting storyteller and as good a writer as I had ever read. As a professional writer myself in my advertising career, I appreciated good writing. The message to me of Norman Maclean's life was simple: he had a purpose and meaning in life until the day he died. He didn't feel it was too late in the afternoon for him. He just kept living a life of research and writing. Norman Maclean gave me a strong sense of hope that it was not too late in the afternoon for me either.

***

Friday at 9 a.m. was a perfect morning for walking. The sky was clear, the humidity was low, and the temperature was in the 70s. As the day progressed, it would be in the upper 90s by mid-afternoon with high humidity, a typical muggy August day in Minnesota. Dave and I arrived at Lake Calhoun and parked Dave's car in one of the parking insets on the west side of the lake, right next to the ball field with the two benches.

We crossed the narrow road, slipping between slow-moving cars, and scampered down to the walking path, one of two paths that circumvent Lake Calhoun. The other is a bike and rollerblading path. I was curious to hear Dave's discussion topic from last Tuesday at Minnehaha Falls.

"Dave, I've wondered for two days what you wanted to talk to me about at the falls. I'm bringing it up now so we don't run out of time again."

"No talk about the weather or baseball first," kidded Dave. "We go straight for the throat? Seriously, I was about to initiate the conversation for the same reason.

"Here goes. Recovering from clinical depression is a three-legged stool. The first leg you have already accomplished—obtaining medication from Zeke to restore the chemical balance in your brain. The second leg is what I wanted to talk to you about today—seeing a counselor or psychologist to discover what is within you that caused your soul to be so out of balance. By soul, I mean your mind, will, and emotions. The third leg is putting your spiritual life in balance. If you don't work on all three, you will always be out of balance in one way or another and could be on medication for the rest of your life. For those who need to be on medication for the rest of their lives, not working on all three could mean never coping with their affliction in a complete and effective way. Think of it as healing for the body, healing for the soul, and healing for the spirit.

"Let me give you an example related to the second leg. A person suffering from strong fear can take anxiety medication, but he or she will not be healed until finding out what caused the fear. Does that make sense?"

I responded, "It makes sense, Dave, but why should I see a counselor when you are my best friend and a counselor? You've helped me so much in the last month, and I'm willing to work on the second leg of the stool with you. But I don't want to see a counselor or psychologist. I'm a private person and don't want to bare my soul to someone I don't know. I don't want to delve into my childhood and what complexes I have. Can't *you* be my counselor, Dave?"

Dave was silent for half a minute, a trait of his that still made me uncomfortable.

"Mitch, it doesn't work to have a best friend as your counselor.

There are many things you're willing to tell me about yourself, but if I started asking the questions I would ask you professionally, you would feel uncomfortable and so would I. It may affect our relationship, and I'm not willing to risk that."

I felt I was being pushed into something I didn't want to be pushed into. "Let's talk about something else. I don't want to see a psychologist or counselor. Let's talk about last Tuesday at Minnehaha Falls. Let's talk about the late-bloomer research I've done on the computer. Let's talk about too late in the afternoon."

Before I could say anything else, we were rounding the south side of the lake and met a man in a wheelchair. It was Daniel. "Mitch, my friend. How goes the battle?"

"Much better," I responded. "My friend Dave here arranged for me to see a psychiatrist for antidepressant medication. The first prescription didn't work, but the second one did. So I'm doing well." I also explained how the benzo I was taking eliminated my worst symptoms.

Daniel gave me a thumbs up and then looked to Dave. "I'm glad to meet you, Dave. Mitch has told me what a close friend you are." He switched his gaze back to me. "Is it all right, Mitch, if I speak frankly to you in front of your friend?"

"Sure," I answered.

***

I arose from my writing desk, looked out the front window, and took in Minnehaha Creek. I no longer believe events in life are accidents. It was no accident Daniel ran across Dave and me. When he saw it was a good-weather morning, he knew I would be taking my 9 a.m. walk. He didn't know, though, that Dave would also be with me. This was a God happening, and Daniel was a friend God sent to me because I needed him. What a humbling thought!

***

Daniel looked seriously at me and spoke as if he were searching for the right words. "You're feeling better because of your two prescriptions. That's wonderful and I'm happy for you, but there's more to it than that. The medication treats the symptoms, not the causes. Are you seeing a counselor?"

I put my head down and gave a "no" shake to Daniel's question.

Daniel's voice took on a concerned but compassionate tone. "That's what I was afraid of, Mitch. Don't you remember when we first met that I told you the Orioles paid for me to see a counselor three times a week for depression? I also was taking antidepressants so I could interact with the counselor. She helped me find the root causes of my depression; I couldn't have found them by myself. If it weren't for counseling, I'd be on medication and feeling flat and joyless, a handicap not visible to people. That's where you are, Mitch. You're feeling better because of medication, but no more than better. Sometimes there's a hint of joy in your life from something you've read or thought, but for the most part you are flat in your emotions. You have a hidden handicap."

"I'm afraid you have it well diagnosed," I responded. "Dave and I have been discussing the same thing. He strongly feels I should see a counselor. However, he's a counselor by profession, and I don't see why he can't be the one to help me."

Daniel didn't even hesitate answering me. "That wouldn't work. You can't have a close friend be your counselor. I won't give you the reasons why it wouldn't work because I expect Dave has already covered those with you. Everything I've heard or read points to a counselor that is a professional to you and not a friend. A counselor can be friendly in sessions, but once a relationship exists, it will adversely affect the counseling. I'm not saying it could never work, but why take the risk? It could even affect your friendship with Dave."

Dave, Daniel, and I talked for half an hour. Daniel asked a load of questions of Dave, and seemed pleased with what he heard, especially the rendering of our three bonds. We said our good byes and headed in opposite directions.

***

From the south side of the lake to the concession area on the northeast, Dave and I talked about our meeting with Daniel and engaged in general chitchat. There were long periods of silence. Dave saw I was thinking hard and let the silence lie. From the concession stand to the west side of the lake, I was fighting a battle in my mind to accept Dave's recommendation to see a counselor or obstinately refuse. I even forgot Dave was walking alongside me. Finally the battle was over. I asked Dave to sit with me on the first-base-side bench at the ballpark.

When we sat down, I opened up. "I've been quiet because I've been pondering the conversation you and I had about a counselor and the conversation with Daniel. There has been a war going on within me. On one side is my mind telling me I don't need a counselor. On the other side is my heart telling me you and Daniel are right. Just as we were approaching the ball field, my heart won. Dave, where do I find a counselor? Do you have a connection?"

Dave smiled. "I do. A guy named Wally was a counselor at Hopkins High School with me. Then he decided to leave education, get a doctor's degree in psychology, and set up his own practice in downtown St. Paul. If you had to make an appointment on your own, it would take five or six weeks. I can call him and see if he could fit you in sometime next week."

"More of your magic, huh, like freeing up Zeke? By the way, do all psychiatrists and psychologists have different names like Zeke and Wally?"

Dave laughed. "They're all a bit different. Why not have different names? Wally didn't start with Wally. He told me the story on a slow day at Hopkins High School. He was born in August 1951 to a family named Fenway. His father loved boxing, and every Friday evening was devoted to the Friday Night Fights. There was a heavyweight named Jersey Joe Walcott that his dad cheered for because he was the underdog in every championship fight. Jersey Joe lost two heavyweight challenges to Joe Lewis and two challenges to Ezzard Charles. He finally became the heavyweight champion of the world on July 18, 1951, when he knocked out Charles in seven rounds.

"Wally's dad was so excited Jersey Joe finally won that he named his new son Joseph Jersey Fenway a month later. They lived in a town in Minnesota, east of Fargo, North Dakota, named Detroit Lakes, a town famous for bequeathing nicknames. My co-worker picked up the natural nickname Joe when he started first grade. When he became a freshman in high school, one of his best friends, who knew about Jersey Joe Walcott, named him Jersey Joe. That name stuck for a year.

"Then his friend went a step further and included the boxer's last name. Thus started Jersey Joe Walcott, then just Walcott. Eventually Walcott morphed into Wally. And that's the name that has stuck with him from a sophomore in high school to this day.

"Wally liked his nickname and began to use it himself. By the time he was in college, everyone knew him as Wally. He still used the name Joseph Jersey Fenway on all official documents, but he told everyone to call him Wally. You'll see his name on his office door as Dr. Joseph "Wally" Fenway. He'll tell you to call him Wally, no doctor and no Joseph."

I was smiling by this time. "Thanks for telling me the biography of his name. I'll make sure to call him Wally."

***

Dave secured an appointment for me with Wally the very next Monday, and that morning I stood before a building just off East Kellogg Boulevard on Cedar Street. Wally had an office with a view of the Mississippi River.

When the elevator stopped on the fifth floor, there on the door in front of me was a sign: Dr. Joseph "Wally" Fenway Ltd., Psychologists and Counselors. I was ushered into an impressive office with rich oak bookcases, a huge rolltop desk that Wally was sitting at in a plush leather swivel chair, a couch with two chairs on either end, and a thick carpet that looked like it was new. Pictures of peaceful settings adorned the walls, and a window looked out over the Mississippi River. I did not feel comfortable calling this impressive man Wally.

"I appreciate your seeing me on such short notice, Dr. Fenway."

Wally turned his chair around and faced me. "First of all, call me Wally. Everyone calls me Wally. I always leave openings in my schedule on Mondays for emergencies and special patients. You fit into the special patients category. Make yourself comfortable and tell me about yourself, starting wherever you want to start and ending wherever you want to end." I chose the couch as my resting place.

What an open-ended directive! I always thought psychologists asked a page-full of questions to start. Apparently Wally had a different approach.

I started with my growing-up years and special friendship with Dave. Then I recounted what happened to me in Chicago, basically what I had told Dave in our catching up meeting and had confessed to him at a later get together. I figured that would give Wally a sense of where my problems lay. Finally I told him I was on a benzo for anxiety and an SSRI for depression and they had pulled me out of a deep pit. Wally busily took notes. When I looked at my watch, I realized I had been talking non-stop for a half hour. "I'd better stop, or I'll use up all our time with your listening to me."

"Don't worry," said Wally. "You're scheduled for two hours, so we have plenty of time. Tell me, Mitch, what goals you have in mind and what you want to be different as a result of our time together."

I thought a psychologist would tell me what he'd to do for me, but I already found Wally marched to a different drummer.

"I want to find the causes of my depression and how I can overcome them. Dave told me there were three parts to recovering from depression. There is the medical part to restore my brain chemistry, and I'm seeing a psychiatrist for that. You are the second part to balance my soul."

"I'm interested what you think is the third part."

I answered, "The third part is putting my spiritual life in balance." It was like I was reading a 1,2,3 notecard written by Dave.

Wally nodded his head. "You have it calculated well; I'd expect that from your association with Dave. So I'm the second part, and you want me to help establish balance in your soul so you can be rid of depression. Let's go for it. I'll be your companion on this journey.

"When you told me about yourself, I noticed your father and mother were absent from the story. What kind of a relationship did you have with your father?"

That was a typical psychologist question—right out of Freud. Next he'd ask me about my relationship with my mother. Wally was looking for a minefield, but he'd only find desert sand.

"We didn't have much of a relationship. My father was in commercial real estate. He owned a number of large buildings in Minneapolis and

St. Paul and was constantly buying and selling properties. It made him very wealthy, but he worked Monday through Saturday from early in the morning to late at night. He had little time for Sam, my older brother, or me. He didn't even have much time for my mother. He treated us decently when he was around, but I felt a gulf between us up to the day he died. It wasn't anger I had toward him. It was apathy."

Wally had his pen in his mouth pondering what I had just said and what I had earlier told him about my life. "Has it ever occurred to you that you are much like your father? What you called your confession revealed that your pattern of dealing with your family was strikingly similar to your father's."

I looked at Wally like he had just aimed a floodlight in my face. The light revealed the truth of his statement. Why hadn't I seen that? I asked Wally how I could have missed such an obvious comparison.

"You missed it because you repressed it. Fathers are meant to be role models for their children, and your role model was missing from the scene most of the time. You patterned yourself after him, but you didn't want to admit you were anything like your father because you had no respect or love for him. You knew your father's behavior to you was wrong, but you didn't want to accept the wrongness of your own behavior. You now understand what you did to your family was wrong and even used the word confession for it.

"Mitch, whether you like it or not, your father is a part of you. I strongly feel we need to work through this right now. Do you think you could forgive your father? He didn't know any more than you what he was doing or how self-centered he was. I think you're carrying more than apathy for your father. I think deep down you are angry with him."

"When you said I'm angry with my father, a wave of hostility rolled through me. I suppose I *was* angry with him, and I suppose I'm still angry. Now that you've described how he messed up my life, why should I forgive him?"

Wally replied, "If you don't forgive him, you'll carry that anger with you for the rest of your life. It's been buried in your subconscious, but it's a big reason why you've treated people the way you have. Kids that have been abused by others often end up to be abusers themselves. Those who live in an alcoholic or drug-addicted family tend to be alcoholics or drug addicts themselves.

"You'd think children would see the harm their parents were inflicting on the rest of the family, but they don't. What they experience in their growing up is what they believe the world to be. Perception becomes reality. This phenomenon is called patterning. A baby duck patterns himself after his mother. It's been reported that a baby duck, mixed up on the farm, found himself aligned with a goose for a mother and patterned himself after her. It was an odd thing to see—a duck acting like a goose. If you don't reconcile yourself with the father inside you, he will always influence how you treat others. You may want to treat your fellow creatures better, such as your children, but you will always hear a voice within you, the voice of your father, whispering that you need to look out for number one."

"I see your point," I said, " but you'll have to help me. I can't right now jump up with enthusiasm and say I forgive my father."

"Of course you can't, Mitch," said Wally kindly. "I will lead you through a process. Just relax and pay attention to my voice. Try to still your mind. Don't let it fight against what we'll be doing."

I relaxed on the couch, closed my eyes, and stilled my mind. Wally led me through a most unusual process. He placed an empty chair directly before me and declared my father occupied it. "What do you want to say to your father, Mitch?"

I didn't want to express to Wally that this was bizarre, but it *was* bizarre. What should I say to my father? Wally stimulated my imagination when he said my father was dead and I couldn't speak to him; but since he was living within my psyche, I could pull him out and visualize him sitting on the chair. "We're not playing pretend," said Wally. "Your father is as much a part of you today as he was when you were growing up. Perhaps more so. See him in the chair as a real person, not someone you're trying to conjure up from the dead."

I looked at the chair and saw my father in a cloud of mist, but visible in a way nevertheless. It surprised me.

"Dad, why didn't you pay attention to me when I was growing up? I felt like I never had a father. Now that I realize how much you have negatively influenced my life, my mind is filled with anger toward you."

"Here's the difficult part Mitch," said Wally softly. "Keep your mind stilled and open, and ask your father what he wants to say to you."

I felt foolish talking to a chair I knew was empty, but the image of my father was still there before me as if in a mist. "Dad, why did you do what you did?" Within the creative imagination of my mind, I heard my father talking to me. Wally knew I was hearing something from my father and so remained passive until it was evident the conversation was over.

This is what I heard from a still small voice within me. "Mitch, I thought I was doing the right thing when I worked so hard to make money for our family. I thought I was doing it all for your mother, Sam, and you. We had a beautiful home on Minnehaha Parkway. You two kids never lacked for anything. You had the best toys, you had the best cars, and you had money to spend on anything you wanted. I sent you to the best colleges. Neither one of you wanted to have anything to do with me after you left high school. Your mother and I kept our marriage intact; it was her strength that accomplished that. Most women would have left me long before. She was a gem.

"When I had my first major heart attack, you were 32. While I was in the hospital and at home recuperating, I realized the terrible mistake of putting my job before my family. One day I went to my knees and begged your mother's forgiveness for the way I had treated her. Charlotte forgave me, and the last 20 years of our marriage were a daily joy. I learned to love her for herself, not for what she could do for me.

"I sought forgiveness from you and Sam, but you two wouldn't give me a chance. I can't blame you. Even when your mother called and told you how I had changed, you couldn't accept it. When we visited you in Chicago, we spent our time with our grandchildren because you were busy with your work. When you were at home, you treated me as if I were a stranger. It was the same with Sam when we visited Birmingham once or twice a year. Neither of you visited us in Minneapolis. You were both too busy. I was so lonely for my two boys those last 20 years! How I longed to have you forgive me. Your mother was diagnosed with cancer just before I died, but even that didn't rally you or Sam because of how I distanced myself from you. It was my entire fault.

"Mitch, can you forgive me? I hurt you terribly. I'm so very, very sorry. Can you please forgive your errant dad?"

I had tears in my eyes as I said, "Yes, Dad, I forgive you. I forgive you. I forgive you. I wish I had been close to you those last 20 years. You could have shown me where *I* was going wrong. Will *you* forgive *me*?" In the stillness of my mind, I heard a yes. And so the session ended. I was surprised to see by the clock on the wall that talking to my father had taken 30 minutes. I felt it was ten minutes at most.

"Well, Mitch, how do you feel?" asked Wally. "You had quite a session with your father, as good as I've ever seen. There was considerable quiet time between what you said to your father and what he said to you. Your creative unconscious must have been working overtime. Did you feel resistance from your conscious mind?"

Tears were streaming down my face. "I feel absolutely great. My anger toward my father is gone. I love him. My conscious mind was constantly trying to discredit everything that was happening. But I kept blocking those interruptions by saying 'Stop.'"

Wally and I continued to talk about what happened. Then Wally turned his attention to my 40-year pattern of always thinking about myself first. "You need to stop spending so much time in your condominium feeling sorry for yourself. You need to become involved in the lives of others. Based on your session with your father, you should try hard to reconcile with your family. It won't be easy, and you have to be more dedicated to the task than your father was. I'd suggest starting with your brother Sam. That should be less complicated than your wife and three children.

"At the same time, find volunteer work where you can be of service to others. Talk to Dave about that. I'm sure he can help you with specific opportunities. Do you want to make another appointment with me in two weeks?"

I said I did. There was more in my soul that needed healing. "I can't begin to tell you, Wally, how much better I feel now than when I first entered your office. I wanted Dave to be my counselor, but he couldn't have accomplished with my father what you did."

"That's because Dave is too close to you," replied Wally. "You required someone at a professional distance from you to engage in something as personal as your feelings for your father. I think you'll discover your thinking will change now that you've forgiven your father. I'll be looking for a good report in two weeks. See you then."

*** *

The rest of that day I reviewed my session with Wally. There was a breakthrough in the hardness of my heart when I forgave my father. Wally introduced that term—"the hardness of my heart." A part of me had been healed, but there was more of my soul that needed to come under a surgeon's knife. I hadn't thought about *healing* coming from a psychologist, but that's exactly what happened.

The next day I called Dave about my exciting visit with Wally and thanked him for kicking me along to see a psychologist. "You were right. It wouldn't have worked for you to be my counselor. But you can be my psychologist's helper. When next we meet, I'll cover in general what happened with Wally and how you can be his helper."

Dave was pleased that my visit with Wally went so well, especially since he had recommended him. "I can hardly wait to learn more about your session and my role as Wally's helper. How about two days from now, Thursday the 18th at the coffee shop on France Avenue? Can you meet at ten? I can pick you up."

"That works for me," I answered. "I think I'll take the short walk over and meet you there. Can you get the meeting room for us?"

"Sure," said Dave. "See you there in two days."

CHAPTER 10
The Start of a New Life

I arrived at Coffee on France at exactly 10 a.m. Dave was already in the meeting room with two cups of coffee. The place was unusually busy for a Thursday, so it was fortunate we had a private room.

"How are you doing, Dave?" I asked as soon as I entered the meeting room. Dave usually asked me that question first, but I beat him to it.

After we engaged in small talk and sipped hot, flavored coffee, Dave asked, "What did you think about Wally? He's quite the character, isn't he?"

This time I was the one who waited 15 seconds before answering. Did I want to discuss my father and the chair with Dave? Why not? "Do you remember my father very well, Dave?"

"No. He wasn't around most times I was in your house. In the 13 years we were friends, I saw him fewer than five times a year. He was always friendly, but we never advanced beyond small talk. I don't remember your talking much about him either."

I nodded. "I didn't talk much about him because he was a stranger in our home. He worked from early in the morning to late at night, and most Saturdays. He didn't have time for Sam or me when he was home, so there wasn't much to talk to you about. That's a sad commentary, isn't it?

"Your house was a different story. Your parents treated me as one of their own. Your father was more a father to me than my own father. Until I met you in kindergarten, my father instructed me that anyone above Minnehaha Parkway, on Nicollet Avenue, was not someone to befriend. Anyone who lived up there and came down to the creek was to be avoided."

"I never knew that," said Dave. "How then was I allowed to hang around you and visit your house?"

"My mother intervened," I answered. "She informed my father that Dave was a nice boy, and I didn't have any friends on the Parkway. Before then, Sam was my only friend, but he was a year-and-a-half older and establishing his own circle of friends. I never told you that because I feared it would affect our friendship.

"My father ended up liking you. When I was in third grade, he let me know he was glad I had such a good friend. I think your friendship helped justify why he spent so little time with me.

"Wally told me I had a stronghold of hidden anger toward my father that I needed to confront. He led me through a strange encounter where I forgave my father and my father forgave me. It was very emotional and broke the stronghold."

I explained the method of the empty chair but avoided details of the conversation. It was too personal.

Dave respected the confidentiality of a psychologist-patient relationship and didn't ask for more information. "Mitch, you said I could be your psychologist's helper. What does that mean?"

I grinned. "Wally instructed me to spend less time in my condominium and more time out and about—like becoming involved in the lives of others.

"He suggested volunteer work and encouraged me to increase social contact with positive, light-giving people who would steer me away from the dark side.

"He insisted I pursue a path of reconciliation with those I've hurt, starting with Sam and then with the rest of my family. He suggested talking with you about his general suggestions because you could be specific. That's why I call you 'my psychologist's helper.' Are you willing to assume that assignment?"

"Absolutely!" said Dave. "Let's start."

Dave's enthusiasm was infectious. We both observed our coffee cups were empty. As we arose in unison—the Washburn Twins—we laughed and left the conference room for the sales counter. I was overwhelmed by the noise of the regular section in striking contrast to the quietness of our room. Safely back in our private haven and bolstered with more coffee, Dave initiated a listing of specific directives to render Wally's suggestions practical.

"There is a volunteer agency named Faith in Action that assists the elderly and disabled to stay in their own homes. The director called last week to inquire if I knew anyone with marketing and advertising expertise for their board. I thought, 'Who would be better than Mitch?' I was planning to ask if you were interested when next we met. That would also fit the volunteer suggestion. You could serve their care receivers with in-home visits and transportation needs. It's a noble cause and fits right into what Wally wants you to do. Here's the phone number of the director. Tell her I suggested you call, and she can contact me as a reference."

"I'll call the director later today or tomorrow. What else do you have for me?"

Dave had written several items on a sheet of paper and rattled through them. "Make a firm commitment to walk around Lake Calhoun this summer and fall. To continue your exercise in the winter, join a health club and schedule four days a week for an hour a day. Do aerobics one visit—like a treadmill, elliptical machine, or stair climber—and do toning and strength exercises the next visit. Start with a personal trainer who can show you what to do. Besides the exercise your body craves, you will also escape your home once a day. You can call that your anti-hermit routine.

"Minneapolis and St. Paul are rich with fulfilling places to frequent. Visit the Minneapolis Public Library once a week for reading and research. Read back issues of the *Mpls/St Paul Magazine* to find fun and interesting venues. Spend time at the History Center in St. Paul to research your ancestors. There's a delightful fellow there who will introduce you to the ins and outs of genealogy. Learning about your ancestors will reconnect you to your family in a non-threatening way.

"Two months remain for golf. Call Jim, the classmate you played golf with when Cathy and I were at the North Shore. Ask him about other classmates who play golf. He'll know. I can play with you on occasion as well. Take some lessons to find your swing again.

"I have one last suggestion: continue attending church. Make it an every-Sunday habit. Join a small group that meets during the week. There's a non-denominational church with a very welcoming spirit less than ten miles from where you live.

"That's enough for today. I've been like a drill sergeant, giving commands without allowing you input. That's my rendition of a psychologist's helper. Did I overwhelm you?"

I was writing feverishly. I finished my last notes and looked up. "Your being a drill sergeant is exactly what was required. Thanks, Dave. You didn't overwhelm me. You have been an impressive psychologist's helper. I'll act on your suggestions and let you know how it's going."

***

One month passed; it was late September. I followed Dave's list with great diligence. The next day after our August coffee meeting, I called the director of Faith in Action. When we met, I showed her my resume, and she immediately asked if I would be on their board. It didn't hurt that Dave had called her to recommend me.

When the director saw my entire career was in advertising and marketing, she asked if I could assist the agency in those areas. My acceptance of that assignment led to a series of meetings with the director and several hours a week developing a marketing plan for the agency. Since I also had expertise in strategic planning, I worked with the board to develop a strategic plan for Faith in Action.

I joined a health club less than ten minutes from my condo. It was in St. Louis Park and featured an inside walking and running path. I didn't particularly like treadmills and the other aerobic equipment Dave had suggested. I walked around Lake Calhoun on good days, and I walked at the club on cold or rainy days. I hired a personal trainer to set up a toning and strengthening program with resistance machines and free weights. We proceeded slowly because of my damaged heart, and I felt better after a month than I had for years.

Dave had forgotten the Minneapolis Public Library downtown was demolished in 2002 to make way for a new library that would be opening next year. So I found a library in Edina west on 50th Street and south on Vernon Avenue. It served the purpose Dave had envisioned, a place where I could spend time away from my condo.

I researched past issues of the *Mpls/St Paul Magazine* and found a treasure trove of spots I could visit in the Cities—such as the Mill City Museum and the Science Museum of Minnesota in St. Paul. In elementary school, we once had a field trip to the Science Museum, but there was nothing about it left in my memory bank. Other places mentioned in the magazine served as a list of outings, quite a list after I read two years of past issues.

The Minnesota History Center in St. Paul was a favorite haunt; the genealogy librarian became a friend. Web sites, records of the Mormon Church in Salt Lake City, birth certificates, death certificates, graveyards, and other tools that were on-line or on-microfiche made searching for my ancestors a fascinating enterprise, and one that gobbled up big chunks of time. It was like a mystery novel, discovering where to proceed with a small amount of information.

At Dave's suggestion, I called Jim about golf. Jim suggested we play Meadowbrook in St. Louis Park. While we were playing this challenging Minneapolis public course, Jim related that he played golf with two other guys once a week. They were looking for a fourth, and I was voted in. I played once a week through the rest of August, September, and a few days in October before the weather turned cold.

Dave's last suggestion became an accomplished fact when I started attending every Sunday the non-denominational church he recommended. I joined a Wednesday night Bible study for people not familiar with the Bible. I fit that definition exactly.

***

Reflecting on the path of my transformation, it becomes clear that following Dave's suggestions at that point in the road was pivotal. I became too busy to spend large amounts of time thinking about myself. Structure invaded my comings and goings. The situational side of my depression was being rewritten with new purpose and meaning. God had mercy on me, though I had not yet drawn near Him. I couldn't have done it without Dave. He saved my soul from relentless and on-going depression.

***

I filled Dave in on my successes through our weekly coffee meetings and on-going phone calls. One day, in a middle-of-September phone call, I said, "I can't thank you enough, Dave. I'm not as busy as I was in Chicago, but I'm busy enough not to be anxious or depressed. My meetings with Wally are healing my soul. My sessions with Zeke are healing my body. He's going to start withdrawing me from the benzo in a couple of weeks. After a few months off that medication, he said he'll start withdrawing me from the SSRI. "

Dave laughed. "You've followed all my suggestions except one. Don't you remember we were going to play golf together?"

Now I remembered, but I had not written it in my notes with everything else introduced that day. "I didn't write that down," I sheepishly replied. "I'm really sorry."

Dave was still chuckling. "Don't let it disturb you. You had enough to remember by the time I finished with you. The fall is not over yet; we can still get in that round. There's a matter I wish to discuss with you that hasn't seemed an appropriate topic for a phone conversation or over coffee. It calls for an outing, like…like…golf."

I was curious what Dave wanted to discuss. The last time he was so mysterious was at Minnehaha Falls when he put off talking to me about seeing a psychologist. "When do you want to play?"

"How about next Tuesday at ten in the morning at Braemar? I'll call and make a tee time. I'll arrive early to hit balls and practice putting and chipping."

I agreed to the time and place.

***

As I walked out of the clubhouse, I saw Dave approaching from the putting green and announced to him. "I've paid for our green fees and cart, so we're ready to go."

"I didn't want you to pay my share," Dave said. "Now I need to remember to return the favor next time. It clutters my mind."

"Don't keep track," I replied. "This is my way of thanking you for all you've done for me. The next time we play golf, we'll split the fees."

"I can accept that," said Dave. "Let's play the middle tees. That will put the course at 6,300 yards."

The first hole was a straightaway par 4. After we teed off and headed down the fairway, I turned to Dave. "All right, what is it you wanted to talk to me about?"

"Be patient, Mitch, this is a conversation to ease into, not one to get out of the way on the first hole. It will be a discussion that will occupy us most of the round."

I was really curious now.

From the third tee, a par 3, I hit my ball into the right trap in front of the green. "That's where I've always been on this hole. It's like a curse."

"I didn't think you played this course before," said Dave.

I was surprised at his assessment. "Don't you recall when Sam and I played golf on Tuesdays in the summer from sixth grade to ninth grade? This is the course we played. We belonged to a junior league and played as partners. Dad was too busy with work to belong to a private country club, so he had Mom drive us to Braemar, which was a public course with a good youth program. He felt we should learn to play golf for business purposes later in life. He paid for lessons during those four years, and we were shooting in the low 40s at the end. Sam was a year-and-a-half older and the better golfer."

"I knew you golfed with Sam on Tuesdays," replied Dave. "But I never paid attention to the course you played, and if you told me, it went right on by.

"Speaking of Sam, where is he now?"

I didn't want to talk about Sam but felt Dave deserved an answer. "Sam was big in real estate in the Minneapolis area, but not commercial real estate like our dad. He represented the residential market, and higher priced homes were his niche. He made so much money from his mid-20s to his early 40s that he bought one of the largest real estate agencies in Alabama and moved down to Birmingham when he was 42. I never did find out why he wanted to move to Alabama; that happened after we stopped talking."

"What happened that you stopped talking?" asked Dave as we continued playing the front nine.

I answered with exasperation. "It's based on an unpleasant circumstance that split us apart when he was 40 and I was 38."

"Have you talked to Wally about it?"

Couldn't Dave see I was uncomfortable with the subject and didn't want to revisit that episode in my life?

"No. That's a sleeping dog that's best left asleep."

Dave did not hesitate; his answer apparently required no thinking time. "Don't you remember how you were healed by talking to Wally about your father? Your estrangement from Sam is bound up inside you, what Wally calls a stronghold. It needs to be loosened. You can't bury bitterness and not suffer consequences. I once said I shouldn't be your counselor. I'm now putting that on the shelf. I remember your brother as a kind and sensitive boy and young man. I won't let you hide behind a circumstance of 20 years ago. If your goal is to overcome your depression once and for all, you must be transparent with all facets of your life."

I had never seen Dave so wound up. He made one final statement with a glare in his eyes and determination in his voice.

"I vowed you wouldn't live a life filled with depression. I intend to fulfill that vow. Tell me about Sam."

It was as if Dave had slapped me in the face to catch my attention. I was taken aback so completely I couldn't respond until we hit our drives on the fifth hole. Slowly my exasperation was subdued. Wasn't Dave looking out for my best interests? Of course I didn't want to be depressed for the rest of my life! As we entered the cart to find our drives, peace and calmness rolled over me.

"You are on target, Dave. I have a hurtful zone inside me I never visit, where Sam is dead. It's time to break into that zone."

I was less than honest when I said I never visited that zone. I looked into it almost every day.

"Twenty years ago, Dad's father died. Since my grandmother had already passed away, there were three people in his will—my father, Sam, and me. Most of his estate went to my father.

"Here comes the hurtful part. Grandfather Jake had a 200-acre piece of land north of Minneapolis that he used for hunting. Sam was his favorite hunting companion, and Sam was the elder brother. Our grandfather bequeathed the land to Sam for those two reasons, and he left me an amount of cash he felt was equivalent to the value of the land.

His estimate of the value of the land was not even close to its actual value. It was worth at least twice what he gave me, and the land would increase significantly in value each year with its proximity to the Cities.

"I called Sam from Chicago and informed him the settlement of our grandfather's estate was not fair to me. He did not disagree. He said I was welcome to use the land whenever I wanted, but that was not on my wish list. I infrequently returned to Minnesota, and I certainly wouldn't drag myself up there in the fall for hunting. I didn't like hunting.

"I demanded that Sam sell the land and combine the money received with the money left to me, and we'd split it. Sam refused. He said Grandfather Jake promised he would will the land to him, but only if Sam pledged never to sell it. It was to remain in the family for all Jasper generations to come. Sam said it was like he signed a contract, and he would never violate its terms.

"I'm ashamed to tell you what happened next. I swore at Sam and proclaimed I never wanted to see or talk to him again—for the rest of my life—and slammed down the phone. That's the last time I talked to him. I saw him twice at the funerals of our dad and mother, and ignored him. He attempted to talk to me, but I turned away. Isn't that despicable?"

The business of Sam was a thread that wove through our conversation as we completed our round. With two holes left to play, I suddenly remembered Dave's purpose for golf was to discuss something that would last most of the round.

"What about the conversation that was to take place today?" I asked Dave.

He looked amused. "We just *had* the conversation—what caused you and Sam not to talk to each other for 20 years?"

Then he turned serious and was a drill sergeant again. "You need to reconcile with Sam, and the sooner the better."

I gulped hard. "Dave, I don't know if I'm ready for that."

"You'd best make yourself ready.

"It's time to consider the third path to heal your depression. First there was Zeke to heal your body. Second there was Wally to heal your soul. Third there needs to be someone to heal your spirit, a spiritual director so to speak. That's the role I can play, if you want."

I quickly answered. "I've been waiting for the third leg of the stool, as you pictured it. When I wanted you as my counselor, I came to understand that wouldn't work. If this will work, yes, I want you to be my—what did you call it?"

"Spiritual director."

"Yes, my spiritual director. I don't want someone new to meet with, and who would be better qualified as a spiritual director than you? When I look at your life, I see something I'm missing—a peacefulness and joy you say comes from your relationship with God. I long for that peacefulness and joy."

"Good, Mitch. I'm pleased to be your spiritual director and will serve you with patience and love.

"Let's begin right now by observing what the Bible says about forgiveness. The Lord's Prayer is a good address to visit. 'And forgive us our sins, as we forgive those who sin against us.' According to your confession last July, you have many sins to be forgiven. Jesus says you must forgive those who have sinned against you if you expect your Father to forgive you. It's not optional. You need to forgive Sam and make your peace with him. There are two parables in the New Testament you should read. I'll look up chapter and verse and send you an e-mail.

"Wally can demonstrate how to accomplish the reconciliation on a practical basis. I'll show you how to bring spiritual healing into the equation."

"As coincidence would have it, I have an appointment with Wally tomorrow. I'll bring the matter of Sam up."

"It's not a coincidence," countered Dave. "God has a plan for your life, and He's directing the outcome."

***

"Glad to see you again," greeted Wally. "What should we talk about today?"

I noticed, not for the first time, the rich mahogany bookcases around three walls of Wally's office. The couch I sat on was close enough to the bookcase behind it that I could grab a book if I wanted. The office was large, and there were enough books to qualify as a small library.

"Let's talk about a matter I should have previously covered with you," I replied. "Dave and I spent 18 holes discussing it yesterday." I stopped there to contemplate how best to present this to Wally.

He gave me a friendly frown. "Am I to guess what the matter is, or are you going to tell me?"

Wally's casual approach made me feel more comfortable and less like I was going to a shrink who was treating me out of a textbook.

I reviewed the conversation from yesterday and added the dark pieces I hadn't revealed to Dave. "I haven't eliminated Sam from my mind. I think about him nearly every day. I have returned to that phone conversation of 20 years ago many times with heightened anger. I have wished something horrible would happen to Sam and his family. I have wished he would die so I wouldn't have to think about him anymore. In my paranoia, I believe Sam is fantasizing the same things about me. It's a battle being fought in my mind endlessly."

Wally looked at me with a serious stare. "For heaven's sake, I'm glad you finally told me about Sam. This is an extremely serious matter that must be dealt with immediately. You have given an imaginative Sam power over your life that no one should be given. You have a festering wound that needs healing—a wound that will fuel your depression until a healing balm is applied."

"I suppose the empty-chair routine is called for again," I said humorously.

Wally was not amused. "No. Your father was dead. Sam is alive. This has to be worked out with Sam face to face."

I was not prepared for that answer. My anger toward Sam was still too strong within me. Wally pressured me to at least call Sam by phone. If Sam were as angry as I was and didn't want to talk to me, then Wally said we could attempt the healing process without Sam.

"Mitch, you've started a new life. Therefore, something that happened 20 years ago must be confronted by the new Mitch, not the old Mitch."

I didn't have an argument to counter Wally; I agreed to at least call Sam.

***

It was now mid-October, and I had not called Sam. I was a reluctant horse at the water trough. The old Mitch strongly influenced me. My mind was a battlefield. The army of the new Mitch wanted to call Sam. The army of the old Mitch proclaimed Sam did not deserve to be forgiven. The Lord's Prayer reinforced the new Mitch, but the old Mitch was winning the battle.

I cancelled three sessions with Wally because I didn't have an argument for not calling Sam other than I wasn't ready. The battle was depressing me.

I met with Zeke on October 25.

***

I highlighted my discussions with Dave and Wally regarding Sam. Zeke noticed I was flirting with depression again, and nixed my coming off the benzo. With my displayed symptoms of anxiety and agitation, he was afraid withdrawal might push me into a downward spiral.

"You're not going to like my telling you this, Mitch, but professionally I have to. I fully agree with Wally. You must call Sam. Until you make an attempt to resolve that dark chapter of your life, I can't recommend coming off any medication.

"The two prescriptions I've written for you—the benzodiazepine for anxiety and the SSRI for depression—don't heal the causes. Until you settle the issues in your life that are behind your anxiety and depression, you'll need to remain on medication—as long as you live if necessary."

That last sentence shook me to the bottom of my feet. Dave had told me much the same thing walking around Lake Calhoun, but it didn't really register until Zeke predicted I'd be on medication for the rest of my life.

I didn't want to be medicated until I died. I didn't want to be depressed and anxious until I died. Suddenly the big picture was before me. There was Dave's sketch of the three-legged stool for healing depression—body, soul, and spirit. There was Wally's depiction of needing to heal body *and* soul. There was Dave's highlight of bringing in a spiritual dimension—the need to forgive Sam if I expected God to forgive me. I desperately wanted peace, and my spiritual director was emphatic how that would happen.

***

The next evening my hand was on the phone. I was nervous to the point of sweating. All day I thought what I would say. I had notes; I had a script. I was starting to feel softer about Sam, and finally at 7 p.m. I made the call without a script, trusting that somehow it would all work out.

"Sam, this is Mitch."

There was a long pause on the other end of the line before Sam said something. "Hello, Mitch." I could tell he wanted to add more but didn't know what to say.

"Sam, it's been 20 years since we've talked, and I think it's time we became reconnected before it's too late." The words came to me from somewhere outside my mind. Suddenly, I felt at ease and was no longer anxious.

"This is amazing," Sam exclaimed. "I wanted to call you and use exactly the same words, but I was afraid of your reaction. I'm sorry for what happened because of Grandfather Jake's will. I think about it every day. If I could turn the calendar back 20 years, I would handle the land issue differently. We both lost a father we were not connected to. To lose a brother has been too much. I would sell the land tomorrow to have you back."

"There's no need to sell the land, Sam. I'm the one who should be sorry, and I am. The land is not more important than a brother. Neither is any amount of money. I thought those were important 20 years ago, and I said things I should never have said. Do you think we could forget the past and start over again?"

"I know we can, Mitch. I hear you're retired now. Why don't you come to Birmingham for a couple of weeks, and we can become reacquainted. We have a large house in Mountain Brook that's bigger than we need with our kids gone. You would have your own private space on the upper level."

We talked for another hour, and reconnecting was well underway. November 3 to November 17 became the date of the visit, and that very night I purchased a plane ticket to Atlanta and a rental car to drive to Birmingham.

I spent the next week thinking about what I'd say to Sam and what he'd say to me. He was friendly when I called, but would that change when he told his wife Mary I was coming for two weeks? She might not share his enthusiasm. Doubts crept into my mind and threatened to take control. I kept the doubts at bay until I headed for the Lindbergh Terminal.

CHAPTER 11
Brothers in Birmingham

On Thursday, November 3, I boarded a plane in Minneapolis for a 2 ½ -hour flight to Atlanta. I had pen and paper to write down my thoughts. This would be one of the hardest meetings of my life. What do you say to a brother you haven't spoken to in 20 years?

When we connected by phone, it seemed everything was right between us. What about when we encounter the nitty-gritty details? It would be important we have a good start, or two weeks would pass like two months.

***

Fortunately, there was a GPS device in my rental car to map me from the Hartsfield-Jackson terminal to Sam's house. Exiting the Atlanta airport to Interstate 20 was not easy for a first-timer. Once on Interstate 20, Birmingham was a straight 2 ½-hour trip. When I entered Birmingham, the way to Mountain Brook and Sam's place on Canterbury Road was yet another challenge. The GPS was up to it.

I sat in my car for two minutes, gazing at Sam's beautiful colonial style, taupe-colored brick, two-level home. I was gathering the courage to walk to the front door. As I headed up the steps, Sam opened the door and walked outside to give me a hug. "That's a good start," I thought. Sam looked like he could still play basketball for Washburn. He was muscled and athletic looking, with a tanned face and all his hair.

"Let's haul your luggage up to your room, and we can talk awhile before you go to bed. I'll bet you're exhausted," began Sam.

Mary gave me a hug when I entered the house. Another good start. Mary and Sam gave me a tour, and we chatted about my trip down and the difference in weather between Minneapolis and Birmingham.

Sam and Mary slept in a main-floor master suite, and there was a second-floor master suite where I would be situated.

Sam was accurate about my having my own space. There was even an office on the second floor that could serve as a base for working on the marketing and advertising I was doing for Faith in Action, and to keep track of investments on my laptop.

Sam and I took my luggage out of the car and up to my room; then we came back downstairs to visit.

***

"You have a very beautiful house here in Birmingham," I declared to Mary. I had known her for 18 years before the blow-up with Sam and wanted to gauge how accepting of me she would be.

"Thank you very much," responded Mary. "We're really not in Birmingham, though. We live in Mountain Brook, just like you live in Edina and not Minneapolis."

There was a smile on her face and a touch of pride in her voice. I soon discovered Mountain Brook was the exclusive place to live in the Birmingham area, similar to Edina being the exclusive place in Minneapolis.

I steered the conversation in a direction other than resolving differences with Sam. That could take place tomorrow, just the two of us.

Mary and Sam must have had numerous discussions over the past 20 years about the estrangement of the two brothers, though I felt Mary was warm toward me and not at all defensive or angry.

"Sam, 18 years ago, you moved down to Mountain Brook." I was careful to specify Mountain Brook in a non-sarcastic tone of voice. I respected Mary's preference as to where she lived. "I've always wondered why you moved so far away, especially when your two sons were in their teens."

"We sometimes wondered the same thing," commented Sam. "It was a career move, something Dad would have done. I was making a ton of money in residential real estate, selling million-dollar houses in South Minneapolis, Edina, Minnetonka, and Wayzata. A million dollars for a house was a considerable chunk in the 1980s, and the commissions put me well into six figures for a number of years. Jake and Justin were both in high school, so there were not college expenditures at the time. I always had the goal of buying a large agency and being the CEO, similar to your wanting your own ad agency. There was nothing on the selling block in Minnesota or any surrounding states, but there was the state's largest real estate agency for sale in Alabama, with its headquarters in Birmingham. Mary and I had come to Birmingham at least ten times to visit friends, and we both thought it was a great city.

"Jake was 18 and graduating from high school. Justin was 16 and a sophomore. They were both prospective Division IA football players, and the opportunity to play for Bear Bryant at Alabama was a stronger attraction than staying in Minnesota. Like a fairy tale come true, they both received full football scholarships at Alabama. Jake started three years at cornerback, and Justin earned his chance to play left guard on the offensive line when he was a junior. It was a blessing that both of them flourished at Alabama. Upon graduation, they both went back to the Minneapolis area to find jobs. I was hoping one or both would join me in the agency and take over when I retired. But that wasn't either one's goal.

"Jake is a mechanical engineer with a testing company in Eden Prairie. Justin earned a law degree at William Mitchell in St. Paul. He's now practicing in Fergus Falls, with a large regional law firm.

"Our pattern at first was getting together seven or eight times a year, either down here or up there. Both boys married in their later 20s and didn't have children until their 30s, so the pattern was easy to maintain. When children came, it was mainly our heading north four or five times a year."

Mary joined the conversation. "Seeing our grandchildren four or five times a year is not enough, but Sam hasn't wanted to sell the agency and move to Minnesota."

"Mary keeps pressuring me," laughed Sam. "One day she'll win. I want more time with our boys' families as much as she does. Right now the agency is making too much money to sell it. Maybe in three or four years."

I noted that Sam and Mary were exceptionally compatible. They just had a disagreement in front of a guest, and it was respectful and loving. I could see they had a relationship together and with their children that I never had with Kathleen or our three children.

Sam continued, "We both love Birmingham. We have a rewarding lifestyle, able to afford what we want and able to mix with friends that are interesting and stimulating."

Mary reinforced what Sam just said. "We *do* have many close friends here. Being closer to our children is my greatest desire, so I pressure Sam to sell the agency. However, another part of me says we'd be leaving much behind. Alabama is an interesting and beautiful state that keeps us forever busy, not to mention the moderate weather in the winter. It would not be easy to leave."

The clock was advancing to a late hour, and they could see I was tired. Sam looked my way. "It's time for a good night's rest for you. Tomorrow morning, when you're ready, we'll hike the Jemison Trail. It's close by."

I replied, "Since my heart attack, I walk most days, but never more than three miles."

"That's perfect," said Sam. "My favorite segment of the Jemison Trail is exactly three miles. It's a winding trail through woods, across a creek, briefly on a street sidewalk, and finishes on a dirt path. The total distance is a mile-and-a-half, and we turn around and return the same way."

I realized this would be our chance to cover what needed to be discussed to become true brothers again. But there was a risk involved. The hike could develop into a tense time when issues related to our growing up might push us farther apart.

***

It was a splendid Friday morning in November when we arrived at the Jemison Trail. The temperature was in the high 60s and would reach the high 70s by the afternoon. Our first quarter mile consisted of small talk. Sam told me the background of Jemison Park, Shades Creek, the Jemison Trail, and the history of Mountain Brook.

Then there was an uncomfortable silence for 100 paces.

I broke the silence. "My mind keeps returning to our phone conversation last week. Do you remember when I said, 'Do you think we could forget the past and start over again?' You thought that was a good idea. I have since concluded it is not a good idea. There are issues besides the land matter we need to discuss. I didn't blow up at you only because of the land. That was just the flash point. There were gallons of fuel stored over the years just waiting to explode."

Sam had a look of total surprise. "I…I really have no idea what you are referring to."

"There is a sound reason why you have no idea. All the issues are from my point of view. I never discussed them with you as we were growing up. And I long ago buried them in the dark recesses of my mind—until a psychologist I'm seeing led me back into my childhood and adolescent years to see what was there. He said my reaction to the land matter was too volatile to have been attributable to that one issue. There had to be a reservoir of other factors, like a man who commits adultery. It doesn't just occur with a single choice. There is a slow build up—a spousal relationship that is not satisfactory, pornography on the Internet, and lots of fantasizing about having a sexual relationship with this woman or that woman. And then one day the opportunity arrives, and he is ready for it. It was that way with the land.

"Sam, you were two years older and two grades ahead of me, yet you often included me in playing football, basketball, and baseball with your friends. You were a good big brother in that way. You never picked on me, were never critical of me when I messed up, were always encouraging to me. So from your point of view, I can see how you thought there weren't any problems.

"Oh, but there were problems, Sam, what I now see as distorted thinking on my part. I was good in sports, better than some of your friends. It was understandable you were better than me because you were a year-and-a-half older. But when I reached the grade you had been in a year earlier, I still could not measure up. I was good; you were great. You made all-conference and all-area in football. I didn't.

"I was closest to you in golf, but you still consistently beat me. One day I shot a 67 at Braemar. Two weeks later you shot a 66. Other golfers complimented me on my low round until you posted yours. Then I was forgotten. That's the way it always seemed to happen.

"You were Dad's favorite because of your sports accomplishments. Grades also were an issue with me. I had As and Bs all the way though 12th grade. You had all As. Dad praised you highly. He never spoke to me with much enthusiasm or praise. Once again, I was good enough, but you were great.

"I saw you as better than me in everything. You had more friends than I did. You were more respected. You were better liked. You were part of the in-group. I envied you. In a way I hated you. I was always in your shadow.

"The most devastating blow for me was the vacation our family took to Gull Lake in Brainerd. I was 12 and you were 14. I was swimming out to a distant raft, when I became exhausted and panicked. You were on the shore, saw me struggling, and swam out to rescue me. You were a hero. I was a weakling. From my way of thinking then, that was a picture of our relationship."

***

I dropped my pen on my writing desk. Comparing myself to someone else, especially an older brother, is one of the most devastating things anyone can do. It poisoned my childhood and adulthood until Wally provided the antidote—facing the twisted lie that possessed me and confessing the truth. God made me in His image and likeness and there is no one else like me. He loves me just as I am and wants to free me from any stronghold that interferes with our relationship. It didn't happen in a flash, but the stronghold of comparisons eventually left me, and I was free. Free to love Sam.

***

"I never realized the mental anguish I put you through," stammered Sam. "Why didn't you bring it up to me? I thought we were close growing up. Did you talk to Mom or Dad?"

"No, Sam, I kept it bottled up inside. When the matter of the land presented itself, it was the final straw. I saw Grandpa favoring you and belittling me. I was actually glad you refused to sell the land. It gave me an opportunity for revenge, a chance to teach you a lesson. I didn't talk to you for 20 years. I thought it would be as if you didn't exist. But you were often in my mind, and the comparisons continued. I couldn't get rid of you."

I could see Sam was shaken. There were tears in his eyes, and I felt compassion for him. "Mitch, I'm so terribly sorry I caused you so much pain. If only we had talked then. Maybe there was something I could have done to make it easier for you. Maybe I could have encouraged you more, praised you more, been more sympathetic to you…or something."

Sam was grasping to recapture the past. I put my head down and spoke softly. "No, Sam, it's not your fault. It's my fault. I should have seen a counselor to work through what existed only in my mind. Now I'm seeing a psychologist, and that's why I'm here talking to you.

"Can you please forgive me for the twisted thoughts I had. You loved me, and I hated you. I understand now how perverted my thinking was… Sam, I don't hate you anymore. I love you like a brother should be loved. I can't change the past, but I can change the present and the future."

"I don't see why you should take all the blame," Sam said. "I should have sensed things were not right between us, but I didn't. I must have been more concerned with myself than our relationship as brothers."

"No, Sam, you weren't. You were easygoing and outgoing. You would not have been able to figure out how messed up my thinking was. I will take all the blame. I insist on taking all the blame. Can you please forgive me?"

"Mitch, you are a different person. You have taken all the blame and attributed none to me. Yes, I forgive you. With all my heart, I forgive you. The last 20 years are erased from my mind, and I want to be your brother again."

Sam and I hugged at the point on the Jemison Trail just before crossing Shades Creek again on the concrete stepping blocks. Tears were streaming down our faces. We held on to each other silently for a full minute. There were about eight-tenths of a mile to complete our walk, and our emotions were so naked on the surface that neither one of us talked on the final leg.

***

Sam and I played golf the next day at a Robert Trent Jones Golf Trail course called The Ridge Course, one of two courses at Oxmoor Valley in Birmingham. Sam informed me The Ridge was carved out of the peaks and valleys of the Appalachians, with scenic forests, numerous creeks, and stupendous elevation changes. He said the 12th hole had a green buttressed with a shelf of exposed shale rock as a reminder of the site having been mining land.

"I have to warn you," mentioned Sam, "that the yardage of this course does not indicate what a tough course it really is. You have to be precise with your drives and many second shots, or have a couple dozen golf balls to replace what you lose."

"I'm up for it," I replied. "It has to be easier than our discussion yesterday."

The conversation of the early holes was about yesterday on the Jemison Trail. On the fifth hole, I told Sam about my renewed friendship with Dave after 40 years. I recounted the kindred spirit experience at the Washburn Water Tower, the friends forever vow after climbing over the arches of the Nicollet Avenue Bridge, and the third bond in our lives—walking from Minnehaha Falls to the Mississippi River.

I could see Sam listening intently as I recounted the bonds between Dave and me. The 40 years separating the first two bonds and the third bond were not caused by a disagreement but by my self-centeredness. The disagreement with Sam was something else. Any bonds between us had to be built now, not renewed from years back.

"Mitch, I felt we made giant steps yesterday resolving our issues of the past."

"You mean issues I had, not we had," I challenged.

"Let's not travel that ground again, Mitch. Where are you today with *your* issues?"

"The issues have flown away, Sam. Wally, my psychologist, helped me realize they were lies, and confessing them to you would be the final step in breaking the strongholds. Truth and confession have set me free. You are my big brother who was kind to me and faithful to include me in your life. My anger has been deposited in a deep valley far away. My hate has flown to the bottom of Death Valley. I'm set to start over again, if you are."

"I am, Mitch. I use a technique of 'drawing the line' with people that has served me well. Here's how it works. I talk to a person about what's happened in the past that has not gone well. Then I tell him we're not going to talk about those things any more. We're going to draw a line in the sand and start with fresh beach. That takes a load off both of us. When you were telling me about your friendship with Dave, I felt envy. I want that relationship between us. My desire is to draw the line right here and start our lives fresh. We won't talk about the past, except the positive parts, and we'll walk into the future as brothers and friends."

I felt a love for my brother that was overflowing. "Sam, I agree with you wholeheartedly, but we can't draw the line here. We really drew the line yesterday when we hugged before crossing Shades Creek. *That* was the bond of being brothers again."

"I see it," said Sam excitedly. "Do you think there will be other bonds?"

"Perhaps, Sam. You never know."

We were playing the 12th hole, a par 5. Each of us hit our best drive of the day, in perfect position to hit the green in two, which we both did. Sam sank a double-break 30-foot putt for an eagle. I followed with a downhill 20-foot putt for the same score. We gazed at each other in amazement.

Then Sam said, "Could this be another bond? It signifies a great achievement and one of equality between us. We can call it 'the bond of the eagles.'"

I was thrilled with the establishment of another bond, especially since Sam declared it. "Yes, 'the bond of the eagles.' Let's use this one to commit that we are brothers and friends forever, no matter who else comes into our lives and no matter where we go."

We finished our round in high spirits, and when we added up our scores, a reinforcement of the two eagles happened—each of us shot 79.

"How interesting," ventured Sam. "We were equals with eagles and equals with total score. Let's always remember this. This round serves as a double bond. No matter who scores lowest in future games, and

I hope there are many more to come, this round forever marks our equality."

"Agreed!" I said, with as much enthusiasm in my voice as I could muster.

***

The next day was Sunday. We went to a church service at Sam and Mary's Anglican church in Birmingham. After lunch we visited the Birmingham Botanical Gardens. We immersed ourselves in an art exhibit in the main building before walking through the many different floral landscapes of the gardens.

Mary was in a high mood during the whole visit. "Mitch, Sam told me about the last two days, without sharing anything he felt you would not want shared. I'm so happy you two have reunited and formed bonds of brotherhood and friendship. I've been praying 20 years this would happen, and now it has. I hope I fit into the bonds of brotherhood and friendship."

I answered, "You two are like one; the bonding between Sam and me most certainly includes you. Thanks for being faithful in prayer."

***

It was not difficult for Sam to take time off work. There was nothing critical happening at the realty company, and it was Sam's management style to have people in place who could run the company and make decisions on their own. It was a "management by exceptions" style. As long as things were going as expected, there was no reason for anyone to update Sam. However, if something really good happened or something really bad, Sam would be informed. That could happen by e-mail or phone, so Sam was always available, even when he was not in the office.

Sam and I left Sunday night for Atlanta and stayed through Thursday morning. A friend of Sam's who lived in the Dunwoody area offered his house to Sam and Mary whenever they came to Atlanta. He was retired and a world traveler, so he was rarely home. This was a chance for me to see some of the sights of Atlanta—Stone Mountain, the King Center (located within the Martin Luther King Historic Site),

Ebenezer Baptist Church (where King's father pastored and Martin was an associate pastor), Kennesaw Mountain (an important battlefield in Sherman's march to Atlanta), the Coke Museum, and the Buckhead area, with some side trips here and there. Mary said this would be a good bonding experience for both of us. And it was.

***

Back in Birmingham, the three of us visited the Birmingham Civil Rights Institute, the 16th Street Baptist Church (where the Ku Klux Klan bombed the church in 1963 and killed four young girls), Ingram Park, Vulcan Park, the Sloss Furnaces, and the Birmingham Museum of Art. We also visited other sites and restaurants in Mountain Brook, Homewood, and Birmingham. We were a sightseeing family for sure, having a great time together.

***

On Monday, November 16, Sam and I drove down to Montgomery, the capital of Alabama. Mary was not able to go because she had a church meeting to facilitate. We left at eight in the morning and arrived in Montgomery 1 ½ hours later. Our plan was to see three sites in Montgomery and then drive to Selma. The first stop was the Rosa Louise Parks Museum and Library, built in honor of the lady who refused to give up her bus seat to a white male passenger on December 1, 1955. A boycott of city buses by the African-American population lasted 381 days until demands were met.

Our next stop was the Alabama State Capitol, which was the first Confederate Capitol for a short time. Down the hill from the Capitol, and in clear view, was the Dexter Avenue Baptist Church, our third stop, where Martin Luther King pastored from 1954—1960. He was the spokesperson for the bus boycott, a very significant event in the civil rights movement. The boycott was important because it captured the attention of the entire nation. Ironically, King's church, a key location for civil rights activities that spanned the 1950s and 60s, was only a short walk from the start of the Confederacy.

When we left the Dexter Avenue Baptist Church, it was two in the afternoon. Sam and I figured we should have lunch before heading to

Selma. We found a cafe on Montgomery Street that looked adequate, not real enticing but adequate. We were the only patrons at that time in the afternoon, so we figured the service would be quick. And it was. A waitress arrived at our booth immediately. We chose off the menu, and she took our order back to the kitchen.

Then it happened. A tremendous blast came from the kitchen. Its walls were blown to the front of the café, and there were flames everywhere. Sam was facing the blast and a small piece of the wall hit him in the head and knocked him unconscious. I had instinctively dropped down in the booth and escaped unhurt. Fear gripped me for Sam. The whole eating area was in flames, especially by the front door. There was no leaving the way we entered. There was no escaping out the back either, for the flames there were the fiercest. The large window in front must have been very strong. It was cracked in a number of places, but not blown out.

There wasn't time to think. I grabbed a chair and hammered the front window until I broke out a large enough section for Sam and me to climb through. I ran to the booth, threw Sam over my shoulder, and carefully carried him through the hole. As I looked back, I could see the café completely in flames. We both would have been killed within seconds. I called 911 on my cell phone from across the street, and a team of medics was there within minutes, with fire engines arriving soon after. It was evident the waitress and cook in the café had been killed instantly. Just as the medics were checking Sam, he woke up.

"How do you feel, guy?" said one of the medics.

"Actually, I feel good," spoke Sam from a blackened face. "I remember hearing a loud blast and seeing a piece of wall coming at my head, and then nothing. I have a splitting headache, but otherwise I feel fine. What happened anyway?"

I explained a blast came from the kitchen, and we were lucky to escape alive. Sam asked questions, and the full story unfolded. I had saved Sam's life, just as he had saved mine at Gull Lake so many years before. The medics finished checking Sam over and one proclaimed, with a serious demeanor, "He may have a slight concussion. I'd suggest you make sure someone is with him until morning and then see a doctor as soon as you can."

There wasn't going to be any Selma trip that day.

***

On the way back to Birmingham, I made sure Sam stayed awake. The next day we found out Sam didn't have a concussion. The piece of wall had hit him a glancing blow, hard enough to knock him out but not hard enough to cause real damage.

I looked over and saw Sam smiling. "Do you know what this means? I'll be indebted to you for the rest of my life. We have secured a third bond that will keep us together as brothers and friends until the day we die, similar to you and Dave coming to the Mississippi River on your walk from Minnehaha Falls."

I agreed. "Yes, we have a third bond, but what a way to achieve it! We will be walking life's path together for the rest of our time on earth."

"And beyond," responded Sam.

Sam and I were brothers again, held together by three bonds.

***

I had a late flight from Atlanta to Minneapolis the next day, so I had time for lunch with Sam and Mary. We mulled over what happened yesterday, and Sam made a surprise announcement. "There's nothing like a near-death experience to illuminate what is important in life. Mary and I talked a long time last night. We're going to sell the agency and move back to Minneapolis/St. Paul. We'll be closer to our boys, and we'll be closer to you. That's the way life should be—families living in close proximity to one another, not a thousand miles away."

I was moved by the announcement and thought to myself, "My life is coming together. I have a triple bond with Dave and now a triple bond with Sam. That's two families that will be with me for the rest of my life."

CHAPTER 12
Withdrawal

By the time I arrived back in Minnesota, I was feeling the best I had in months. I had just doubled my close friends from one to two and had gained a brother back in the bargain. I looked at my calendar and noted a meeting tomorrow, Friday the 18th of November, with Zeke. On Monday I noted a meeting with Wally. Though these two had greatly helped me, I thought I was well enough to make it on my own now.

***

What a mistake in judgment that was! I believed circumstances had dragged me into depression, and circumstances would lift me out again. I had somehow forgotten situational depression had changed into clinical depression that required medication, regardless of circumstances. The chemical composition in my brain was out of balance, and medications were prescribed to return the balance. At the time, I felt great and wanted to come off the benzo. How naïve I was about my emotional condition.

***

I continued my pattern of talking to Dave at least four days a week by cell phone, from a few minutes to an hour a call. We met religiously for coffee once a week. I purposefully chose the word "religiously." Dave taught me that depression was a three-legged stool—a psychiatrist for the body, a psychologist for the soul, and a spiritual director for the spirit.

Dave was my spiritual director, and he started to ramp up the time we talked about God, not in an overbearing but in a caring way. I was attending a Bible study that was a broad study of Scripture. Dave's Bible study for me was specific. I couldn't imagine how God fit into my depression when it first engulfed me. How could He be so cruel to allow such a horrible affliction? Dave taught me God was involved in everything that happened. We went through a series of Psalms that showed how God intervened in the life of David and other psalmists, and how David's depression turned into triumph. The Psalms opened my eyes to God's mercy and compassion to those in mental anguish.

One day Dave surprised me with a gift—a book called *Streams in the Desert* by L.B. Cowman. The consistent thread running through 366 daily devotional readings was that spiritual growth and strength come out of hardships, anguish, and suffering. It was another eye-opener.

***

When I told Dave about the fiery explosion in Montgomery and the bonds with Sam, Dave was elated. He told me a major healing of the soul had taken place, something he had been praying for since our golf match at Braemar two months earlier.

"Yes, I feel healed," I said. "I have an appointment with Zeke tomorrow to start withdrawal from the benzo. After that will be the SSRI."

Dave cautioned me to let Zeke guide the withdrawal process and not go too fast. It was unfortunate I didn't listen to him.

***

"How was your trip to Birmingham?" asked Zeke when I came into his office.

"It exceeded my expectations by a mile," I replied, and then proceeded to fill in Zeke's ledger with the details. "This is the best I've felt for six months. I feel ready to stop taking the benzo."

Zeke put on his professional face. "Benzodiazepines are highly addictive drugs. You don't just stop taking them. There is both a physiological and a psychological dependence. You've been on your prescription for more than three months. You need to come off slowly. I'd suggest a one-fourth milligram drop every week."

I did a quick calculation in my mind: three milligrams of the benzo multiplied by four equals twelve weeks. "That would be closing in on three months," I said with exasperation in my voice. "That's too long. I respect your caution to come off slowly, but I don't want to proceed at a snail's pace. I feel great and can handle a quicker withdrawal."

Zeke flinched. "This should be a team decision, so I'm listening to you. How about your going down one-fourth milligram today and another one-fourth milligram in four days and follow that pattern."

I did another quick calculation. "That would be beyond a month and a half, still too long. Everyone is different, aren't they? Can't I be the one able to withdraw quickly, especially with how outstanding I feel? What if I came off one-half milligram today and another one-half milligram in four days and followed that pattern? I'd be off the benzo completely in 20 days. I should be able to handle that."

There was a pained look on Zeke's face. "Yes, everyone is different in how they react to withdrawal, but there are upper and lower parameters to those differences. You're pushing the envelope with what you are suggesting. Do you remember when we covered my numbering system of 1-5?

"Five is normal. Four is mild to moderate depression. Three is severe depression that affects your thinking, eating, sleeping, and socializing—and initiates the onset of hopelessness and tears of anguish. Two is major depression that is not sustainable without relief. One is a mentally horrific depression that is life threatening.

"It won't kill you to withdraw at the pace you want, but you will drop into at least the 3s. Why do you want to do that? If you follow your plan, you'd better have plenty of things to keep you occupied, including a very rigorous exercise program in which you break into a sweat, releasing endorphins that are natural chemicals in the brain to help withdrawal.

"What you eat will also be important. Get plenty of carbohydrates and proteins. Force structure in your life for the next month. Try meditation and imagery, or prayer if you are so inclined."

I felt confident my withdrawal plan would not be as drastic as Zeke thought. My life was coming together. I no longer had the ingredients to cause depression. I didn't believe Zeke when he said I was going to slip back into the 3s. Maybe the 4s, I thought, but I could handle that, a half-bubble off level. Zeke said my SSRI covered anxiety as well as depression. Wouldn't that help the withdrawal? That very day I went from three milligrams of my benzo to two-and-a-half milligrams.

***

Saturday I did fine on the reduced benzo. I didn't miss a beat. I felt well Sunday also. Monday I met with Wally and experienced no ill effects. Our discussion started with my trip to Birmingham and the reconciliation with Sam. I sheepishly explained to Wally I had cancelled three appointments with him because I had not called Sam.

"You were on target with not facing me," responded Wally. "It was so obvious to me you needed to reconcile with Sam that I would not have let you off the hook. You're paying me to heal you, but if you reject being healed, there's nothing I can do.

"Now that you've reconciled with Sam, major healing has taken place. I can see it in your face. I'm proud of you."

"Wally, I feel better than I have in months. My life is coming together in so many ways that I feel like a new man. I no longer need to be on a benzo. The SSRI I'm taking should be enough. I met with my psychiatrist last Friday and we agreed on a withdrawal rate of one-half milligram every four days until I'm off the benzo completely. I dropped the first one-half milligram the very day I met with Zeke, and I'm feeling no withdrawal symptoms on this my third day. I'm so committed to be medication-free that I'm thinking of dropping another one-half milligram today instead of waiting until tomorrow."

"I wouldn't do that if I were you," said Wally. "Withdrawal has a cumulative effect. The lower the dose of the benzodiazepine, the greater the withdrawal pain. You may not feel much withdrawal now, but when you're down to one milligram, you'll feel *really* bad. The last one-half milligram will be the hardest."

We finished the session with Wally dispensing some of the same advice as Zeke—watch what you eat, exercise often until you sweat, put a lot of structure in your life, and think about something else other than yourself.

I left the session feeling both Zeke and Wally operated with a model of what normally happens. "Everyone is different," I reflected. "The way I feel, I'll be the one who withdraws from a benzo with mild symptoms."

And so I dropped to two milligrams of the benzo that very Monday, one day early. When I had a phone conversation with Dave later that afternoon, we talked mainly about the momentous journey to Birmingham. Dave asked how my meetings went with Zeke and Wally, and I said they were fine. I didn't want one more person telling me I was withdrawing from my medication too fast. Dave was not aware I had decided to sail my own ship, against the advice of two doctors.

*****

The next day, Tuesday, November 22, the withdrawal hit me hard. I had dropped one milligram of the benzo in three days. It was now the fourth day, and my body was telling me it wanted three milligrams, not two. I had my own simple interpretation of Zeke's scale of 1 to 5. I couldn't always remember his exact definitions. For me, 5 was feeling good, 4 was half a bubble off level, 3 was severe emotional pain that brought me to my knees, 2 was dropping into a pit where I couldn't move, and 1 was a place so treacherous I didn't even know who I was. I was at a 3 and miserable.

I called Dave that morning in desperation. "Dave, I've gone back to the emotional pain I was in last July and early August. It's not as bad as the day I crashed on the first antidepressant, but it's bad enough to be a 3, and I'm afraid I'm heading toward a 2. Help me, Dave. I don't know what to do. I didn't think I'd be in this condition again."

*****

I asked Dave as I wrote this to give me his first reaction when I called him that November day. I felt there must be more behind what he said than what he actually said.

*****

I realized when Mitch told me how fast he was coming

off the benzo that he was coming off too fast, much too fast.

I also realized Mitch had a character trait of persistence that was a blessing when he was striving for success in business but a curse when it became stubbornness that eschewed logic. The French have a saying that one's faults lie in one's virtues.

If Zeke and Wally could not convince Mitch to come off his medication more slowly, I would inherit the same fate, even though Mitch knew he was in for a more difficult time than he originally thought. His bravado was weakened but not defeated.

Mitch was asking for help, not advice. So I elected to embrace the role of being an encourager rather than a critic.

***

"Mitch, you're withdrawing from the benzo unusually fast. I think you know that. Is it your goal to maintain the same withdrawal rate?"

"It is," I answered, with as much conviction as I could muster. "For better or for worse, when I make up my mind to do something, I follow through. It's my goal to come off the medication and get on with my life, the sooner the better. Do you think I'm making a big mistake, Dave?"

"Your regimen will certainly result in completing the benzo withdrawal more quickly. What you're doing will cause you more than a little physical and emotional pain, but it won't kill you. There are people who withdraw from narcotic drugs by quitting all at once. It's called 'cold turkey.' I wouldn't suggest you try that; you may wish you were dead again. Keep your present rate of withdrawal if you want, but don't speed it up like you did the last step-down. What you're experiencing is normal for what you're attempting. You'll feel even worse further down the withdrawal road, but you'll get through it. I'll help you.

"The keys to lessening the pain are putting in as much heavy-duty exercise as you can and not thinking about the withdrawal. Stop thinking about yourself and how terrible you feel. Try your technique of saying, 'Stop!' You won't drop as low as you did the time you crashed on that first antidepressant Zeke prescribed. Keep reminding yourself of that. Tell yourself you've been this way before, and you're going to make it through. You can do it, Mitch. You can do it."

We continued talking. Dave encouraged me and gave me hope. I felt better when I closed my cell phone. The rest of that day I was at a high 3 and slept reasonably well that night.

****

The morning of Wednesday the 23rd of November was wretched: I was at a low 3. I choked down my breakfast and gagged as I cleaned up the dishes. Dave's advice to exercise briskly dropped into my mind, so I dragged myself to the health club.

I changed into exercise clothes in the locker room and headed for the track. It was about nine in the morning. After circling the track three times, I heard something behind me. It was not the sound of someone running or walking but more of a whirring. I looked back and there was Daniel, the friend I had met three times walking around Lake Calhoun. The whirring sound was his wheelchair.

"How are you doing, Mitch?" asked Daniel.

What was Daniel doing at my health club? Then I remembered he belonged to a health club with a track around it. Not many health clubs have walking and running tracks, maybe only one in St. Louis Park. So it was not unlikely we belonged to the same one.

"Mitch, this morning's prayer time ended with a strong discernment that you were in trouble and needed someone to talk to. I usually complete my exercise routine in the afternoon, but you are a morning person. I checked the list of members a few weeks ago out of curiosity, and there was your name. I came here after nine to find you. And here you are. What's the trouble?"

I was amazed. Was Daniel a modern-day prophet? I'd have to search the definition of a prophet to see if he fit the criteria.

I said to Daniel, "To use your words, we're not here by accident. You keep popping up when I need you most. And, yes, I'm in trouble."

As we went around the track, I explained the struggle I was having coming off the benzo. When I laid out the pace of my withdrawal, Daniel's eyes opened wider, but he didn't say anything. "So what do I do now, Daniel?"

Daniel answered, "I know your struggle first hand. I came off pain medication and depression medication, both faster than recommended; I was passionate to be drug-free. My withdrawal from pain meds was similar to your coming off a benzo.

"Here's an important thing for the front of your mind: you're not feeling miserable just because you are anxious and depressed. You are experiencing the physical symptoms of withdrawal. Until you stabilize without any benzo medication, you will have both physical and emotional pain.

"Even though the physical symptoms are inevitable, you can make the emotional pain more tolerable by following three suggestions.

"First, you are afraid you won't get any better, that you are heading into a deep pit from which you'll never escape. That creates a pit of emotional pain. You can counteract that by telling yourself you will be better when you have completed the withdrawal. Trust me when I tell you that's the truth; don't believe Satan's lie that you'll never be better.

"A second issue is that you're focusing on yourself and your withdrawal with every waking breath, and that creates even more emotional pain. You must stop thinking about yourself. Move beyond yourself."

"That's easier said than done," I responded. "When I'm in so much physical and emotional pain, all I can think about is myself. I've tried to think beyond myself, but I can't."

Daniel maneuvered his wheelchair in front of me, stopped, and looked straight into my eyes.

"Oh, yes you can, if you follow the third suggestion. You have to turn your pain over to God, trust He knows what He's doing, and believe He will not let you fall into a pit. He will not abandon you. He is with you even now. I'm not suggesting you pray; you're probably not able to. But you can say to God, 'I trust You will bring me through this, I believe You love me, and I rest in that love to strengthen and encourage me.' Keep repeating that over and over, and focus on God's mercy instead of your miserableness.

"I have a meeting in less than an hour. Let's meet here tomorrow at the same time, and we'll talk more about what you can do. In the meantime, trust me and take hope you will eventually be better. Can you do that, Mitch?"

I nodded my head, and we both left the club. It was remarkable Daniel knew exactly how I was feeling. It's not that I felt exactly the way he had; in fact, he told me that wasn't the case. It's that he *knew*. Daniel the prophet.

***

I was at a high 3 when I left the health club. Within five minutes after I stepped into my condo, a dark cloud of angst overwhelmed Daniel's hopeful words. The dark cloud followed me to bed Wednesday night, and the next morning I was at a low 3 again. And this was the day I withdrew another half milligram, bringing me to one-and-a-half. Oh, how my body wanted more of the benzo. I was in a downward spiral. I wanted to flop into my recliner and lay like a corpse all day, overwhelmed with how miserable I was.

But I dragged myself to the health club because I promised to meet Daniel. I was on my second circle around the walking path when I heard the whirring of his wheelchair.

"Not feeling too well today are you Mitch? You thought about not coming here, but I'm glad you did."

Once again, Daniel the prophet. He didn't ask me how I felt. He told me.

"I didn't *feel* like coming here today, Daniel. I *had* to. Something has to change. I can't continue like this."

"You could always up the dosage of your medication, Mitch."

" If I did that, I'd be a failure. I'm halfway there. I'll tough it out and hope my condition doesn't become worse."

"But it *will* become worse," Daniel said, "unless you do something positive to lessen the pain."

I replied, "You gave me three suggestions yesterday, but I wasn't able to follow any of them by the time I arrived home."

Daniel suggested we go downstairs to the coffee room and try again to gain a positive outlook on my depression and anxiety.

***

We bought our coffee and found a table secluded from everyone else. Daniel looked at me with empathy in his eyes and spoke softly, pulling a pad of paper and a pen from the back of his wheelchair and giving them to me.

"I have some important things to tell you, Mitch, and I want you to write them down. Are you ready?"

I nodded yes. I was feeling better just being with Daniel, but I was still at a high 3 at best.

"Let's set the groundwork first. You are not able to think clearly enough to recall what I said yesterday. That's how I was withdrawing from the pain medication. A counselor told me the same things every time we met, as if I had never heard them before.

"You are made up of body, soul, and spirit. Your soul is made up of your mind, will, and emotions. You are letting your body take control of your mind and emotions, and that doubles your pain. You are fighting a losing battle right now, with your mind on the defensive and your emotions screaming 'poor Mitch.' Your spirit is not even in the battle."

Dave had emphasized the same thing.

"How do I win the battle, Daniel?"

"Remember when I spoke to you about Ann, the wife of a friend, who taught me to say 'Stop!' whenever I felt sorry for myself. I still use that technique. There were times I said 'Stop!' a thousand times a day, and it worked. We'll call that Strategy Number One: whenever you begin feeling sorry for yourself, say 'Stop!' as many times as you need to. You can't say stop to your body, but you can say stop to your mind and emotions.

"The basis for the next two strategies is to think of something or someone other than yourself, which will bring your spirit into the battle. How *is* your spiritual life?"

"It's stronger than it has been at any time in my life, but I have miles to go before I become a saint," I answered.

"You don't need sainthood, Mitch; you need to be grounded in your spirit. Do you have a Bible at home?"

"I bought a Bible two months ago, but it's rarely been out of my bookcase."

"Here's what we'll call Strategy Number Two. Read the psalms and the gospels for at least an hour each day. But don't just read them; pray them. Take five psalms a day and two chapters of the gospels and read them slowly, praying verse-by-verse with what the Word is showing you. When you come to one of God's promises, praise Him for that promise and confess it for yourself. Do that every day at least once a day, more if you can. This may seem strange to you at first and difficult to do on your own. But the Holy Spirit will be with you, guiding you. Depend on Him to show you how to follow this strategy.

"Put an asterisk by Strategy Number Three in your notes. Every time you think of yourself, think of someone else instead—Dave, me, your ex-wife, your kids, your brother Sam, or someone you admire. Think of something else besides rehashing all your mistakes—playing a game of golf, lying on a beach at one of your favorite resort spots, climbing a mountain, going on a hike, whatever. Extricate yourself from the negative strongholds in your mind and embrace the positive. I call this neutralizing your mind. It won't be easy, but you'll become better if you stay with it.

"The last strategy, Strategy Number Four, is to do those things that will refresh your mind. Visit the health club every day and use your exercise time for affirming how good you'll feel when you no longer take a benzo. See as many movies as you can at a movie theater, so you can be around other people. Take car trips to cities like Duluth, Northfield, Red Wing, and Mankato. You'll be on freeways, which will force you to concentrate on driving. Schedule day trips so you sleep in your own home. Take your Bible along for praying the gospels and psalms. Talk to Dave and me often. We can help share your burden and encourage you. Discover the roots of your fears, anxieties, and depression with your psychologist.

"Do you have all that down, Mitch?"

I asked Daniel for clarification on two of the strategies to make sure I had them down correctly and completely.

"I'll follow all four strategies, Daniel. I'm not capable of developing a plan for myself. You have given me practical hope, not platitudes. I appreciate your concern for me."

I had risen from a low 3 when I arrived at the club to a low 4, a considerable improvement. I knew I'd drop down when Daniel and I parted company, but I had positive ways to avoid a downward spiral into the pit—Daniel's four strategies.

* * *

Three days later on Sunday I dropped to one milligram. The past three days had been rough, but not as rough as they would have been without Daniel's four strategies. His advice was more than that of a friend. He had an authority in the way he looked and the way he spoke. I don't know how to describe it other than at the health club his demeanor and voice seemed to be something beyond himself. I was still a novice in reading the gospels, but I saw a striking similarity of Daniel to Jesus, who spoke with authority at all times. He even looked like I imagined Jesus, with long hair, a medium-length beard, and steely eyes that bore right through you.

And so I followed all four strategies with diligence. They were precious to me. They kept me out of the darkest den of depression.

Since last Thursday, I said, "Stop!" hundreds of times a day when I felt sorry for myself. It worked better than I expected.

I prayed the psalms and gospels, verse by verse, for an hour on Thursday. I didn't obtain much out of it, other than to take my mind off myself. On Friday, the technique was more meaningful. Saturday was a breakthrough when I realized this was not a technique to master, but a way of communicating with God. I found that praying Scripture only worked if I concentrated on God and not myself. On Sunday I prayed Scripture for two hours, and I branched out to the Old Testament and the Epistles. My outlook changed from the setting of the sun to the rising of the Son.

* * *

As I wrote that last sentence from my struggle journal, I had to laugh to myself. It was a great line that came into my mind, and Christians may say, "Only a Christian could write those words." However, I was not a Christian by a long shot; perhaps this was my first step on that journey. The sentence sounded good at the time, like one of my best ad slogans.

***

Strategy three became intertwined with the first strategy. When I shouted, "Stop!" my mind often took me someplace else. Many times I returned to the Washburn Water Tower where Dave and I became kindred spirits, to the Nicollet Avenue Bridge where we became friends forever, and to the path from Minnehaha Falls to the Mississippi River where we cemented our friendship. Other times I envisioned the Jemison Trail in Birmingham where Sam and I first reconciled, the golf course Sam and I played, and the explosion in Montgomery.

I lived the fourth strategy by talking to Daniel and Dave every day, and seeing Wally once a week. I met Daniel at the health club every morning except Sunday. I met Dave weekly at the coffee shop on France and talked to him on the phone other days.

I journeyed to Northfield late Friday morning, after working out at the health club and talking to Daniel, and had lunch at a unique restaurant. Driving down and back and around the town was enjoyable, but eating by myself, with everyone else there being a couple or a group, was not uplifting.

I didn't stay away from my mind and emotions at all times, but I succeeded often enough that a high 3 was my lowest boundary. I even managed to live in the low to mid-4s some of the time. Most of the withdrawal was coming from my body, as Daniel said, not my soul or spirit. And that made all the difference.

I couldn't thank Daniel enough for being my rescuer. Daniel seemed to show up when I had depleted my own resources and hope. In Daniel's words, "It isn't just an accident I'm here, you know." Sometime, I would need to ask Daniel exactly what he meant. For now, I just accepted it as fact.

***

By Wednesday, the 30th of November, I dropped to a half milligram of my benzo. Just one-half milligram left. I was feeling awful. I remembered Wally telling me the last half milligram would be the hardest—and it was. I tried to follow the four strategies Daniel had given me, but they didn't lift me up as they had before. My body's withdrawal was flooding my mind and emotions. I was close to being defenseless. Saying, "Stop!" and thinking of something positive was being negated by my body's screaming at me in pain. I could not focus on Scripture or prayer. Going anyplace was out of the question. The only thing I could do was call Dave and Daniel. Both of them encouraged me that this was the worst of my struggle, and it would eventually pass.

I was now at a low 3 and even invaded the 2s when a wave of hopelessness and fear overtook me. If it weren't for Dave and Daniel to talk to, I would have been lost in the pit. That was my greatest fear—that I would descend so low I couldn't come back up again. Both Dave and Daniel told me that wouldn't happen; "God is with you all the time." Their words kept me from the depths of no return.

***

The next day was even worse. I was hanging on by the skin of my teeth. Dark thoughts pervaded my mind and emotions. I couldn't stop them. I couldn't stop thinking how bad I felt. I was immobile in my recliner at 10 a.m., wondering how I would make it through the day, when the phone rang.

It was Kathleen from Chicago. Jane, our youngest daughter, had been in a terrible car accident the night before, and her life was hanging in the balance.

"Mitch, I don't know what you'll want to do. I felt I had to call you. She's your daughter too."

The effects of the withdrawal were buried by the news of Jane. Adrenalin raced through my body. I forgot about my physical and emotional pain. All I could think about was Jane. It was all about her. It was not about me.

"Kathleen, I'll pack up and head down to Chicago within a half hour. I can reach Chicago faster by car than making plane arrangements. It's all freeway from Minneapolis, and I'll be there in six hours. Thank you for calling. I'll talk to you again when I'm on the road."

Kathleen informed me what hospital Jane was in. I knew exactly where it was. I packed quickly and was out the door in twenty minutes. All I could think about was that Jane might not live. I almost forgot to pack my medications.

CHAPTER 13
A Vigil in Chicago

The highway to Chicago was like a railroad called Interstate 94, filled with cars instead of trains. Once I passed the eastern suburbs of St. Paul and entered Wisconsin, the traffic eased considerably. I grabbed my headset and called Kathleen to obtain more information about Jane.

Kathleen was in the hospital cafeteria having an early lunch when I called. Suzie was in the Intensive Care Unit (ICU) with Jane.

"Are you on your way, Mitch? Where are you?"

"I'm in Wisconsin," I answered with worry and fear in my voice. "I should be there in five hours. Please tell me more about Jane? How did the car accident happen? What is Jane's condition?"

Kathleen responded with the matter-of-factness of a person overwhelmed with tragedy and inundated with medical information. You see a similar posture at funerals, where the newly widowed wife is strong beyond belief at the wake and collapses after the funeral.

"Jane took a day of vacation from the bank where she works, and we were together all day Christmas shopping. By the time we returned to my condo, the roads were becoming dangerously slippery. I begged her to stay put. She said no every time I asked her to remain safe with me. Finally, with a smile on her face and a determined look in her eyes, she set out by car for her apartment near Millennium Park, where she could walk to work the next day. She didn't want to use up any more vacation days because she was planning to use all of them to spend time with Mike, Susie, and me between Christmas and New Year's.

"On the way down North Shore Drive, just before the Chicago River, a semi-trailer truck jackknifed, with the front of the truck facing north. Jane was driving faster than she should have and following too close. The road was so icy that she apparently applied the brakes and did a 360 before she hit the truck with the driver's corner of her car. She was unconscious when a Chicago policeman, who had seen the whole accident, checked her condition and called an ambulance. She was pried out of the car with the Jaws of Life, but still made it to the Northwestern Memorial Hospital within 40 minutes of the accident.

"We now know both her legs were crushed, and she experienced trauma to her head. She's in a coma, and the doctors need to determine the extent of the damage. Without her seat belt and air bag, she would not have survived."

My eyes were filled with tears, and I could barely breathe. When I started talking, my voice was shaking. "Oh, my daughter Jane, my daughter Jane. Is she going to live?"

"The doctors said she will live, but her life won't be the same. They want to wait a few days to make an accurate assessment of her injuries. Right now they are hoping the swelling goes down."

"I want you to know I'll be there for her, whatever the outcome," I said.

"You haven't been there for her for years," replied Kathleen, with more resignation than anger. "Why would I think you would be now? Why would Jane think so? And you're not going to have a great welcome from Mike or Susie. They are very upset you are even coming, after all these years of being a detached father. I can understand their feelings, but I told them you are Jane's father after all, and it's better you are coming than not coming."

"Thank you, Kathleen," I said with a catch in my throat. "Your telling me I can't expect anyone there to be thrilled with my coming is nothing more than I deserve.

"It's only words right now, but I hope you all will see changes for the better in me. I'm asking for a chance I don't deserve but desperately want—to be on friendly terms with you, Mike, Susie, and Jane.

"Last month, I visited Birmingham for a couple of weeks and reconciled with Sam. I admitted that our estrangement was my fault, and I wanted my brother back. So did he. That was a big step for me, but I felt so much better the day we settled our differences.

"My next goal was to draw closer to my family, but not under these circumstances. I wish I had been in that car instead of Jane."

"Let's see what happens when you get here, Mitch," Kathleen replied in a voice softer and more compassionate. "I forgave you long ago; yet, there is still lingering pain left from the divorce. You'd better concentrate on your driving. I'll see you in a few hours. Jane is in the intensive care unit on the eighth floor, west wing. Ask for directions at the information desk right inside the main door. Good-bye, Mitch. I'm glad you're coming."

I closed my cell phone and entered into deep thought. I had been so concerned about Jane that the dynamics of meeting my family was at a decibel level lower than I could hear. Would my arrival cause more harm than good? It was confusing. What posture should I take when I arrived? Dave would help me sort it out. Thankfully, he answered on the first ring.

"Dave, this is Mitch. My youngest daughter Jane has been in a bad car accident, and I'm on the road to Chicago now." I related to Dave Jane's injuries and the comments Kathleen made about the hostile feelings of my children.

"How do I approach this, Dave? I'm in a fog and need light. Can you help me see what I should do?"

There was a minute of blank time before Dave spoke.

"Mitch, I'm not seeing clearly myself what you should do. Give me ten minutes to pray and frame the issues. I'll call you back."

***

How slowly ten minutes passes when you are awaiting word from your commanding officer. Finally, the phone rang.

"Mitch, pull off to the side of the road and prepare to take notes."

I was 500 feet from a roadside rest area, pulled in, and equipped myself with pen and paper.

"Mitch, you reconciled with Sam first because it was easiest, but the battle plan was for you to reconcile with your family next. I was perplexed how that would take place, but the opportunity has come in the guise of tragedy."

"Do you think God engineered a tragedy for the opportunity to reconcile?" I asked.

"Absolutely not," replied Dave emphatically. "God doesn't work that way. We live in a fallen world where bad things happen. God may allow them, but He doesn't cause them unless His will can't be accomplished in any other way. I don't see that as the case here. He does work within tragedy, though, to bring about good. You need to trust that good will come from this. Keep that as your overriding focus no matter how bad things become.

"Here's the frame as I see it. You have not contacted any members of your family since you came to Minneapolis; to them you are a missing person, and one they are not anxious to find. Your children have bitter feelings not only for the pain you caused them but also for the pain you inflicted on their mother. Kathleen says she has forgiven you, and I don't doubt that is true from what you've told me about her. I do doubt, though, that there is much trust in you on her part.

"Now they are collectively huddled in the midst of a family crisis, and you are an unwelcome intruder to their family enclave, one who will breach the boundaries of their solidarity."

"What a bleak picture you paint, Dave. How can I ever reconcile with the family you have just painted?"

Dave's response displayed a map I could follow in navigating my way through the difficulties awaiting me in Chicago.

"Most importantly, focus on Jane. You are her father and have a right to be by her side, no matter what you have done in the past. You don't have to apologize for being there.

"If your kids ask why you came or challenge your being there, be humble and always give this answer: 'I'm not the person you knew in the past. I deeply regret how I treated you, but I can only be a different person in the present and the future. When your mother called about the accident, I left Edina in 20 minutes to be with Jane. She's my daughter, and I love her. I love you too.'

"If your kids challenge your love for them, don't engage in an argument. Look them directly in the eyes and sincerely say, 'I love you too.' You'll find that will curtail the challenges, and there *will be* challenges.

"Ask first to visit Jane with Kathleen. Let her see how deeply you love Jane. Then, when the opportunity presents itself, tell her how miserable you feel about the pain you've caused her. Talk about whatever Kathleen wants to talk about.

"Next, ask to go into the ICU with Suzie. She's probably not as hostile to you as Mike, from what you've told me about her. That will give Kathleen a chance to talk to Mike to lessen his anger toward you. Talk to Suzie about her life, not about yours, and talk to her about Jane.

"Finally, go into the ICU with Mike. Let him see how much you love Jane, and talk to him about her. Ask him about his family and life, and don't start into apologies. Tell him about your reconciliation with Sam. As I remember, he was very fond of his uncle. Sam was a surrogate father to him, taking him hunting, fishing, to ball games, and other events a boy needs to be initiated into by an adult.

"Wait a day and arrange to have coffee one-on-one with Suzie and Mike. Let them be initiators of the conversation so they don't feel you are lecturing them. Seek to understand them first; then seek to be understood as their changed father. You must at this time make a strong confession, so they know you are truly sorry for the way you raised them.

"Do you have all that?"

I had been taking notes feverishly as Dave was talking, stopping him a few times to catch up and ask for clarification.

Dave's suggested strategy resonated within me like a piano string to a pitch pipe.

"Yes, I have it. Thank you, Dave. Without you, I would have been uncertain how to proceed. Now I have a map. I'd better hit the road again to arrive at the hospital when I said I would."

"Give me a call when you can," said Dave, "and let me know how the battle is going, and if any changes to the map are needed. I'll wait to hear from you."

* * *

I parked my car in the hospital ramp and walked through the main entrance of Northwestern Memorial Hospital. I saw the information desk ahead of me and asked for directions to Jane Jasper's room in the ICU.

***

As I exited the elevator doors, I could see a waiting room before me. Mike and Suzie were slumped in reclining chairs, looking like they hadn't slept in 24 hours. They looked up when they saw me and fixed me to the elevator door with their eyes. I approached them cautiously.

"I wish we were meeting in different circumstances, Mike and Suzie. You two look tired. Jane's accident must be terribly hard on you. We can talk more later. Right now I'd like to see Jane. Is your mother with her?"

Mike ignored the question and answered instead with a fury seething inside him. "What are you doing here? You don't deserve to see Jane? You don't deserve to see Mother or Suzie or me." I was taken aback by the force of his anger. I had expected hostility, but not to this degree.

It was time for me to depend on Dave's road map. If I didn't have that, I would have been frozen by Mike's onslaught.

"I'm a different person than you knew before I moved to Minneapolis, Mike. I don't expect you to accept that at face value right now. Your mother called me this morning to tell me about Jane, and I left my condo in 20 minutes to drive here. She's my daughter, and I love her. I love you too."

Mike sneered. "You have a funny way of showing love. You wrote us kids off during our growing-up years. Mother suffered in silence with being mid-level in your list of importance. It was work, work, work for you at the ad agency. When you weren't at work, you were mixing with your high-profile friends. We rarely saw you. You were not interested in what we were doing in school or in our athletic or social lives. After high school, things became worse. We haven't even seen you for two years."

Mike was just getting wound-up, when I interrupted him.

Quietly and with my head bowed, I said, "You're absolutely right, Mike, in everything you said. Lately I have been convicted of what a huge mistake I made, thinking my work and high-profile networking were more important than my family. How I wish I could change the past with what I now know about myself, but I can only deal with the present. I love you and Suzie and Jane, and I have great pain for what I have done to your mother. Now, Mike, can you tell me if your mother is in the ICU with Jane?"

It's not easy to continue fierce anger when the person you're attacking concedes your argument. Mike calmed down and answered my question in an even voice.

"Mother said you'd be here about 2:30 this afternoon, and so you are. She asked if you would come to Jane's room when you got here. Suzie and I have been with Jane for an hour, and Mother has been with her for the last five minutes."

***

I walked into the ICU and found Jane's room. I remember once stepping off a plane in Orlando, Florida, in mid-July. It was so hot and humid it took my breath away. I had that same feeling when I entered Jane's room. All hope was drained from me. My daughter was unconscious, with several monitoring devices attached to her and two intravenous tubes invading her veins. She was pale and fragile, hanging on to life tentatively. Kathleen was staring at her with blank eyes and holding her hand.

Kathleen looked up at me with the blank stare intact and exhaustion in her voice.

"Hello, Mitch. You arrived when you said you would. Traffic must have been light on the freeway."

This was the woman I had married. I felt sadness and a sense of love for her that had never been present in our marriage. She was so vulnerable. Jane was so vulnerable. I spoke in a low voice.

"It was, Kathleen. It was. I talked to Mike and Suzie before I came in here. You were right about my not receiving a great welcome when I arrived. I didn't deserve a warm welcome. I have a lot to make up for.

"Would you mind if I sat where you are for a few minutes? I would like to hold Jane's hand and talk to her."

"I've read that unconscious patients can sometime hear a person talking to them," Kathleen said. "I've talked to her all night and all day."

Kathleen sat in a chair at the foot of the bed and watched a Mitch she probably had never seen before.

I sat down and held Jane's hand. I started talking to her, but then broke down and started weeping. When I regained control of my emotions, I whispered to Jane, "Oh, Jane, I can't bear to see you like this. I wish I had been in the car instead of you. You're such a beautiful girl, such a beautiful person. I am in agony over what a poor father I was. I hope you can forgive me. I wish we could start our lives over again right now. I would draw a line on the edge of your bed separating the past from the present and the future, and we would go on from there."

I continued to hold Jane's hand and softly prayed for her. I forgot Kathleen was in the same room. I prayed for healing: that her head injuries would not be life threatening or debilitating, that we could be reconciled to each other, and that our whole family could still become a real family after all the pain I had inflicted.

"Do you really mean that, Mitch?" asked Kathleen with disbelief in her voice.

I was suddenly awakened from my reverie. It was no longer just Jane and me.

"Do you really want us to be a real family? How could that ever be possible with all the pain you have caused us?"

"Yes, I really want that, Kathleen. I plan to spend time with you and each of the kids separately and let God fashion how we can become a healthy family.

"I want to start the process by apologizing to you. You said you've forgiven me, but I'm haunted by the pain I inflicted on you. I was so insensitive. I made colossal mistakes throughout my life. Divorcing you was undoubtedly the worst. In Minneapolis, I thought it was too late in the afternoon to have a meaningful family life. I was mired in helplessness and hopelessness. A friend I grew up with helped me see it was not too late in the afternoon, it was never too late to change. He pushed me to see a psychiatrist and a psychologist. How I view the world has changed 180 degrees. I'm on a path to becoming a new Mitch."

I had forgotten how beautiful Kathleen was, both on the outside and the inside. She walked over and put her hand on top of my hand that was holding Jane's hand.

"It's going to take a lot more than words, Mitch. I've been praying for two years that you would change. It may take that long for you to demonstrate what you've just now said. What I've seen and heard from you today is a good start, but only a start. I question you can change as much as you want to, but I'll give you the chance. I won't shut you out. Call it acceptance with reservations. If you stay here with Jane, I'll slip out and talk to Mike and Suzie, and ask one of them to come into Jane's room with you."

"Thank you, Kathleen," I quietly said with head down. "I know I don't deserve a chance, so I am thrilled by acceptance with reservations."

***

Suzie entered the ICU five minutes after Kathleen left. I was still sitting beside Jane, holding her hand and talking to her. I looked up when Suzie stepped into the room.

"Hello, Suzie," I ventured. "Thanks for coming in. I'm overwhelmed with Jane lying here so helpless. If you might lose a daughter, you realize how much you love her.

"And it's not only Jane. I realize now how much I love my whole family and what a fool I was in not appreciating what I had. That might seem uncharacteristic to you right now, but could you judge me for who I am, not who I was. I'd like to start over again if you all will let me."

Suzie seemed moved by my attention to Jane.

"Mom talked to Mike and me in the waiting room. She asked us to give you a chance. If you're different, we'll know it. If you're not, we'll know that too."

"Thanks, Suzie. That's all I want—a chance. Could we talk about your life and how things are going for you?"

"S-Sure," answered Suzie.

I could tell by her stuttering and the look on her face that I had surprised her by asking about her life. When Suzie was growing up, I either wasn't there for her or talked about myself.

"We're living in Wheaton now. Jeff purchased a car dealership there last year, and we moved to be closer to it."

Suzie continued with an outline of her life, telling me about their two children—how they were doing in school, in athletics, and in their social lives. She was now working most days as an artist. There was an art gallery in Wheaton where she took her pictures to sell. I asked questions here and there, and revealed that I saw promise in her as an artist when she was in high school. Even with that glimpse of her budding talent, I was too involved with my work to tell her what I felt. If only I could go back in time with what I now knew....

Suzie looked at the clock in Jane's room. "I can't believe an hour has gone by. I'd better leave and let Mike spend time with you and Jane. He'll not be as easy as I've been."

"I know that," I responded.

***

Mike entered the ICU room five minutes later and found me as Suzie had, holding Jane's hand, talking to her, and weeping softly.

Mike started the conversation. "Mom said we should give you a second chance. All past evidence about you precludes my giving you that chance. However, Mom said she had been praying for two years that you would change and somehow re-enter our lives. I can argue with evidence on my side, but I can't argue against prayer. She spent the last hour softening me up. So, I'm going to give you a chance, but it's going to be like a courtroom. You'll need to present the case that you've changed, not just talk about it."

"Spoken like the lawyer you are," I responded with a smile.

Mike couldn't help smiling either. And then he started laughing.

"Dad, I guess I've some of you in me. You used to talk like an advertising executive, and here I am talking like a lawyer."

Such a small thing that broke the ice. When Mike started laughing, I started laughing, and the hostility Mike felt when he came in vanished.

"Oh, Dad, I've always wanted a real father. I've wanted to have a grandfather for my children. I'll give you a chance, and I hope I lose the case I came in here to argue."

"I hope so too," I said. "I'd like to catch up on what's been happening in your life. How is your law career going? How are Monica and my three grandchildren doing? Are you still living in Naperville?"

Mike talked non-stop for an hour, except for a few questions I asked him. He told me his family still lived in Naperville, and he still commuted into Chicago. He was with the same corporate law firm, but he was now a partner and a very high-profile lawyer in the corporate world. He sounded like me, taking pride in his accomplishments.

Monica was a stay-at-home mom. With the three kids now in school, she was about to pursue a law degree. She wanted to help the poor, and this was her avenue.

Mike talked about his three children and how they were growing up. I could sense Mike was more like me than he thought. I could see he was spending too much time at the law office and not enough time at home, especially not enough time with his children. Perhaps we could talk about that some day, but not now.

I told Mike about my recent reconciliation with Sam. It was evident he was pleased. Sam had been a favorite uncle, but Mike lost touch with him when Sam went down to Alabama.

"Let's go to the waiting room," I said, "and give your mother and Suzie time with Jane. Then I can find a hotel room close by."

****

I crossed the threshold of the hotel room I found exactly one block from the hospital. After unpacking, I called Dave.

"How are things going down there?" was the first thing Dave said.

"Better than expected," I replied. "I followed the plan you gave me on the interstate and have been given a second chance by Kathleen, Mike, and Suzie."

I covered the family conversations with Dave and related that the emotional landscape was considerably warmer now than when I first arrived. "We're talking respectfully, if not entirely cordially yet. If we continue to draw together, I feel we're on the way to becoming a family again. I only wish it were under better circumstances."

"Mitch, you still have a critical part of the plan to accomplish. You need to meet with each one alone, maybe in a coffee shop, and make a full confession of your faulty past. They won't completely trust you until they know you are aware of your mistakes and are willing to repent of them. Repent meaning you will not make those mistakes again. Then seek their forgiveness."

"Do I really need to, Dave? Shouldn't we become re-acquainted first? And I can make a confession when the time seems right."

"No!" answered Dave emphatically. "You agreed to the plan, and the last step is probably the most important one. You have arrived at that step. Don't falter now. Finish strong."

"Dave, I put myself in your hands because I didn't know what to do on my own. I will follow through. I'll return to the hospital tonight, but that may be too soon for confessions. Maybe tomorrow would work better."

"Tomorrow it will be," responded Dave. "You're doing great, Mitch. They're seeing the new you and responding positively. Keep to the plan, and you'll have a new family to add to your life."

I returned to the hospital for the rest of the evening, engaging in small talk with Kathleen, Mike, and Suzie, and spending time in Jane's room. I didn't say anything about getting together tomorrow on a one-to-one basis. When I had a chance to doze, I felt more at peace than I had in years.

***

At the time, I was caught up with the quest to earn my family back. I see now what a critical time this was for the healing of my anxiety and depression. To say "no" to feeling sorry for myself, there had to be a greater "yes," the yes of focusing on my family. To stop looking at myself, I had to start looking at others.

Given that I was still in clinical depression, the changed circumstances were not going to heal me instantly. But it was a start. I was discovering the underlying reasons for my depression and changing my thinking and behavior, so there was less stress on the biochemical make-up of my brain. And less stress meant I was starting the journey back to normal. But a new normal, not the old Mitch.

CHAPTER 14
Building Family Relationships

On Friday morning, December 2, 2005, I walked into Northwestern Memorial Hospital and rode the elevator up to the eighth floor. It had been six months since I left Chicago, and I had often thought about returning for perhaps a week to recapture the familiarity of a city I lived in for 40 years. Especially when I was lonely and deeply depressed in Minneapolis, the thought of returning to Chicago was alluring. But something deep within me resisted the call, even for a week. Dave had told me Minneapolis was my true home now and reinforced that a trip to Chicago would set me back in what I must do to escape unrelenting depression—carve out a new life for myself that would be a 180 degree shift from the paradigm of my old life.

In the elevator, for no reason I could think of, a wave of anxiety and depression came over me. Anxiety and depression are so intermixed, I didn't know where one left off and the other started. I usually used the word depression as encompassing both.

Fear returned, and I was close to panic. My body was craving more of the anti-anxiety benzo than the one-half milligram it was getting. The antidepressant SSRI that I was taking offered no cushion for withdrawal of the benzo. With no one else in the elevator, I yelled "Stop!" a half-dozen times. The panic released its grip, leaving me at an uncomfortable low 3. How could I have felt so free of symptoms yesterday and be on the edge of the pit today? I wanted to go back to my hotel room.

However, I knew what Dave would say. "Pray to God and stick it out. You can't let your depression and anxiety keep you from interacting with your family."

I breathed in and out deeply several times. I prayed that I would have a sound mind today, that God would give me the strength to make it through. By the time I stepped off the elevator, my rating had risen to a high 3. Funny how that level, which previously had been the threshold of severe depression, now seemed almost like a blessing. I was not going under. I could survive the day.

***

As I entered the waiting room at 8 a.m., there were Kathleen, Mike, and Suzie. They had slept in the waiting room, insisting about four in the morning that I go to the hotel room and sleep.

"Hello, Mitch," said Kathleen with a weak smile, but a smile nevertheless. "I hope you slept well."

"I did sleep well," I replied, as energetically as I could after what I had just gone through in the elevator. I had to fake a smile. "My room has two queen-sized beds. I slept in the one closest to the window. Why don't one of you head over for a more restful sleep than in a waiting room? We can stay in contact by cell phone if anything changes here."

"Hello, Dad," said Suzie, with a more pronounced smile than her mother's. "The doctors are checking Jane now to see if the swelling has gone down in her brain and to assess the swelling in her legs. I'd like to take your offer of some more restful sleep. I don't think I've slept at all here, worrying about Jane. I can catch up on the doctors' report later, unless the news is something dramatic."

Mike also welcomed me, without a smile but without anger in his voice.

"Hello, Dad. I'm glad you were able to get some sleep. When Suzie returns, we'll send Mom over." Not a lot of words but with an entirely different attitude than yesterday.

Twenty minutes after Suzie left, one of the doctors came to the waiting room.

"The x-rays we took of Jane show severe bruising from her left hip down to her foot, and several significant breaks in the femur, tibia, fibula, and ankle. Her right leg looks much better, with multiple fractures of the ankle and some bruising of muscles, tissue, and veins. The bruising will take as long to heal as the broken bones."

"Will she be able to walk again?" I stammered.

"I think so," the doctor answered. "We'll better know the full prognosis when we operate."

"When will you operate?" Mike asked.

"First the swelling needs to go down. The best orthopedic specialists available will perform the surgery. The likelihood of Jane walking again will be in good hands. We have been administering steroids to reduce the swelling in her legs and brain. Scans of her head show an intense concussion and multiple contusions. The swelling almost reached the point where we had to operate to relieve the pressure. We have given her anti-seizure medication as a preventative as well.

"The swelling has diminished enough in the last 24 hours that we are past needing to operate. However, she will be in a coma or semi-coma for somewhere around a week. She has what we call mild traumatic brain injury. There may be symptoms that last a year or more: such as fatigue, headaches, mood changes, getting lost or confused, irritability, feelings of depression, memory loss, and poor concentration.

"For today and tomorrow, not much will happen. Sunday will be a critical day, the day we hope to operate on her legs.

"I almost forgot to tell you. We did an MRI on her brain and back. That's how we determined she suffered mild traumatic brain injury and not a more severe injury, which would have been a whole new ballgame. The MRI on her back showed no breaks and no damage to the spinal cord. She could have ended up a paraplegic if the lumbar 1 or lumbar 2 were severed or crushed. She has movement and sensation above the waist, but we were concerned there may be another reason for her legs not moving besides being crushed. You have much to be grateful for."

That was a file cabinet full of information to take in. We *were* grateful she would be able to walk again; we were afraid she might never be able to. We *were* concerned about the brain-injury symptoms exhibiting themselves after the coma lifted.

We decided to let Suzie rest and bring her up to speed when she returned. Mike had taken extensive notes, like a good lawyer. Kathleen and I walked back to Jane's room. Mike departed for the hospital lobby to return law-firm phone calls from the last two days.

***

I asked Kathleen if I could be the first one to sit by Jane's side. I held Jane's hand and told her how much I loved her and how much I wanted to be a part of her life as a real father.

Then silence set in, and I was lost in thought. When I expressed my love to Jane, something inside me lit up. My depression had diminished, going from a high 3 to a low 4. That may not seem like much, but it's the difference between the shadows of darkness at twilight and the first glimpse of sunlight in the morning. Energy and alertness returned.

***

Once again, seeing my depression from two years out is like a clear picture in color compared to the hazy black and white portrait I saw in the hospital. Clinical depression, the biochemical imbalance in your brain, can grab you at any time for no reason, such as in the elevator. If your only defense is taking medication, then more medication seems the only answer to relieve on-going mental anguish.

I see now in living color that a three-pronged approach is the best way to escape living in depression the rest of your life. The first prong is the medication so you can think and function again. But you can't stop there. You need to engage the soul to discover the causes behind the symptoms and treat them with inner healing. Many people will find some success with these two approaches. The third prong, healing of the spirit, will bring you to a higher level of recovery than the first two approaches alone.

To complete the picture, I must color in two more images.

There are some people for whom a biochemical imbalance in the brain is a chronic condition, without being precipitated by hidden causes. The two approaches beyond medication will help alleviate the depression, but total healing may never happen. However, you'll never know if you are that person unless you at least try the other two approaches.

The second image is people with mild or moderate depression who can be healed without medication, sometimes by just seeing a doctor to discuss symptoms and learn about depression. Seeing a psychologist or counselor will accelerate inner healing, as will having a spiritual director. Dave was my spiritual director. I have talked to people for whom the Holy Spirit was directly their spiritual director.

Do I sound like an expert on depression? I am, in a way. Those of you who have had a critical illness, like diabetes, have become experts by living through it, as well as by talking to doctors, talking to other people with diabetes, searching the Internet, and reading everything about diabetes you can get your hands on. That's what I did. I'm not an expert on depression through credentialing. I am the depository of information gathered from my own experience; from Dave, Zeke, Wally, and Daniel; from depressed people I talk to (we seem to find each other by instinct); and from much research.

***

After ten minutes talking to Jane, I looked up and saw Kathleen watching me. When she saw she had my attention, she spoke.

"Mitch, when you arrived yesterday, you walked into a den of lions, ready to tear you apart. I'm talking about Mike and Suzie, not myself. I don't know how you did it, but they are now more like lambs."

I responded, "Without you, they'd be lions yet. Mike and Suzie told me you had been praying for me and asked them to give me a second chance. They told me that during all their growing-up years, when I was not there for them, you kept saying I loved them but just didn't know how to express it. You presented a Dad to them they could live with. Even after I divorced you, they said you would rebuke them when they unleashed their anger against me. You would say, 'I don't want you talking that way about your father.' You kept them within the range of reconciliation."

Kathleen smiled, "Well, I might have had *something* to do with it." Then she turned serious. "If you were the same old Mitch, any conversation with them would not have been helpful. They realize you are not the person they grew up with, and their initial coldness has thawed. If the thawing continues, which will be a result of what you call your new personality, they'll eventually warm up to you."

"Oh, how I hope so," I said with a catch in my throat. "The friend that I talked to you about—Dave, a retired high-school counselor—was emphatic that I confess to Mike and Suzie what a terrible father I was, and Jane when she emerges from her coma, or the healing will not be complete. He suggested I do it today, which frightens me. I am uncertain what to say or how to say it."

"Today wouldn't be a good day, Mitch, especially with the information we just received from the doctors. Mike and Suzie are thawing out, but they aren't warm yet. Give them a chance to rediscover you. In a couple days, your talking to them about the past will have better results, probably after Sunday when we receive a report on Jane's legs."

I nodded my head. "What you're saying makes sense. I'll call Dave later this morning. Right now I want to visit the small chapel down the hallway from our waiting room and give God a chance to help put my thoughts in order."

I could see the surprise on Kathleen's face. When we were married, we went to a large church attended by business and professional people, among others, but for me it was just a cog in my social networking and a source of potential advertising clients. Kathleen knew that was my motivation, not part of any spiritual walk with God. She was just happy I went, for the sake of the kids.

***

I felt out of place in the chapel. This was God's territory, and I was a stranger seeking Him in a strange land. I don't remember ever looking to God for answers before, even though I was now attending church again with a new attitude toward Him. He was real to me, but out there somewhere in the distance.

"Help me, Lord," I pleaded. "I don't know what else to say to You."

I sat for an eternity with my head bowed in silence. I did not think about my depression, and it did not think about me. Then in a flash, the strategy of meeting one-on-one with Mike and Suzie was revealed to me. I left the chapel for the lobby to call Dave. When I turned my cell phone back on, I saw a message from Dave at 9 a.m.

"Mitch, call me as soon as you can. I hope you haven't talked to

Mike or Suzie yet. I'll explain why when you call."

Dave answered right away.

"Hi, Dave, I have not talked to Mike or Suzie yet. What's up?"

"I'm still certain the advice I gave you about making a confession to Mike and Suzie was correct," Dave answered, "but I believe the timing of talking to them today was wrong. Sometimes I'm so convinced a particular path is true north that I lack the patience to let it unfold naturally in God's timing, not mine. I've become much better at that, but sometimes I regress. You should wait a few days to let your being there settle in."

"I'm glad to hear you say that." I told Dave what Kathleen had said about timing, which was my purpose in calling him.

"Follow what Kathleen suggested," Dave said. "Wait at least a day after the leg surgery or until she tells you the time is right. Do you have any idea how you're going to go about the confession?"

"Actually I do. I just spent an hour in a hospital chapel asking God to sort my thoughts out, and a plan unfolded before me."

"Let's hear the plan!" said Dave with marked enthusiasm in his voice.

I started slowly because I hadn't written anything down. I wanted to hear what Dave had to say first.

"Dave, my natural way of implementing this would be to analyze how I failed each of them and apologize for those failures. Then I realized that was the old Mitch. I'd be able to check off the confession, but it would be ineffective. A light flashed within me. 'Listen to what your children have to say first, and you'll know you are addressing their needs, not yours.'"

I started writing down the conversation points, as did Dave on the other end.

"Here's the dialogue I'd use:

1. 'Mike/Suzie, over the years what have been your greatest disappointments with me?'

2. I'd ask them each questions for clarification if necessary and explore other issues that might be important, issues each may not have thought of on the spur of the moment.

3. Then I'd make a confession of how I failed them so miserably and seek forgiveness for every issue brought up.

4. The last step would be to ask, 'What can I do now to be a true father, the father you want me to be?'

What do you think, Dave?"

"That's a wonderful plan, Mitch. Seeing everything from their point of view in itself will send an unmistakable message. My one suggestion would be to have an introduction first, to prepare them for what's coming, such as, 'Mike, I want to ask forgiveness for being such a poor father to you, not on my terms, though, but on yours. I want to hear specifically how you have suffered because of me.'"

"That's an excellent addition, Dave. I've written it down."

The rest of our conversation covered how Jane was doing and some specifics of my interaction with Kathleen, Mike, and Suzie

***

The landscape of the waiting room, Jane's room, and the rotation of four people to my hotel room for sleep defined the remainder of Friday and Saturday. I was in moderate to mild depression over the two days—anywhere from a low 4 to a high 4. I talked to myself often. I was at my highest point in Jane's room when I was not thinking about myself. I was at my lowest point sitting in the waiting room with everyone else sleeping, when depression saw its chance to attack me.

Sunday was the appointed day to experience how zero milligrams of the benzo would affect me. I didn't want to jeopardize my one-on-one meetings with Mike and Suzie, so I decided to hold off on that final withdrawal until I was doing better. It was important that my thinking remain clear.

Hospital rooms and waiting rooms are wonderful places for people to come together. The focus on Jane became a shared passion, relegating everything else to a distant second. Without the tension of visiting past wounds, I was able to gather enough information about the lives of my ex-wife and three children to fill a magazine.

At a time when only Kathleen and I were in the waiting room, I prayed and took the opportunity to see how the four conversation points of seeking forgiveness resonated with her, even though she said she had forgiven me. She told me she never felt loved; she was more of a companion for me when a particular situation called for a couple. She told me I treated her with cold indifference, rarely asking her opinion about anything, even important family matters like moving to the Gold Coast. There were many times she wanted to remind me there were other people in our home besides me but didn't feel it would do any good. I was writing furiously as Kathleen pointed out my past sins. There were some smaller items, which I also recorded. I first confessed how badly I had treated her, and then asked forgiveness for each issue she had raised. Finally, I asked what I could do now to be a friend.

"You are relating differently to me now than in the past. Just be the Mitch you now are, and let's see what happens. I have been praying you would change. Yet, we've only been together here two days. Valleys of deep pain within me are crying to be healed. It will take time, Mitch. It will take time."

For over ten minutes, I told Kathleen how my friend Dave finally convinced me I was not too old to change. I related my changed thinking and behavior in Minneapolis the past few months.

After a period of silence, while Kathleen was absorbing my stated life changes, she said, "I'd like to meet Dave sometime. He sounds like a good man."

"I hope you meet him too, Kathleen. Without his influence, I don't know where I'd be."

Kathleen replied, "People are brought into our lives when we need them. That's God's way of taking care of us."

***

On Sunday, December 4, orthopedic specialists performed surgery on Jane's legs. The operation took hours, and as each hour ticked by, we became more and more anxious. I believe the anxiety would have overwhelmed me had I stopped taking the benzo.

"Why is it taking so long?" I asked with frustration.

Kathleen was steeped in prayer, so Mike answered my question.

"I think it's a good sign, Dad. They're putting her together again so she'll be able to walk. Otherwise, they would have patched her legs as best they could and brought us the bad news by now."

After another hour passed, one of the surgeons came to the surgery waiting room with a smile on his face.

"I have mostly good news for you. Jane will walk again."

We all breathed a sigh of relief.

"We wish that could happen in a month or so, but it won't. Her rehabilitation will take six months to a year. In two weeks, we'll change the cast on her right ankle to a walking cast, and she'll be able to go home in a walker, if the swelling in her brain is down and she's alert. We expect that to happen. You'll find out the details from the rehab people. Any questions? I need to return to the operating room for casting."

We were so elated with the good news that there were no questions.

***

The rest of Sunday and Monday followed a familiar pattern—visiting Jane in her room in twos, taking turns sleeping in my hotel room, and drawing closer together in the waiting room. We waited expectantly for Jane to exit her coma. She was starting to progress from a coma to a semi-coma. Occasionally her eyes would open, unfocused and in obvious confusion

I felt now was the time to meet with Mike and Suzie. Kathleen agreed. Where would be best? Dave's suggestion of a coffee room would not be secluded enough for an open discussion. The chapel seemed the obvious place. No one was ever in there other than me. I felt the prompting to start with Mike this time.

***

Tuesday morning, Mike agreed to meet with me in the chapel, almost as if he knew what would take place.

I was nervous. Friendly small talk helped me regain my courage. I was precise in following the framed questions I had rehearsed at least a hundred times.

"Mike, this conversation will not be easy for either of us. I want to apologize for being such a lousy father, but I want to do it from your point of view, not mine. What have been your greatest disappointments with me?"

From the quickness of Mike's answer, I realized he had rehearsed this conversation in his mind thousands of times over the years. It's probably where he was heading when we tangled Thursday afternoon as I stepped off the elevator.

"Dad, since you asked this question with sincerity, I'm going to answer with sincerity, though it may hurt you. My greatest disappointment was growing up without a father to care about my life, to show his love and acceptance of me, to help guide me from boyhood through high school and through becoming an adult. I grew up in a family with one parent. You only came to a few of my athletic events, you never took me hunting or fishing, you didn't even take me on vacations. That really hurt."

I recorded everything Mike said.

"What about my giving you money and not time? Was that hurtful?"

"Extremely so," answered Mike. "I couldn't express it at the time; I can now. I was a commodity, not a real person. Your buying me bikes, nice clothes, cars, and paying for college and law school was hurtful. I was not grateful. You made me feel cheap, going through the motions of being a father without commitment, without ownership, with money and no feelings. I would have ridden a used bike, worn old clothes, walked to high school, and worked my way through college if only you had treated me as a beloved son. That about sums it up."

Tears streamed down my face. My voice cracked when I spoke, like a cell phone with a bad connection.

"Mike, I am crushed by shame. All you have brought up is tragically true. I confess to your indictment on every point. You have made your case as well as any lawyer could—precise, clear, and complete. I was not there for you when you were growing up. I was a miserable excuse for a father, distant and cold. My throwing money at you was a slap in your face. I can't change the past. I can only promise you a better future with me."

I next asked forgiveness for each issue Mike brought up. In addition to the two general matters, there were several specific sins he pinned on me, all painfully accurate. There was no anger or emotion in his voice, only a somber matter-of-factness. For all the years he had struggled with these thoughts, I sensed a great relief on his part to finally present them to me.

"Mike, I'm begging your forgiveness for everything you brought up. Heaven knows I don't deserve it. If you will let me, I will be your true father, and you will be my beloved son. I will love your wife as my own daughter. I'll be a grandparent to your three children and give them time, love, and care. What else can I do? What else do you expect of me?"

Now Mike had free-flowing tears. He asked me to stand up so he could hug me.

"Dad, this has all been so sudden. Five days ago, I was ready to tear you apart. I have been numb for years without having a father. I never thought I'd say I forgive you, but I do. I'm sure you can understand, though, it will take more than five days to absorb that I have a real father. Let's call this the first day of our new relationship, with many days to come.

"You asked what I expect of you. I want a dad who will always be there—by phone or in person. A dad who listens to what I care about and embraces my family. A dad who loves me unconditionally, through all my mistakes and challenges.

"There's one more thing I didn't list: I want you and Mom to become at least friends. I hated you for divorcing her, but my forgiveness includes even that. Treat her with the respect she deserves. She stuck by you when she shouldn't have. She defended you to us kids; she never said anything negative about you. You had a wife any man would be grateful to have."

"I know that, Mike, and I have asked her forgiveness."

We stood in the chapel without talking for five minutes. It was a blessed time. We hugged each other often. We cried often. And then we left the chapel, two different men than the ones who had come in.

***

Back in the waiting room, Mike and I were mostly quiet for an hour, pondering deep thoughts. Suzie realized something special had happened and allowed us our silence. When I asked her to visit the chapel with me, she was ready.

I followed the same pattern with Suzie as I had with Mike. Many of her disappointments were similar to Mike's, but there were two very different general ones.

"Dad, a girl needs a father as a role model for boys she will date and the man she will marry. I didn't have a role model. I experimented when I was dating in high school and college. Some were good experiences; most were bad. In my confusion, God led me to Jeff. He was everything you weren't. That's why I first loved him. He is very attentive to me and to our children. He loves us more than his car dealership.

"Then there was my artwork. How I longed for you to say my art had promise. Mom told me that, but it wasn't the same. My high school and college teachers were very encouraging—I had what it takes to be an artist, a real artist, not just a hobby-time artist. I drew from that encouragement, but it wasn't the same as if you would have said to me, 'Princess, your art is beautiful. It's good enough to be sold in an art store.' How many times my mind dwelt on those words, those exact words. But you never said them, and I was crushed."

I recorded what she said. Once again my voice was cracking and tears ran down my cheeks. I confessed that everything she said was true, just as I had with Mike.

"I understand what you're telling me, all of it so true. I wish I had been hit over the head with that realization while you were still growing up."

I asked her forgiveness for each and every point, one by one.

"The past is gone. The future is before us. I repent for being such a disappointing father. If you'll allow me the chance, I'll be the father you deserve from this day on. Tell me how I can be a real father to you, one that meets your expectations."

Suzie was crying and couldn't speak for half a minute. She arose and hugged me, just like Mike had.

"Daddy, I forgive you for everything. Please love me and become part of my life and my family's life. My children need a grandfather they can look up to. My husband's father left his mother when Jeff was five. He needs a father-in-law to ask private questions about his car business and to experience those things a man needs a father for. Mom needs a friend too. Will you be her friend?"

Suzie was more desperate for a father than Mike. She did not stipulate any time frame for accepting me. She wanted a father right now. Her life had a hole in it that needed to be filled.

"Suzie, I promise I'll be there for you. I hope there are 20 or 30 years left for me to be the father I never was. Mom and I have already started being friends. It will take time to earn her trust back. I will be patient but committed."

We stood hugging each other for what seemed a very long time. We had joy, we had tears. I kissed Suzie on the forehead, and we walked back to the waiting room, two different people than those who had entered the chapel.

***

My depression soared to a low 5 after my meetings with Mike and Suzie, and I thought about dropping the last half milligram of the benzo. However, the next day I slipped back to a 4 and stayed with the same dosage. I needed to remain strong.

It was at this time that I visualized depression as an enemy, as a live entity to fight against rather than just an illness in my body. I became convinced I would fight a good fight, that I would not let depression defeat me. It may try to grab me, but I would triumph in the end.

On Thursday, one week to the day since I arrived, a doctor stepped into the waiting room.

"Can you all come to Jane's room with me? I have a surprise for you."

When we entered the room, Jane had her eyes open and was talking coherently to another doctor. We were so elated, we didn't know what to do. We laughed. We cried. We hugged Jane.

The doctor who had come into the waiting room said, "Jane is out of the woods with the swelling in her brain, but healing will take time. There may be some residual symptoms for up to a year or more. Some may be permanent. We don't know that yet but are optimistic for complete recovery.

"In the next few days, you'll find her sometimes alert, like right now, and sometimes confused. She'll be leaving the ICU to a room on the fifth floor. She'll stay there for at least two weeks as we assess her cognitive and behavioral functioning from traumatic brain injury. Her legs will have a chance to heal for the two weeks before she starts using a walker. We'll change to a walking cast on her right ankle so she can start putting some weight on that foot; that will occur near the end of the two weeks. Our goal is to send her home for Christmas."

The doctors left Jane's room, and Jane seemed excited to speak. Amazingly, she was not surprised to see me.

"Daddy, the doctors told me I was in a coma for a week, but I could feel you holding my hand and telling me how much you loved me. You asked for my forgiveness for being less of a father than I needed and deserved. You kept using the same words over and over. I felt warm inside when you were holding my hand and talking softly to me. I forgive you, Daddy, with all my heart. I'm ready to accept my new father."

I gazed on Jane and then Kathleen, Mike, and Suzie. We were a family for the first time.

"I know I need to prove to all of you that my changed heart is not just for this hospital. I have new meaning in my life, and I'm not going to blow it. You all will be seeing me often in the weeks and months ahead. Chicago is not that far from Minneapolis."

And so the reconciliation I was praying for charged off the starting line. I was amazed it happened so effortlessly. I thanked God for preparing the hearts of the Jasper family. Now it was time to wait again, to observe how Jane would function after the brain injury and how her legs would heal. Two weeks the doctor said.

CHAPTER 15
Between Chicago and Edina

Jane had been recovering in the hospital for one week from the accident that easily could have killed her. In two weeks, she might be able to go home. It was a miracle. Yet there were questions. What would be the temporary and permanent effects from her brain trauma? Would she be her old self again, mentally astute and able to work? How long would it take her to walk again? Would she ever walk normally? Would she be able to run?

Mike returned to his Chicago law office, visiting the hospital every evening before driving home to Naperville. On Saturday and Sunday, his whole family descended on Northwestern Memorial Hospital—Mike, Monica, and their three children. What a joy it was for me to interact with Luke, Matthew, and Joseph. They seemed entirely comfortable with their "new" grandfather. Why do children adapt to new situations so much easier than adults? Maybe because their baggage is small and light.

Suzie returned to Wheaton. She visited Jane every other day, with her two children in tow. Sometimes her husband Jeff was with her. I immediately fell in love with Maria and Ruth, my other two grandchildren. And they returned my love. What a marvelous awakening for me.

I noticed that Mike and Suzie watched with great interest the time I spent with their children. Their eyes told me, "You really have changed Dad. You're not just pretending." You can't fake it with children. They instinctively know the real thing from a sham.

Kathleen and I were with Jane every day. After a few days, Kathleen returned to her condo every evening to sleep. I stayed in Jane's room sleeping on a cot a nurse brought in. Jane often awoke during the night with a start, anxious and fearful. She was reassured when I arose and held her hand.

When Kathleen returned in the morning, I'd go back to my hotel room for four or five hours of uninterrupted sleep. I didn't have commitments other than talking to Dave daily, updating him on what was happening. I called Faith in Action to let them know I'd be in Chicago for another two weeks at least. If they needed me for anything, they could call my cell.

For two weeks, Kathleen and I fell into a habit of having supper together, either in the hospital cafeteria or at a nearby restaurant, while Jane was busy with late-afternoon medical routines and her supper ritual. When we left, Jane was happy because, as she said, "you two need a chance to become reacquainted." Maybe Kathleen was becoming reacquainted; I was falling in love. Kathleen was beautiful on the outside and beautiful on the inside. What a gem I had, what a gem I lost. I was seeing her full loveliness for the first time.

***

With one week left before Jane was scheduled to be released, Kathleen and I were eating at a restaurant, when I introduced the topic of care for Jane after she left the hospital.

"The doctors told us, if everything proceeds as expected, Jane will receive a walking cast on her right leg next Thursday and leave here Friday with a walker. That will be December 23. Christmas is on Sunday and rehab starts on Monday. If you don't mind, I'd like to be present the first week of rehab to see what progress Jane makes and what the prognosis is for the weeks and months ahead."

Kathleen, with an edge of warmth to her matter-of-factness, replied, "I've talked to Mike, Suzie, and Jane. They all want you to celebrate Christmas with us at my place. You've made a breakthrough with them, though I didn't think that would be possible. They suspect they have a father for the first time. And I welcome your staying for the first week of Jane's rehab. Quite frankly, I was worried how I'd be able to manage until I knew how to transfer her into and out of my van, and how to meet her needs at home. You can be a great help."

We finished the meal talking about Jane—how she was not showing the symptoms of mild traumatic brain injury, except for periodic confusion and a sense of anxiety and depression as she assessed her future.

I understood the anxiety and depression because I had been and was there. One of her doctors suggested a prescription medication to help her. I was opposed to that unless Jane became more depressed. Presently she was in mild depression that was, to my observation, totally situational. She didn't need to face withdrawal down the road with all the other obstacles she would be facing. I finally won that argument.

I was in mild to moderate depression myself at the time, living in a world of 4s. Thank God I was able to function, and I saw life through a misty gray screen and not a dark cloud enveloping me. It had been 12 days since I had been scheduled to be off the last one-half milligram of the benzo I was taking. Although committed to following my ill-conceived withdrawal plan, I could not risk dropping into the 3s of severe depression. Too much was at stake in Chicago.

If only I felt better, I would have explored where a future relationship between Kathleen and me might go. It would be too drastic to reveal that I was in love with her. Perhaps she would consider dating me and see where things went. However, the mist of depression took my courage away. I was too fragile to face rejection. When we left the restaurant, I walked over to my hotel and reserved my room for two more weeks.

***

I looked up from reading my "Struggle Journal" and writing about that dinner in late December. How frustrated I was that I still had not escaped my depression. Why wasn't the 60 milligrams of the SSRI holding me up? Yet again, time made clear what was a dusty road to me in the restaurant.

Not dropping that final one-half milligram of the benzo was a brilliant move that, at the time, I saw as failure. My physical and emotional being could not have withstood total withdrawal. My brain was telling me it needed time to stabilize; it needed time to adjust to only the SSRI. Staying where I was on medication allowed me physically and emotionally to avoid heading back into the pit and allowed me to heal gradually. My chemical imbalance was not going to be corrected in four months, and putting myself under major stress again would only set me back.

God was in charge here, not me. His grace kept me from doing what would harm me. Truly, He wanted only good for me. But it would take time. He worked through the circumstances in Chicago to allow me to eventually come back out of the darkness and into the light.

I also see now that talking about "dating" to Kathleen would have been absolutely the wrong timing, love her though I did. She was not ready for that discussion. She would have pulled away from me. I was thinking about me and not her. The depression affected the clarity of my mind. My growing love for her required patience.

***

Christmas Day announced its presence with a blue sky and radiant sun. The whole Jasper family was at Kathleen's condo. Jane had come home two days earlier in a walker. It was good I stayed because Jane needed two people to get her in and out of Kathleen's van. The Walker family was the first to arrive—Suzie, Jeff, and their two girls; Michael, Monica and their three boys were next. Counting Kathleen and me, there were an even dozen.

Kathleen asked me to say grace. I did so with thankfulness and love, ending with, "I am thankful we are here as a family. Six months ago, I would have thought this scene to be impossible. But God is the God of the impossible, and we praise Him today, the day of the birth of Jesus." Twelve people bowed their heads in silence after I finished. Then there was a boisterous digging into the feast before us.

After dinner, we gathered for presents. Kathleen had instituted a tradition of giving only one present to Mike and Monica, to Suzie and Jeff, and to Jane; one present to each of the five grandchildren; and one present to her from the Walker family, from the Jasper family, and from Jane. She delighted in being more of a giver than a receiver. It was agreed I would follow the same pattern of giving and receiving. What a great tradition! There wasn't the usual feverish tearing of wrapping paper off scores of presents. Each gift was cherished and applauded by the twelve.

We visited four hours before the day ended. I listened much and spoke little, learning more from observation than exposition. Occasionally, a question would be tossed my way, which I answered courteously but briefly. This was a big change for me. What my family was used to was my talking about my advertising agency, my important friends, and myself.

***

Monday morning I drove back to Kathleen's condo, arriving at 8 a.m. Jane's first rehab session was at nine. We clumsily pushed and pulled Jane into the van and headed to the rehabilitation center, less than ten minutes from Kathleen's.

When we entered the facility, an inch of documents to read and sign awaited us. Abby was the physical therapist assigned to Jane.

Abby brought us into her office and explained the protocol for Jane's rehabilitation. She gave us a copy of the chief orthopedic surgeon's instructions for Jane's recovery. "I'll work with Jane every day for four weeks. When that time is completed, I'll send a progress report to the surgeon and await further instructions. Will you both be with Jane the first week?"

"Yes," each of us responded.

"That's good because you two will be significantly involved in a learning process the first week. You probably had trouble getting Jane in and out of your vehicle this morning. I'll show you how it can be done with just one person. To start off, Jane will learn how to use her right leg as leverage to walk in her walker. The cast on her right ankle will protect that leg. It's important she keeps weight off her left leg, which has one break in her femur and multiple fractures in her fibula and tibia, as well as a pin in her hip.

"Next week we'll start exercises to help keep her leg muscles from atrophying. Massage therapy and motion exercises can be used on the right leg. With a full cast on her left leg, we can only electrically stimulate that part of her leg above the cast. When the cast comes off in about two months, we'll work vigorously on that leg."

Kathleen and I asked questions until we felt we had a good assessment of Jane's condition, and what she could and could not do. We had been overly protective up to this point because we didn't know any better.

***

The following Friday morning completed the first week of rehabilitation. When we entered Kathleen's condo, she said to me, "Mitch, I feel confident I can care for Jane myself now. I'm not chasing you off, but you've been here for a month, and you must have a pile of mail, bills, and things that demand your personal attention. Why don't you head back to Edina for a couple weeks and then come back to see Jane, Suzie, Michael, and their families. It's important that you show them a continuity of presence."

I was disappointed Kathleen did not include herself to see when I came back. It felt like a slap in the face. I knew first-hand now what she must have felt when she loved me, and I treated her like a commodity. Sadness permeated me.

Softly I said, "I do have to attend to the matters you listed, Kathleen, especially the mail. I need to pick it up today or tomorrow, or make other arrangements. I have Mike's and Suzie's phone numbers and will call them on my way out of Chicago."

I said goodbye to Jane and Kathleen. "I'll stay in touch by phone and be back within two weeks."

***

The first part of the trip back was hard. With all the activity in Chicago, I didn't have time to think much about my anxiety and depression. For the first 50 miles out of Chicago, the black dog of depression attacked me. The black dog was a term Winston Churchill used for his life-long affliction. It was fortunate I needed to focus on a task—driving a car—or I would have been more vulnerable than I was.

I didn't feel up to calling Mike and Suzie, but I forced myself to put on the headset and dial their numbers. I tried to be as cheerful as I could with the dog chewing on me. Those calls lifted my spirits, and the black dog retreated into the shadows.

Mike and Suzie were happy to hear from me and happy to know I would be coming back in two weeks. To have my children excited to talk to me was a joy I had never experienced before, a joy that was unexplainable. Each of them said their children would miss their grandfather. Another joy.

The rest of the trip went much better than those first miles. I was lifted out of the 3s and into the 4s, a number I was getting used to. Half a bubble off level can be a good place. You become more sensitive to your surroundings and able to interact with other people. I was elated to be mildly depressed and out of the grip of severe depression, teetering on the edge of the pit. When I entered my condo, I was still thinking about the wonderful discussion with Mike and Suzie and not thinking about myself.

The next morning, I called Dave and asked if we could meet for coffee.

***

I walked into Coffee on France and asked if the meeting room was open, knowing Saturdays were a prime time for scheduling that room. It had been booked all morning for a business meeting and suddenly cancelled. We had it. Funny how things seemed to happen like that lately. I would come to a closed door, and suddenly it was opened from the inside.

My emotional state was high just knowing I'd be meeting with Dave. He was a beacon of light to me. Dave walked in at 9:05 a.m.

"Sorry I'm late, Mitch; the roads were slippery and traffic was crawling."

Since we had talked Thursday afternoon, I brought Dave up to speed on the happenings of yesterday.

Dave laughed, an odd response I thought. I gave him a quizzical look.

"I'm sorry for laughing, Mitch, but I can't help remembering the time in this very room when you said it was too late in the afternoon for you to change."

Dave had a good reason for laughing. "How wrong I was when I said that, Dave. I have changed. I'm no longer the same person. You've played a major part in that change, as have Daniel, Sam, and my family. I've mentally and spiritually matured three years in the last six months.

"I'd like your perspective on an important matter before we dive into other topics. Two years ago, my oldest son, Michael, became a partner in his law firm. From what I observed when we were in the hospital, he's on a path of too much focus on work and not enough focus on family, heading toward the same destination I arrived at with my family in Chicago. He works in his office late and often has supper with clients or his firm's partners. He claims it's a way of building relationships. Those are nearly the same words I used to justify my behavior. He's consumed with his work, and his family is becoming a distant second. I'm concerned he will eventually become like me. How can I talk to him, given I was worse than he now is? I'd feel like a hypocrite."

"Well," mused Dave, "It looks like we need another map. Actually, using yourself as an example will be more a plus than a negative. I suggest you use an 'I' message, putting the focus on yourself instead of Mike. You want to keep from overusing 'you,' which is accusative and puts others on the defensive. There are four parts to the 'I' message.

1. <u>I have a concern</u>: Use yourself as an example of behavior you see in Michael. Tell him you love him and want to prosper him and not harm him.

2. <u>Here are the facts</u>: Tell him you have observed his behavior and have concerns about where he is heading. Notice the focus is on your concern and not pointing a finger directly at him.

3. <u>Ask Michael how he sees it</u>: This is the key to an 'I' message. It's important that he has a chance to express his views. He might respond in a way that surprises you.

4. <u>What might be a path forward?</u>: Hopefully, he will suggest a solution rather than dismissing the concern. Don't you offer anything. He needs to own any solution.

Does this make sense?"

"Yes, it does, but I have a few questions."

I had taken good notes and asked for clarification in a few spots. We discussed the "I" message for another 15 minutes, and I caught up on what was happening in Dave's life, which meant what was happening mostly with those around him. Dave was the most humble person I have ever known.

"It's 11:30 and I need to get home for lunch," Dave said. "Cathy has invited neighbors over, and she'll use the 'I' message on me if I'm late."

***

I felt marvelous when I left the coffee shop and stepped into bright sunshine. All was right with the world. Saturday evening was New Year's Eve. I celebrated by calling Kathleen and Jane and talked to them for over an hour. Because my depression was now at 5, normal, I decided to totally withdraw from the benzo. I had been 27 days on one-half milligram, 23 days more than scheduled. I skipped the evening dosage and was still at a 5 when I went to bed shortly after midnight.

***

I awoke Monday morning with mild depression, an upper 4. I could handle it; my life was on an upward climb. The health club was beckoning to me for a vigorous workout after a month in Chicago. I arrived at nine in the morning and started walking around the track so briskly that I was a half step short of running. After three circuits, there was a whirr behind me, and there was Daniel.

"Daniel, just the person I wanted to see."

"Yes, another accident," replied Daniel with a chuckle. " By the way, thanks for calling me from Chicago so I didn't worry about you. I felt in my spirit you would be here this morning, so I adjusted my schedule to your schedule. Why am I just the person you wanted to see?"

I explained the happenings in Chicago since calling Daniel, including that Jane was suffering from a mild depression I was afraid might grow into something more serious.

"Mitch, she must be concerned about what the future holds for her with such extensive damage to both legs and her traumatic brain injury."

"I'm sure you're right. Do you have some ideas how I can help her?"

"Mitch, this isn't something you can do. It's not good practice for one family member to counsel another family member. Jane sounds like a sensitive young woman who needs to express herself in a manner she couldn't with you.

"I think she needs a Christian counselor from what you've told me about her faith, someone who could provide the greatest comfort level for her. Let me search my contacts in Chicago and see if I can find someone near the Gold Coast. I'll call you with what I find."

The rest of our walk embraced a lively discussion regarding Daniel's faith and my faith. Not much similarity was evident; both of us knew it. Daniel told me to trust God in everything, and my faith would grow.

"Just look what God has done in your life already," Daniel said. "You could never have accomplished what has happened under your own power."

***

Once again, I didn't understand that clinical depression, in a way, transcends circumstances. My life was turning around, and I felt confident with total withdrawal of the benzo prescription, especially since I still remained on my SSRI antidepressant. I had learned by this time that the benzo was mainly for anxiety but also alleviated depression, and the SSRI was mainly for depression but also alleviated anxiety.

Anxiety and depression were crouching close to me, waiting for an opportunity to leap. I gave them the chance when I totally withdrew from one prescription. My brain was telling me, "You should have stayed on the benzo. You have denied me, and I'm going to strike back." And it struck back with a physical reaction only people who have withdrawn from a highly addictive drug can appreciate.

I vividly remember that Tuesday, Wednesday, and Thursday. I was back into the 3s, in severe depression. I couldn't believe I was there again. When I looked into the mirror, I didn't recognize myself again. I had no appetite and was sleeping fitfully, if at all. My body was adjusting to total abstinence from the benzo, trying desperately to stabilize. For nearly a month I had been improving, now this setback.

To be on the rim of the pit again was depressing in itself.

And then it happened. I was watching the 5:30 news Thursday afternoon, when, for no reason at all, the heavy cloud of depression and anxiety lifted. I was back into the 4s. I dropped unto my knees and thanked God. I was in business again, mildly depressed and functional. The SSRI was enough.

***

The next day, January 6, exactly one week after I left Chicago for Edina, all that needed to be accomplished was accomplished, even though I was in severe depression for three days. The focus on getting things done probably kept me from descending into panic.

I thought, "Why not head back to Chicago sooner than two weeks?" It would send a message to my family that staying involved was rooted in action, not words.

With the "I" message script and the name of a psychologist given me by Daniel safely tucked away in my briefcase, I called Kathleen to see if flying into Chicago on Sunday would work for her.

She seemed pleasantly surprised I was returning in a week instead of two. It would work for her.

I called Mike to tell him my plans. He quickly checked with Monica and invited me to dinner January 15, a Sunday. I called Suzie, and she invited me for dinner on January 16. Two intensive days in a row. I would have preferred more of a separation for some re-energizing time. I felt somewhat fragile after being clawed by depression for three days. But it was what it was, and I'd have to make it work.

I booked a flight, reserved a rental car, and made reservations at the same hotel, close enough to Kathleen's for convenience, but far enough for strategic separation.

***

I parked my car in front of Mike's house in Naperville. A week had passed through Chicago since the day I returned. Jane's physical rehabilitation was positive and her moments of confusion were minimal. Depression lingered around her, reminding her how long rehab would take, and sowing seeds of doubt that her condition wouldn't improve anywhere near normal. I made an appointment for her to see the psychologist Daniel recommended. After one session, she had the start of hope, and three-times-a-week sessions booked for a month.

My own depression remained in the 4s the whole week, moderate to mild. I understood clearly now that focusing on something or someone other than myself was a key to keeping depression at bay. Given how self-centered I was for 40 years, looking without was more difficult for me perhaps than for most people. And looking outward was nearly impossible in severe depression—the dreaded 3s. Two prescriptions, the benzo and the SSRI, had first lifted me out of the 3s. Most recently, last Thursday evening, the grace of God was my strongest medication.

A light dawned. All three prongs of combating depression were medical—medicine for the body, medicine for the soul, and medicine for the spirit.

"Welcome, Dad," said Mike when he opened the front door. "Tell me how the week has gone for you." He looked like he wanted to give me a hug but hesitated, and the opportunity was lost. Monica and the children hugged me.

We all talked about Jane for five minutes after I took off my coat and sat down to warm up. A bitter wind from the north was blasting Chicago with an icy chill. I deflected any discussion about myself.

"Monica, can you show Dad our house?" So the tour commenced, with three boys tagging along close to their grandfather, and concluded 15 minutes later. I told them what a beautiful home they had, marvelously designed and finely decorated. It could qualify to be featured in *Better Homes and Gardens*.

After the tour and before supper, we all talked for three hours in the family room—once more about Jane, before expanding the topics. I asked about Mike and Monica's activities since they were first married. I asked for a biography of Luke, Matthew, and Joseph, as each of them sat by me on the love seat while their lives were unfolded. It was fun to see the pride each had in his accomplishments.

After supper, the boys removed themselves and Monica cleared the dishes. At just the right moment, when Mike and I were alone at the table, I asked if we could talk somewhere in private. Seconds later, Monica returned.

"Monica, I'm going to show Dad my office and talk to him about my law firm."

"That's fine, Mike. Just like a Victorian novel—'and then the men retreated to the drawing room for brandy and cigars,'" she said in a husky man's voice. "I'll keep the kids out of your hair."

***

When Mike told Monica we would be talking about his law firm, little did he know that was my primary intent. Mike *did* start telling me about his law career, and I asked him how much time he was spending at the office lately. A 60-hour week was the norm, sometimes more. That gave me the opening I was waiting for.

Mike was sitting in a large leather swivel chair, with his back to an enormous mahogany roll-top desk piled high with small mountains of legal research documents. It was a desk begging to be organized so it could see light again. I was facing Mike in an identical chair. Two walls of the office were bookcases from the floor to the ceiling, one wall filled with books related to corporate law and business analyses. It was his law office right there at home. That wall also contained all the books purchased for his business degree from Northwestern University and for his law degree from the University of Chicago. There were a few novels and non-fiction books. In a prominent spot were a Bible, a concordance, and a number of Bible commentaries.

The second wall was a markedly different collection of books, evidently Monica's library. Several Bibles, a wide assortment of religious books, a treasure trove of novels, children's books, and numerous books about world history and prophecy caught my attention. The two walls were a formidable collection of books.

"Mike, you know what a workaholic I was when you kids were growing up. I left home early in the morning and returned late at night. Even the weekends were spent working or building what I said were strategic relationships. It wasn't until this last half year that I realized how destructive my career was to our family.

"I love you, Michael, and I'm concerned you're traveling the same unfortunate path I did. When we talked in the hospital and just now, you told me how much time you were spending at your law office since you became one of the partners. And you told me you were working and building relationships on weekends, just as I did.

"Tonight, I noticed there was not the banter of a close family except between Monica and the three boys. You were not a part of that warm relationship. You seemed present at a distance. That's the way it was with me as the head of our family, though I didn't see it then."

I had expressed my concern and listed the facts. Now it was time for the third step of the "I" message.

"How do you see it, Michael?"

Mike thought a long time before answering with a sigh of resignation. "Dad, you're right. I have thought a great deal about what I've been doing to my family, but I haven't done anything about it. I understand your concern. I *don't* want to do what you did." He made that last statement with a smile on his face, as if to show he was not attacking me but acknowledging what I said about myself was true.

"There yet is hope. My negative behavior has only been this past year, since I became a partner. It hasn't been 40 years. I believe the damage I've done is fixable."

"How are you going to fix it, Michael?" I asked, relieved he had accepted my concern as legitimate.

Mike thought a minute before answering again. It seemed like a week.

"I'm going to apologize to Monica and to Luke, Matthew, and Joseph separately. I'll tell them I've been heading in the wrong direction and neglecting them. I'll promise to start spending quality time with the four of them, starting with supper. I'll do networking and relationship building mainly over lunch, with an occasional supper. Whatever work I bring home will be for after the kids go to bed and Monica is studying for her law courses. She started law school part-time this fall at Northern Illinois University College of Law.

"Thanks, Dad, for waking me up. If you hadn't brought this up, I may have gone on this way until…until…."

"Until you became just like me," I interrupted.

"I was going to say something like that, but I chose not to. That's why I hesitated."

"That's OK," Mike. "It would have been factual, not mean-spirited.

I've painfully realized my mistakes. That's why I wanted to have a talk with you. You might have figured all this out on your own one day, but I couldn't take the chance."

This time Mike hugged me as I left for the hotel.

***

The next day I parked my car in front of Suzie's home in Wheaton. I hoped this day would unfold as well as yesterday. I was amazed how smoothly the time with Mike and his family had passed. My talk with him couldn't possibly have been better. I had been redeemed from persona non grata to a father able to give advice to his son without resentment.

Suzie opened the front door and gave me a hug. Jeff and the two girls were lined up behind her. Suzie hung up my coat, and we all sat in the living room and visited. After 30 minutes, there was a lull in the conversation. That's what I was waiting for. "Suzie, can you show me your artwork?"

Suzie explained that when they built their house, a large porch in the second level was converted into an art studio, with sunlight streaming in from windows on three sides and from a skylight in the ceiling.

"This is my artist's loft," remarked Suzie proudly. Everything was neatly displayed or stored. There was a wall rack that held hundreds of paintings, and there was a partly completed landscape on her easel. I looked at the pictures and was stunned to see how professional they were.

"Princess, your art is beautiful. It's good enough to be sold in an art store."

"Oh, Daddy, you remembered what I told you my wish was growing up."

"I did, Suzie, but I didn't say your art is beautiful because that's what you wanted to hear. I said it because your work *is* beautiful. How unfortunate I didn't recognize your talent in high school and encourage you to become the best artist you could be. I can't change the past. I *can* change the present and the future. I'll help you market your paintings, if you want me as an unpaid consultant."

"I'll take you up on that, Daddy," answered Suzie. Once again I had bridged the gap from a non-responsive father to an interested and supportive dad.

The rest of the afternoon and evening went much the same as at Mike's, complete with Maria and Ruth sitting next to me and telling me all about themselves. I listened mainly and asked questions. The two girls loved the attention.

I observed Jeff was a real family man, dedicated to Suzie and the girls. No advice was needed for him.

***

I had spent most of the previous week with Kathleen and Jane, other than Sunday and Monday. The following Tuesday and Wednesday were more of the same. Jane was emphatic that Kathleen and I have dinner together at a restaurant most evenings. I was not confident enough to be that insistent. Jane achieved more for our relationship than I could have accomplished. My little matchmaker.

On Thursday morning early, I received a call from Dave that Jim, a mutual friend who had become my trusty golf partner, died of a heart attack Wednesday evening. The wake was Friday and the funeral Saturday. Because his entire family came to Minneapolis when he was taken to Methodist Hospital, a speedy funeral worked best.

With all planes from Chicago to Minneapolis fully booked Friday morning and early afternoon, I needed to fly out Thursday. I immediately called Kathleen and relayed the information. She was most understanding and wished me a safe trip back. I said I'd call and let her and the kids know when I'd return to Chicago.

Dave told me he'd give me the details about Jim when he saw me. And he wanted to share a thought he said cascaded into his mind as soon as he heard Jim had died.

CHAPTER 16
A Spring and Summer of Contentment

I met Dave at the wake Friday night at a funeral home in St. Louis Park. It was a massive white-stone building, decorated inside with soft, calming colors. I needed the peacefulness of the décor because I was feeling anxious. Why was that so? I had been off the benzo for almost three weeks. Perhaps my brain was telling me I wasn't healed yet. I was still fragile and vulnerable.

***

In reading this part of my "Struggle Journal," it was evident I was starting to understand anxiety and depression for what it really was—a malady of the mind that would take many pages of a calendar to heal. The relationship of brain chemistry, circumstances, struggles of the soul, and spiritual well-being were so intertwined that re-establishing balance in my life was complicated and time consuming. It was a struggle, a fight against a powerful enemy threatening to destroy me. I had to be ever watchful, ever wary, keeping my enemy at bay every waking minute, patiently waiting to come out on the other side.

***

Before viewing the casket and visiting with Jim's family, we staked out a corner in the lobby where we could talk in confidence. Dave told me Jim was well until late Wednesday afternoon, when pain in his chest gripped him like a vice.

"As you know," said Dave, "he was living alone since his wife died some years back. He thought the pain was indigestion or muscle cramps, and he decided to wait it out. He called me around suppertime because the pain was not getting better and had spread to his arms. When he told me the pain had started two hours earlier, I urged him to call an ambulance immediately. Just then the phone dropped to the floor. I called 911, and an ambulance arrived at his house seconds before I arrived.

"Jim was unconscious. The medics said his heart rhythm was erratic; they couldn't stabilize him. Methodist Hospital was minutes away. There was a frantic effort in the emergency room to establish a normal rhythm. After a half hour, the doctors were successful, and Jim was awake. Ten minutes later his heart went into tachycardia, racing like the engine of a car revved up to its maximum rpm—and then it broke. He was dead in the snap of a finger."

I was somber as Dave related the details.

"Dave, you mentioned on the phone yesterday that you wanted to share a thought you had when Jim was dying."

Dave answered deliberately, "Yes, I had a thought that led to other thoughts. I don't know if Jim was saved or not before he died, but he went so quickly I didn't have time to ask him if he was all right with the Lord. I pray he is in heaven, but there is not strong evidence in his life that gives me that assurance. I deeply regret I didn't talk to him about salvation when I had opportunities. It's easier to talk to total strangers about the Lord than someone you have been friends with for years.

"Mitch, you've had one severe heart attack; you could go as quickly as Jim. I won't make the same mistake with you. Do you feel you have a saving relationship with Jesus?"

I hesitated. "I have heard enough sermons on being saved that I know what is required. I'm glad salvation is not based on good works, because I have precious few of those in the last 40 years. The short answer to your question is that I don't think I'm saved. I keep putting it off because I'm not ready. I'm closer now than six months ago, but there's still something missing, something unknown. I see what happened to Jim, and I get your point. Let's talk more soon, but not today. I can't make what you call a commitment until I process all this."

***

It was now Wednesday, April 19, and much had passed through me in the last three months. The funeral on January 20 reinforced what Dave had told me about salvation the evening before. The sticking point for me was that I was afraid of losing my identity, of losing control over my choices. The idea of Christ living through me just didn't calculate.

Zeke had weaned me slowly off the 60 milligrams of the SSRI. This time I listened to him. On March 15, I dropped to 40 milligrams; on April 15, I dropped to 20 milligrams. My brain chemistry was starting to stabilize. I was in and out of mild depression but on the mend.

Wally worked with me to stabilize my soul as well as my body. Dave urged me to strengthen my spirit. The two of them helped me assemble a sturdily built three-legged stool.

My life was coming together in ways I could not have imagined. There were a confluence of purposes that enveloped me in a vivid light—my family, volunteer work, new friendships, my church, and my health.

I visited Kathleen, Mike, Suzie, and Jane twice a month for three days a visit, sometimes four. I was investing 20 percent of my life in Chicago. My children were experiencing a real father for the first time in their lives, and my grandchildren loved me. I was truly blessed. Kathleen had forgiven me in her mind but not deep inside. Her forgiveness was gradually inching that direction.

Faith in Action was burgeoning at breakneck speed. Besides time as a board member, I was helping with marketing and the intricacies of managing a growing agency. That made up another ten hours a month.

Dave and Daniel were my stalwart friends. Beyond them, I became close with my two golfing partners, a fellow board member on Faith in Action, and a friend from Washburn High who reintroduced me to chess (he and I were fierce competitors in high school).

I joined Dave and Cathy's church in Hopkins—an Anglican Church with a charismatic pastor who showed me God was a magnet drawing us toward Himself, a God big enough for all our problems. I believed in a loving God. I believed in Jesus Christ with all my heart, and understood He was to be my Lord and Savior. I knew the gospel of salvation backward and forward.

***

And yet I was not a Christian, and I knew it. How can that be you may say? All the ingredients seemed to be in place. However, I was still 12 inches away from being a Christian—the distance from my head to my heart. I was struggling with wanting to be someplace I could not reach. I see now that God was waiting to fill me with His Holy Spirit, but it would be in His timing, not by my grasping and striving.

***

I was committed to an exercise regimen my personal trainer developed for me. One day I worked out with weights and resistance machines. The next day I did aerobic exercises. When the weather was clear and warm, Lake Calhoun beckoned me for an easy run. As my mind was being transformed, my body was becoming a portrait of good health.

***

Four weeks passed, and it was now Friday, May 19, 2006. I was playing golf at Minneapolis public courses once or twice a week with my two golf buddies; Dave took the place of Jim in our foursome.

The overwhelming meaning of my life was in Chicago. I kept in close contact with Kathleen, Mike and his family, Suzie and her family, and Jane. They were the 11 stars in my universe. Those 11 relationships were roots growing ever deeper. The funny thing is that Kathleen, who said from the start that she forgave me, was the most difficult to draw close to. She was amicable but still distant. I must have hurt her terribly. She seemed afraid to let herself enter into more than a friendly relationship. There was no love there. I couldn't blame her.

Ironic. When she loved me, she was at best a friend. Now that I loved her, I was at best a friend. Of the 11 stars in my universe, Kathleen was the brightest. My love for her had been growing since the three weeks I spent in Chicago five months ago. I was smitten. Unrequited love.

Jane's recovery was remarkable. The cast on her left leg was removed in March, and after two months of rehab, it was wonderfully close to normal. She graduated from a walker to two crutches.

The healing of her traumatic brain injury was even more remarkable. She exhibited no sign of confusion or any other symptoms her doctors had warned us about.

I hired Daniel's suggestion of a counselor in the Gold Coast to see Jane three times a week for a month, and then twice a week, and then once a week. Her depression had disappeared and her outlook on life was positive. The counselor achieved for her what Daniel's counselors had for him—changing her paradigm from seeing a loss to beholding a new season of life, one that would be more exciting than the last.

I was now medication free, yet feeling a bit fragile from the onslaught of the last year. I was healed of depression but knew it was not far from me, waiting for its chance to grab me again. I wasn't going to let that happen. I sensed deep within me that I would never go that way again. I trusted God would not allow it. I embraced quiet time each day to read and pray Scripture. It rejuvenated me now more than any medication. I was at last on the other side of depression.

***

A week later, the Friday before Memorial Day, Dave and I drove to a golf course named Albion Ridges, 50 miles west of Minneapolis, near Annandale. It was a links-type course with wide fairways and roughs devoid of trees for the most part. We teed off at 2 p.m. There were some ominous looking clouds in the west. If we had seen them from Minneapolis, we would never have traveled one-and-a-half hours to play the course. But we were there and determined to make the best of it. After all, the sun was shining brightly, and we hoped the storm clouds would pass to the north. That was wishful thinking.

Sharing the same golf cart was conducive to on-going discussions.

"How's it going? Are events in Chicago meeting your expectations?" asked Dave.

How was it going? What happened to me happens to those who have weathered extreme emotional stress. I entered one side of a black box, where confusion, anxiety, and mental anguish were waiting. I was tossed around in that box, unable to find a way out. I needed others to guide me to the other side. And four formidable guides came into my life—Dave, Daniel, Zeke, and Wally.

A year later, I finally came out on the other side of the box. I was no longer anxious, no longer depressed. Was I healed of depression forever? Not quite. Dave told me depression was not far from me. I needed the distance of several months to be able to finally say, "I have triumphed over depression." I had listened to Dave from the start. I was not cocky. I respected depression with a silent humility. I would not let my guard down. I would triumph.

"I am doing well, Dave. I am doing well. You know what I went through. How do you think I'm doing?"

"I think you're a new man, Mitch. I can see it in your eyes, hear it in your voice, observe it by the way you walk. You have turned the corner. God has blessed you by bringing you out of a terrible depression. You will never be the same.

"This may seem a strange perspective to you—depression, which has seemed like an arch-enemy, has in a way been your friend. It has brought you out of your isolation and self-centeredness. It has given you your family back. You have learned to connect with others as a true friend. You have started a meaningful walk with God."

Dave's portrayal of depression as a friend was a novel thought. He was right. Without depression, I would have continued on as the old Mitch—self-sufficient, without deep friendships, without a family, without a God, in poor health, without meaningful volunteer work, trying to stay active by shallow pursuits and a focus on my investments. I would have been a lost soul.

"That's a fascinating thought, Dave. Depression *has* been a friend as much as an enemy."

Dave respected my silence for the next two holes, as I meditated on what he just said. Depression as a friend? I would never have thought that. As Dave was replacing the pin on the 12th hole and gathering up his clubs, I bowed my head in the cart and thanked God for His great grace in allowing depression to run its course in me and change me forever.

"You asked if events in Chicago are meeting my expectations. The answer is no. They have exceeded my wildest expectation. The 11 stars in my universe are shining brightly on me. Kathleen is moving toward me slowly, but that's to be expected. She's wary of being deeply hurt again. You're aware of all that has happened in Chicago. How do you read it?"

"I read that you are seeing things backwards. I see that ten of your stars have brought you into their world, without your knowing it. You have not brought them into your world; it is not attractive to them. The old Mitch still exerts its influence on you, the Mitch that saw everything from his point of view. I think that's what's happening to Kathleen. She feels you are trying to draw her into your world, and she doesn't want to go there. Meet her in her world, and I believe she will eventually accept you there."

Dave's words were a hammer to my head. I was looking at reconciliation with my family from my point of view, not theirs. What a misguided fool! If I were going to form a true and deep relationship with my 11 stars, a 180-degree change in my perspective was required. Otherwise I risked my children and their families turning away from me at some point. I was not a new and wonderful Dad and Grandfather presenting myself to them. I was a beggar asking for their love. And Kathleen would continue to accept me at a distance. I saw an image of her pushing me away with one hand, while motioning for me to enter her world with the other. Dave's perspective would be my guide from here on. I was excited to think what difference this might make with Kathleen.

"Dave, I thank you from the bottom of my heart. You have humbled me, and I accept it. You have turned my thinking from error to truth. You are not done with your job of being my spiritual director. The mist of my faulty perceptions requires more work."

Dave laughed. "I'm glad you realize that. It makes my job easier. I never thought I was done. Maybe a year from now you'll be able to say, 'Dave, I have forgotten about myself. I am seeing the world from God's perspective.'"

For the next two holes I thought about Chicago from a new vantage point. Jane's recovery was a miracle. She had progressed from crutches to a cane. She limped when she walked, but her doctor said she would be walking normally by the time the cane was no longer needed. She still lived with Kathleen.

I visited Mike and his family and Suzie and her family every time I was in Chicago. We were a close family. Yet…yet, it seemed we had reached a plateau. I hadn't fully entered their worlds, and more depth was not available in my world. That would change.

The relationship with Kathleen and Jane had also plateaued. Although my world had greatly expanded, we were now at the edge of it. Now I had new hope. I would step out of my world into theirs. My heart beat with anticipation.

We were standing on the tee of the 16th hole. It had been a slow round because of Memorial Day weekend. It was past six, and we still had three holes to play. The clouds from the west were passing over us. Suddenly, the heavens opened up. A deluge of rain poured on us, and a fierce wind made the weather even more unpleasant. Everyone on the course ran for the clubhouse.

All except us, that is.

"Well, Mitch," yelled Dave as the wind and rain battered us so badly we couldn't stand up straight. "We have three holes to play. I say we do it. We can move fast with no one in front of us. Are you game?"

"I am, Dave. This is where we separate the survivors from the quitters. It may seem stupid to go on, but it will be a round we'll never forget."

How true that was.

The par 5 sixteenth hole called for a drive over a winding creek. But there was a cross wind, so we hit 3-irons around the creek and all the way to the green. This was not a quest for a good score. It was an adventure to finish the round, no matter what. We didn't even count our shots.

The 17th hole was a par 3 directly into the wind. We each hit three 4 irons to the green and five putted from there. We were soaked, our clubs were soaked, our spirits were determined. We found it difficult to catch our breath.

At last we stood on the tee of the 18th hole, a par 4. The wind was directly behind us. This would be interesting. The landscape was so dark that we didn't dare hit drives. If we had, we might have been able to reach the green. We hit seven irons so we could see where the ball went, just barely. I've never hit a seven iron 240 yards before.

From our drives, we just punched the ball to the green. It was too dark to see anything in the air. We certainly didn't want to be looking for a ball. We putted with seven irons because there was so much water on the green. Finally the last putts were holed. We made it.

We drove to my car and threw our clubs in the trunk. From there we parked the cart by the front door and stumbled into the clubhouse. Warm showers and clothes off the merchandise racks took three holes of beastly weather out of us. We drank hot coffee, ate hot dogs, and recounted our feat.

"We made it, Dave. Boy, am I glad we did that. Most people would say we were morons, but I say *we made it*! We conquered the wind, the rain, and the darkness. We'll remember this round for the rest of our lives."

"And there's something else we'll remember for the rest of our lives," added Dave.

"Everyone else on the course gave up. For them, it was too late in the afternoon, too wet, too windy, too unimaginable to keep playing. But not us. We never gave up. We persevered. We met our goal of finishing the round. Courage went with us. Let's mark today with a stone of remembrance. If we could accomplish what we did today, we can accomplish anything, God willing. I felt Him out there with us. I felt His pleasure."

"Dave, I took heart because I saw you plowing ahead. I know I couldn't have made it on my own. I didn't think we'd survive the 17th hole. We must have made quite a picture out there. I can't remember the last time I had so much fun, once we were finished."

I was babbling on I was so excited.

***

On Sunday, the 4th of June, I flew to Chicago, this time for a full week. I was trying to get my arms around what it meant to live in the world of my family. I thought I was doing that, but Dave said I wasn't. Wasn't I listening to them more than talking about myself? Wasn't I interested in their lives? Wasn't I meeting them on their turf?

***

I assumed I could think my way through this. How wrong I was. Everything I did with my family, up to this point, was from my perspective. I was inside looking out. To experience their lives from their perspective was a subtle adjustment I couldn't make in my mind. Little did I know that a change of perspective would come crashing down on me this trip. And little did I know how my spiritual life would be changed. God is good.

***

Jane maintained a steady progression toward full recovery, almost a half year since her accident. All therapy was now done at home. She still used a cane because of her fear of falling, a common feeling for one who has mended from serious injury. Her casts were all off, and she was feeling vulnerable.

On Monday afternoon, while I was spending time alone with her, the unimaginable happened. She fell. As she was lying on the floor in pain and tears, I too was lying on the floor with her—in my heart. It was not something I thought about. It just happened. I was in her world, experiencing her frustration and fear.

"Darling, are you all right?"

"I think I am, Daddy. I'm crying because I'm so afraid."

"I know, Jane, I know. Let me put a pillow under your head and play your favorite Steve Green album. Just rest until your fear is spent. Just rest."

How remarkable! My mind told me to help her up and dispel her fear. My heart told me she needed comfort and care just where she was. She needed to ease out of her fear before anything else happened. I had moved from my perspective to her perspective in a flash. I knew now what Dave meant.

When Kathleen came home, Jane was lying on the couch, asleep from mental exhaustion. No physical damage had been done. She rested in peace. I told Kathleen what had happened. Her face turned white.

I wanted to inform her that the fall caused no damage and let her know she had no reason for anxiety. However, something inside me said, "Her anxiety is real. Don't dismiss it. Bring her into Jane's peace slowly. Enter into her world."

"Kathleen, see how peaceful Jane is. Why don't you sit by her side and hold her hand."

She looked at me with tears in her eyes, as if to say I had read her mind. She sat on the couch beside Jane, with the color returning to her face. By the time Jane awoke, Kathleen was calm and loving. She and Jane hugged. No words were required. I felt that love within me also, the love of a mother toward her daughter.

Once again, Dave's instruction was realized without my thinking it through. What a great spiritual director. I had entered the world of two of my 11 stars. Great joy was in my heart. Jane and Kathleen seemed to look at me with new eyes. And I looked at them with new eyes. From the plateau we had been on, there was a path before us leading upward. Could this mean love was possible from Kathleen? I hoped so.

***

The following Wednesday evening, I took Mike and Monica out to a steakhouse in Chicago. I was attuned now to living in the world of others, so I sought an opportunity to do so with Mike and Monica. Backward thinking again. I was seeking what *I* wanted to accomplish. How about waiting on God? How would He accomplish his purpose through me?

***

That question started me on the road to salvation. I was blocked from being a Christian because I viewed it from my standpoint. What did I have to do to be saved?

Backward thinking. Not what I had to do for God but what God had already done for me—gave me His Son. My role was to accept His gift in my heart.

So I became a Christian right there? You might think so, but I didn't. It was an awakening of my mind, but not a regeneration of my spirit. There were more miles to walk on the path of salvation. It was a start.

***

I didn't have to wait long. Mike was attempting to reveal a deep side of himself to me, but was nervous and hesitant. I felt his uncomfortableness and considered what I would do if I were him.

I gave him a diversion to collect himself, relating to him the golf round Dave and I played at Albion Ridges. He and Monica were laughing so hard they had tears in their eyes.

"Dad, I can just see you out there with your face set against the wind, determined to conquer the forces of nature. When you decide to do something, you do it."

With that, they laughed even harder. The picture in Mike's mind must have been humorously vivid.

When Mike stopped laughing, he turned suddenly serious. "Dad, I want to tell you what I have done since you talked to me about my workaholic ways and how it was affecting my family.

"I apologized to Monica and our three boys."

Monica came into the conversation at this point. "Mike said what we were all feeling. The boys missed their father. I missed my husband. I was praying he would change. My prayers seemed to be lost somewhere in space, until Mike said how sorry he was to all of us. It was a miracle. I'm so glad you talked to him, Mitch. He said he wouldn't have come to his senses otherwise."

Aha, I had come into Mike's world and didn't even recognize it at the time. I felt joy. No, to be more exact, I felt the joy of Mike and Monica, and that gave me joy.

"Dad, I hired a business coach to help me. He analyzed my workflow and pointed out many timewasters. The amount of work to do didn't diminish, but he showed me efficient ways to handle it, allowing me to spend more time with Monica and the boys. I was receptive to his advice at 28 years old, more so perhaps than I would have been at 40 or 50, when my habits would be more deeply ingrained. I've almost completely stopped having dinner with colleagues and clients. I've been eating lunch with them instead. As a result, I feel more energized for the afternoon and look forward to reaching home early. My coach showed me how certain tasks I completed at work could be better done at home, just as we talked about, when the boys went to bed and Monica was studying."

Instead of thinking how helpful I had been, I stepped into his shoes. "Mike, I'm so proud of you. You have done what was best for you and your family. You have done what I should have years ago. You appear to be more relaxed. You act like a man who has undergone transformation. Is it now family first and work second?"

"Absolutely," said Mike.

"Absolutely," said Monica.

***

On Thursday, Kathleen and I were sitting down at a restaurant on North State Street, not far from her condo.

"Mitch, you've been coming down to Chicago for over five months. I'd like to come to Minneapolis for a week to see your world. Jane encouraged me to make the trip. I can stack the refrigerator with food and leave money for taxis if she needs to go someplace."

I nearly fell off my chair. She caught me by complete surprise. "I'd love for you to come to Minneapolis," I stammered.

She saw I was surprised.

"You've been different on this trip, Mitch. Jane has noticed it too. Whatever we are thinking or doing, you seem to be on the same frequency. Jane said I should let myself trust you without fear. That's not easy for me to do, Mitch. This last week has given me the courage to step out in faith. I hope I'm not making a mistake."

"I am thankful to God that you can trust me. I will not betray that trust. I will never abandon you again. You are not making a mistake."

***

On Friday, I met with Suzie at her home to discuss marketing her paintings.

"Suzie, from what you've said, I calculate your greatest desire is to sell your paintings to customers who will appreciate them, rather than earning a pile of money. Am I correct?"

"You are, Daddy. You have captured exactly what I wanted to present to you as my motive for selling pictures. I appreciate your seeing it from my point of view."

***

I had already been helping Suzie with establishing distribution channels for her paintings. But I had projected the old Mitch's point of view in selling them—trying to get top dollar for a small selection of paintings. She didn't seem to be excited about that.

When I was able to understand her reason for selling paintings, it opened up a whole new marketing position. She was doing what she wanted to do. Her new message became, "Gorgeous landscapes at a modest price." Soon she couldn't keep up with the demand for her art, and her enthusiasm for painting blossomed.

***

Kathleen arrived in Minneapolis the third full week of June. I had reserved a hotel room for her near the Ridgedale Mall.

Monday was our day for exploring the Twin Cities. Tuesday we stopped by my church in the morning and visited with the pastor until noon. Kathleen was pleased by his humility and his confidence, a powerful combination. In the afternoon, we swung by the Faith in Action office and spent time with the director and her assistant. Wednesday she met my two golf buddies as we played golf at Meadowbrook. She drove the cart and had a blast.

***

Thursday morning, I picked up Kathleen and took her to Coffee on France. It was a beautiful summer day in Minnesota, like the day one year ago, less three days, that started this story. That day a year ago was bright on the outside but dark on the inside—I mean the inside of me. Today it was bright on the outside and bright on the inside. What a difference one year brought.

Dave was waiting for us at the coffee shop.

"Well, Kathleen, I have heard much about you. What do you think of Mitch's Minneapolis world?"

"I see this is Mitch's city. He has good friends here, meaningful volunteer work, a spiritually sound church and pastor, and the remembrance sites of three bonding experiences with you."

"Yes, the bonding experiences. Mitch and I have a friendship so deep nothing could tear us asunder."

I saw a wistful look on Kathleen's face when Dave said, "a

friendship so deep."

Could she be hoping for the same depth between us, but more than just friends? Could she be looking at the relationship of love between us that I was praying for. This stepping into someone else's world made me sensitive to what was important to them. I couldn't read minds, but I was coming close.

We stayed in the coffee shop for three hours and then had lunch at a café nearby. True to form, Dave told Kathleen all about his family and little about himself. She had to pull personal information out of him. Dave's eyes told me he liked Kathleen.

***

From lunch, we headed over to my health club. I had called Daniel to meet him there. Kathleen was taken by his deep spiritual moorings and his electric personality. We laughed at how Daniel always showed up when I needed him most.

I hadn't spoken to Kathleen about my struggles with depression because I didn't want to focus on my problems, given Jane's serious health issues.

Dave and I had talked freely about my struggles in front of Kathleen. Daniel and I talked openly as Kathleen listened. I told Kathleen how important Dave and Daniel were to my transformation. Without them, who knows where I'd be. I could tell that Daniel was impressed with Kathleen.

Two hours later when we left the health club, Kathleen said to me, "*Now* I know you are a new Mitch. I have seen it with my own eyes. I have heard it with my own ears. I have experienced it. I am sorry you went through major depression, but if the new Mitch emerged from the ashes of suffering, depression was good for you."

Interesting. Dave had said much the same thing at Albion Ridges: depression as a friend.

As I glanced at Kathleen in the car, her eyes were misty. She put her hand over my hand on the steering wheel and spoke softly. "Mitch, you seemed different in Chicago, but I couldn't bring myself to accept you had changed as much as you said. I kept my distance. This week in Minneapolis has shown me how completely you have changed. My heart has replaced the Mitch I couldn't bring myself to trust with a Mitch I might learn to love."

"A Mitch I might learn to love." Those words were like the first rain after a drought. I was overjoyed. I was lifted off the earth into the heavenly realms. My prayers had been answered. I had never wanted something so much in all my life as I longed to hear those words. I thought owning my own advertising agency was the pinnacle of my life. How wrong I was. How deliriously wrong.

***

It was now the first week of September. I thought, "This has been a wondrous spring and summer of contentment. What an unimaginable contrast to the spring and summer of 2005."

When Kathleen was first in Minneapolis in June, she said she might learn to love me. It was a breakthrough in our relationship. I had fallen in love with her in Chicago; now she was falling in love with me. Subsequent visits to Chicago reinforced that love. At the end of August, Kathleen visited Minneapolis again, this time with Jane. She wanted Jane to experience what she had in June. I was going to say it was like old times, but it wasn't. It was like new times—a caring family with mutual respect and growing love.

Though I now had deep friendships and a family to love, there was something missing. Relationships and activities kept me busy, but it was a piece here and a piece there. There wasn't a major endeavor to pull everything together. My volunteer work with Faith in Action was meaningful but not significant in time spent. I longed for something I could embrace with a passion. I asked God to send an opportunity where I could serve Him and others and not myself.

CHAPTER 17
A New Venture

The trees were starting to change colors. Some leaves were lazily drifting down from the branches that gave them life to lawns that would soon be massive graveyards. The evenings were brisk. The final tentacles of summer exerted their waning influence of warm and fresh days without the heat and humidity of July and August. The Master Artist was giving us a brilliant landscape prior to the bleak white and gray of winter. It was mid-September in Minnesota. Dave and I were overdue for a coffee meeting.

***

At precisely 9 a.m. on a Friday morning, Dave and I linked up at Coffee on France. The main room was especially loud for some reason. Fortunately we had reserved the meeting room. We closed the door and captured a welcome quiet.

Dave started the conversation. "Mitch, you have your life wonderfully full right now with your family, Faith in Action, our church, golf, exercise, and new friendships. To say I am pleased with your life would be an understatement. Are you fulfilled with where you are?"

"Dave, I am very busy. For sure, I am happy with where I now am compared with where I was a year ago. My planner has something significant on it every day. And yet, there is something missing. I feel fragmented. My family has become the most meaningful part of my life. The other pieces you mention are a bit of this and a bit of that. What I need is a mission for my life that will become an ocean of passionate pursuit, next to my family. This may sound morbid, but I'd like an endeavor in which my last day of work and my death are the same day."

Dave laughed, a strange response I thought. "Mitch, you are in for a huge surprise. I wanted to talk to you about a matter that may exactly fit what you desire. Have you ever met Theresa Voight who goes to our church?"

"I've talked to her and her husband a few times over coffee and rolls after the service. She seems interesting, but it's hard to discover much about a person who is part of a couple. I remember she said she works for a large CPA firm in downtown Minneapolis."

Dave filled in more of the picture. "Theresa and I are on the vestry together, and we've become friends in the bargain. She is very unsatisfied with her career as a Certified Public Accountant at a large accounting firm. Service work for God is her passion; she feels she is being called to serve the poor. Theresa has a concept she thinks is viable and needed: helping the poor access available government and private programs. Some programs are well known, others are little known. In either case, the poor have trouble finding and accessing existing ways to help them, and trouble with applications and job seeking skills when seeking meaningful work.

"Theresa informed me she's ready to start her new venture, but she doesn't possess the business, marketing, and fund raising expertise to pull it off. I thought of you immediately. However, I didn't say anything to her until I could talk to you. You can provide exactly what she's missing. If this is of interest, you two should meet."

***

I had asked God for an opportunity where I could serve Him and others with commitment and passion, an opportunity that would be a purpose for my life until I left this earth.

I recently read a book entitled Letters by a Modern Mystic *by Frank Laubach in which he had such a purpose. Dr. Frank Laubach was a Christian evangelical missionary who became famous for his method of "each one teach one" to teach some 60 million people to read in their own language. His life mission was to combat poverty, injustice, and illiteracy. During the last years of his life, he traveled worldwide speaking about literacy and world peace.*

That's what I wanted in my life! And the meeting with Dave that 15th day of September brought it to me.

***

"Dave, I'd like to meet with Theresa and learn more about her new venture. A piano string within me vibrated as you were telling me about her idea."

I didn't want to be too effusive with Dave, but I was absolutely giddy about the prospect of working with Theresa's project. Something within me said, "This is it." I wasn't sure where that something was coming from; that's why I was reserved with Dave.

"Here's her phone number, Mitch. Tell her I talked to you. I know she'll be excited to hear from you."

I called Theresa that very afternoon. We agreed to meet at Coffee on France Tuesday morning. I reserved the meeting room for three hours.

***

Tuesday morning, September 19, 2006, I arrived early and stood by the front door waiting for Theresa. While I waited, I reviewed the questions I was prepared to ask her. I didn't have long to wait.

"Hello, Theresa. Thanks for meeting with me."

"No, thank you for meeting with me. I was pleased to hear from you, Mitch, and I'm excited with what may happen today. What do you want from the coffee counter? I'm buying."

There was no waiting line, so we were soon in the meeting room.

"Do you mind if we pray first, Mitch? Our time together will turn out for the best if God is guiding us."

And so she prayed for our meeting time, a short and simple prayer that was moving. This was a good start. With God in charge, we started the discovery process to see where His path led.

***

Theresa and I exchanged backgrounds and aspirations for half an hour. She had been in the same accounting firm for 20 years, ever since she finished college and passed her CPA exam. She was 42 years old. Her husband George was a dentist who had practiced the past five years in the downtown slums of Minneapolis. He left a lucrative private practice to serve others. This was a major change in his life, and Theresa was looking for a similar path of service. She needed a salary, not as much as a CPA earns, but something to augment her husband's minimum income. They would be a couple of missionaries, a family of four with their children.

This was a solid individual—humble, committed, and intellectually brilliant. I felt comfortable with her and decided it was time to broach the topic of why we were there.

"Theresa, why don't you share with me your concept to help the poor, the full picture so to speak."

"I don't have a big picture to present, Mitch. It's hard for me to envision everything. I'm hoping that's why we're meeting. After you called me, I called Dave to thank him for sharing my idea with you. Everything he told me about you is exactly what I need to complete the picture. His testament about your character was impressive. I thought, 'anyone that close to Dave is someone I can trust.'

"Let me lay down a few dots and hope you can connect them.

"My husband explained to me that the poor he works with are unaware of what's available to them through city, county, state, federal, and private sources. Even when they are shown a program that can assist them, they are confused by the paperwork that needs to be filled out.

"Many of the poor George works with want a job, but they don't know how to search for what's available or how to present themselves. I've found a few grants that would fund an agency with a mission to help the poor, but I need a business plan to submit. I researched agencies that are in this arena; they mainly refer people to other agencies and don't spend enough time with a population who need handholding and confidence building to extricate themselves from the poverty that hangs on them like a shroud.

"Those are the dots. What do you think?"

Being a marketing, advertising, and businessperson trained me to take good notes. I listened as Theresa spoke, and I wrote out what I envisioned as the big picture. It was clear to me by the time she was halfway through her explanation. Theresa had the idea. I had expertise in fleshing an idea out. We complemented each other well.

"You have an outstanding concept, Theresa. I am fascinated. If you'll pardon my boldness, I saw a name for the agency in my mind: Equality of Access, Inc. Are you ready for the big picture?"

I could see Theresa was excited. "I love the name, and I'm eager to see the picture."

I drew on a sheet of paper and explained what I was drawing.

"This is you, Theresa, the president of Equality of Access, Inc. You would receive a salary and be responsible for the mission and vision of the agency, and the procuring and management of volunteers. From what you've told me about yourself, you would also write grants for funding.

"This is another person who would be a chief operating officer—responsible for managing the business, marketing, advertising, and fundraising. He or she would have experience in strategic planning and business planning for grants. This would also be a paid position. The remainder of the staff would be unpaid volunteers, maybe retirees, to work closely and personally with the poor."

I did not want to be overeager. Although I was describing a person with my expertise for the COO position, it hardly would have been proper to advance myself.

"Let's look at a list of steps to establish Equality of Access once the two positions are in place:

1. Form a board of directors for accountability

2. Write a business plan

3. Develop a mission statement, a vision, and a strategic plan

4. Write grants and solicit individual and corporate donations

5. When enough money comes in, the two main positions would receive a salary

6. Find office space

7. Find volunteers and train them

8. Establish channels of communication to find clients

"Many of these steps would take place at the same time. Your husband could help with the eighth step."

We discussed in depth how all this would take place, who would be responsible for what, and details of each of the eight steps.

"That's the big picture as I see it. There will be a wheelbarrow of details to accomplish each step. What do you think, Theresa?"

"I understand the big picture for the first time. I am as elated as an author who suddenly sees a new novel from beginning to end in her mind's eye. This may seem premature, Mitch, but as you were drawing the picture of Equality of Access, I heard a still, small voice within whispering, 'Mitch will be the chief operating officer.' I know it must sound outlandishly presumptuous to you...."

"Theresa, I sensed the same thought."

Theresa was more spiritually advanced than I was. I wanted to say "a still, small voice" also, but I wasn't sure what a still, small voice was. I do know the thought came from outside me. Normally, I would need time to process all this, maybe a couple of days. But the normal did not happen.

"Really," said Theresa. "That's what's called a confirming message. God works in strange and mysterious ways. I came here looking for advice, not a working partner. I prayed for God to take control of our meeting, and He did. As you were showing me the big picture, I thought: 'Are you the one or should I look for another?'"

"I am the one, Theresa. This is exactly what I've been looking for. It's happened faster than either of us envisioned, but, as you said, we were not the ones in charge. For me, there is the conviction of God's calling more so than any conviction I could conjure up on my own.

"I have the resources to work without a salary; I would not want to be paid. Yours would be the only paid position."

Theresa raised her coffee cup and said, "Here's to our partnership."

I raised my cup with her. "Here's to our partnership."

***

I was so energized after meeting with Theresa that I called Dave ten minutes later.

He listened intently and gave me his take on the newly agreed-upon partnership.

"Would you like another confirmation of what happened at your meeting? When Theresa first unveiled her idea to me, I heard the same still, small voice within me saying, 'This is an opportunity for your friend Mitch. He will be a perfect complement to Theresa.' And now it has come to be."

We talked for a few more minutes about Equality of Access, when a thought jumped into my mind. I asked Dave if I could call him back. I dialed Theresa, and she was thrilled with the idea.

A phone conversation with Dave followed. "How would you like to be the first member of our board of directors?"

"You two certainly act quickly. Yes, I would take great pleasure in being involved in your new venture. Count me in. When do I start?"

"Right now, Dave, as we speak. Welcome aboard."

***

During the next three months, step by step, Equality of Access evolved from a concept to an entity. Seven board members in all were selected; Dave was elected chair. One board member, Matt, was a professional grant writer. Board Treasurer Laura's job was fundraising for the United Way. Theresa worked closely with Matt, and I worked with Laura. By the end of 2006, we raised $100,000, the amount the board recommended to have in the bank before launching the agency. Theresa resigned from the accounting firm on January 15, 2007, and started full time as Equality of Access president the next day.

My goal of working half time and having a central focus in my life was realized. There were eight months separating me from all medication. Depression was no longer crouching nearby, waiting to devour me. The black box was so far from me that I could no longer see it when I turned around. I was healed, first in my body, then in my soul, and finally in my spirit. The three-pronged approach to depression brought me though. God would not be bringing me down that path again. In my spirit I knew that being whole for the rest of my life was a fact. He brought Dave, Zeke, Wally, my brother, my family, good friends, and Equality of Access into my life. Most importantly, He pursued me until He had my utmost allegiance.

***

So finally I was a Christian, right? And yet I was not. What was missing? He was waiting for me to embrace Jesus with all my heart, with all my soul, with all my mind, and with all my strength. He was waiting for me to come into His world and see the cross radiant before me, beckoning me to come to its foot and see Jesus as my all in all. He was waiting for me to be aligned to His True North. Be patient, dear reader, for it will soon come to be.

***

As I continued my visits to Chicago, I reconnected with lost friends from my previous life. They were dumbfounded and embraced with fondness the new Mitch, and generously donated money for Equality of Access. These were not the shallow people I thought they were. I had been the shallow one. They took to me with a warmth I had never experienced. They parted with large sums of money for Equality of Access because they trusted me and were committed to helping the poor. By the end of January, I collected a quarter of a million dollars for the coffers of Equality of Access. It exceeded my greatest expectations.

***

The 14th of February peeked out its head, free from the below zero temperatures of the last week. The sun was bright, no clouds were visible, and the temperature soared into the 20s. Today was Valentine's Day, and love was in the air. Equality of Access was up and running. I had never felt so positive about something in all my life. I had a passion for the work of the agency and a purpose that stretched before me as far as the eye could see. I thanked God that He had brought me out of depression and into His world.

From wondering how I could stretch out my responsibilities for the agency to encompass 20 hours a week at the beginning, I was now wondering how I could possibly get done what I needed within the parameter of 20 hours a week.

The marketing and advertising I was responsible for brought in as many clients as we could handle, brought in enough volunteers to match up with the clients, and brought in enough money to comfortably run the agency, with a surplus rapidly building. With grants and donations totaling over a million dollars, we were able to help the poor not only with care but also with money to lift them out of abject poverty. Most of our donations and grants were not one-time gifts but a commitment for the long term. There was money for food, money for housing, and money for clothing to instill confidence when job seeking. Twenty people were no longer on welfare. Those who couldn't work were lifted up from the depths of hopelessness.

I continued my regular visits to Chicago.

***

I was so thrilled with the rapid growth of Equality of Access that I did not apprehend Kathleen was falling more genuinely in love with me. For me, she was the love of my life, but I thought my love for her was on a different level than her love for me. How could she ever deeply love me after all the pain I put her through?

***

One month later, Dave and I met at the coffee shop on France Avenue. Our main topic of discussion was the success of Equality of Access. I lifted my coffee mug in a toast.

"Dave, I never imagined how successful this venture would be. God has blessed Equality of Access richly. I believe our service to the poor pleases Him. I lift this toast to Him, to Theresa, and to you for all you have done to encourage us."

After fifteen minutes of bringing Dave up to speed about the agency and my visits to Chicago, he interrupted me.

"From what you've told me, Mitch, you have a major work purpose in your life and a real family, something you've never experienced before. There's just one thing missing."

That confused me. Something missing? "What, Dave? I couldn't be much happier than I am now. Equality of Access is what was missing in my life. My family relationships are fulfilling. I talk to my brother Sam every week. Sam and Mary are planning to return to Minneapolis soon. Sam sold his real estate agency in Birmingham and bought another agency in Edina. Two title closings are forthcoming. The housing market is considerably stronger in Birmingham than here, so he'll get a better price for his agency there than what he will pay for the agency in Edina. So what is missing?"

"Mitch, have you ever thought of remarrying Kathleen? That's what is missing."

Dave caught me by surprise. Marry Kathleen? That was a dream that would take a miracle.

"Dave, I would marry Kathleen tomorrow, but I don't think she'd ever consider putting herself at that much risk with me. I can see she loves me. But enough to marry me? I don't think so."

Dave hesitated, as if pondering whether he should tell me something or not. Finally he did. "Kathleen called me last week. She has fully forgiven the old you and is deeply in love with the new you. She feels you have come up against a wall and are not allowing yourself to draw closer to her. She doesn't know why. That's why she called me. She hesitatingly asked if I would talk to you."

I felt like I had been zapped by a stun gun. "She…she loves me that much?" I muttered. "I would give a million dollars to be married to her again. No, more than that, I'd give everything I have. Did she say she would be willing to remarry me?"

"Yes," answered Dave smiling broadly. "She wants that as much as you do. I strongly urge you to haul yourself to Chicago as soon as you can and propose to her. Don't let on why you are coming when you call. Just say you're heading down for a usual visit—then make a dinner appointment at her favorite restaurant."

I had been to Chicago a week ago. I couldn't wait another week; I couldn't wait another day. I finished the meeting with Dave abruptly. There was a phone call to make.

Dave laughed. "Don't you think I know why you are shoving me out the door? Go with God-speed my friend. Tell me the good news as soon as you can."

Good news hardly described what I was hoping for. I was looking for a 144-point headline, twice the size of a newspaper masthead, twelve times the size of newspaper copy.

CHAPTER 18
It's in the Box

My heart was beating as if I had just stepped off a treadmill. Prayer calmed me down, and I took several deep breaths before picking up the phone.

"Kathleen, this is Mitch. Do you mind if I come to Chicago this week instead of next? This week is a slack week, and next week will be a full-plate week."

"You're welcome anytime, Mitch," answered Kathleen in a warm and inviting voice. My pulse quickened.

"When are you thinking of coming?"

"How about tomorrow, if that works for you?"

"That will work very well," replied Kathleen. "When will you be here?"

"I could take a mid-morning flight and be at your place in the afternoon. The three of us could visit; then you and I could have dinner out."

It had been 15 months since Jane's accident. She stopped using her cane months ago, but she continued with rehabilitation because she walked with a pronounced limp, which was improving week by week, slowly. Not able to be on her leg for half a day or even to walk a block, she gave up her job and her apartment downtown. Her doctor said she might end up with a slight limp in the end, but it would not hamper her from doing anything, except maybe running in a marathon.

It was a comfort to Kathleen for Jane to live with her and a comfort to Jane. The two of them became as close as a tree with one of its branches.

***

We were at Kathleen's favorite restaurant, a reservation I made before leaving Minnesota.

Kathleen asked me to explain again the bonds of friendship between Dave and me, and I did so. Then I recounted to her the bonds of friendship I had with Sam — the time on the Jemison Trail in Mountain Brook before crossing Shades Creek, the round of golf at Oxmoor Valley, and the café explosion in Montgomery.

Kathleen was enthralled with the bonds narrative.

"I wish some day we could have a bond of friendship, Mitch."

Kathleen didn't say so, but there were no bonds between us in the past. You'd think that getting married would be a bond. I'm not sure what it meant to Kathleen, but to me it was just an event.

"You never know when bonds will arrive," I replied. "The only planned bond for me was when Dave and I climbed over the arches of the Nicollet Avenue Bridge. The others arrived without announcement. A bond may present itself to us soon. You might say, 'It's in the box.'"

"Whatever are you talking about, Mitch?"

Kathleen had a quizzical look on her face. I had a lump in my throat. My hands were shaking. I reached into my sport-coat pocket and pulled out a jewelry box. Kathleen gasped. I think she suspected what might be in the box.

I put the jewelry box in front of her and opened it to show a diamond engagement ring. I felt I was in a stuffy room with little oxygen. I could hardly talk. My 60th birthday would be in one month, and here I was feeling like a teenager on a first date.

"Will you marry me Kathleen? I made too many mistakes to count in our first marriage. I was a horrible husband and father, and I repent of all the sins I committed. I desire with all my heart to be a real husband to you and a real father to our children. Please accept me as I now am. God has changed me into a new creation."

***

"I repent of all the sins I committed." This was an awakening. To repent, to accept that Jesus died for my sins, to bury the old Mitch, to

accept that God was in charge of the new Mitch—ah, finally, this is what it meant to be a Christian. The Holy Spirit had plowed my soul and spirit. The seeds had been planted. The harvest was soon to come.

***

Kathleen was transported into the same low-oxygen setting I was already in. She had trouble catching her breath. She started to cry and fought to compose herself.

"Oh, Mitch, yes I will marry you. I have been earnestly praying for this moment, yet fearing it would never come to be. I have seen with my own eyes that you have been transformed and will be the husband I have always desired. And I will be a loving and true wife to you. "

She pushed her chair back, arose, walked to my side of the table, and kissed me tenderly. The people at the tables around us had been watching the proceedings. When Kathleen kissed me, they applauded.

Kathleen returned to her chair and said to me, "I will live with you in Minneapolis. That is where your work is and your deep friendships. It would not be right for us to live in Chicago. A fresh marriage, a new location. There is one favor I'd like to ask of you. Could Jane live with us in Minneapolis?"

"I wouldn't have it any other way, Kathleen. You two come as a package. Jane needs a sheltered environment for her healing, and I need her loving face to look into every day. Do you think Jane is receptive to leaving Chicago?"

"I'm almost certain she would, Mitch, but we'd have to ask her. We can talk to her when you take me home."

"Two more things I'd like to cover with you, Kathleen. We would not make our home in the Edina condo. I want to give you and Jane the house I denied you when we moved to the Gold Coast, and room for our whole family when they come to visit. Would you mind if I worked with Sam's new agency to find a home for us in Southwest Minneapolis, in the area where I grew up?"

"I've always loved that area, Mitch—the wooded areas in Minnehaha Parkway, the four lakes in close proximity, the uniqueness of Tangletown, the beautiful homes, and the quiet and safe neighborhoods. I often went for long walks and short drives when I was spending time with your mother in her last days."

How it was all coming together was exciting! The thought of a home and flourishing family stretched my imagination to its outer limits. Was this possible? It was like a dream of utmost joy, a dream where everything turned out right.

"You mentioned two more things, Mitch. What is the second one?"

"I thought we would keep the condo in the Gold Coast as a second home when we come to Chicago to visit our family. We'd be here often enough to make good use of it."

"Mitch, I can't believe this is happening. If I were to paint a picture of how I wanted our life to be, everything we have just talked about would complete the picture."

"There is one rather important detail you need to add to your picture, Kathleen: the date of our wedding."

Kathleen replied, "It would be silly for us to have a long courtship. I know with all my heart that I want to marry you. I don't need time to 'test you out.' I've done that over the past year and three months. I've witnessed your transformation. I've met your friends. I've consistently seen the man I want to spend the rest of my life with.

"Let's go for the middle of June, at your Church in Hopkins. Is that too soon for you?"

"Tomorrow is not too soon for me, Kathleen. The middle of June would be wonderful. We'll need about that much time to make all the arrangements. Let's talk to the kids tomorrow and ask for their endorsement."

Leaving the restaurant, we stopped in a large and warm entryway before heading outside. We were alone. Spontaneously, we moved toward each other and hugged tenderly for a long minute. "That seals the bond," said Kathleen.

***

I arrived at Kathleen's the next morning, and together we talked with Jane. Kathleen had said nothing to her last night.

Jane was close to yelling. "You're going to get married? I thought this might happen, but not so soon. I'm thrilled beyond words. Where are you going to live?"

We explained our plans to her.

Jane said, "That's cool. I can live in the condo here until I'm able to find a place for myself, if that's OK with you."

I moved forward in my chair and gazed intently into Jane's eyes. "No…that's not OK with us."

She looked dismayed.

"We want you to live with us in Minneapolis, in a big house we're going to buy. You can complete your rehab in Minneapolis and stay with us as long as you want. Would you like that?"

Jane started crying. "I was so happy when you said you were getting married. I'm even happier, if that's possible, by your including me in your life. That is so generous of you. Yes, I'd like that. No, I'd love that."

Jane went to her room and left us alone. I kissed Kathleen and said, "One announcement down, two to go."

***

We traveled to Naperville Saturday morning for the second announcement. Michael and Monica were overjoyed.

As we walked out the front door and stood by the passenger door of my car, I kissed Kathleen again and said, "Two down and one to go." With that we headed to Wheaton.

***

That evening before supper we told the Walker family of our plans. Suzie jumped off the couch and hugged both of us, appropriately together on the love seat. Jeff sat in his favorite chair with a grin on his face. Together we celebrated a Thanksgiving dinner in March. The two girls were a bit bewildered by the celebration, but they were happy because everyone else was happy.

***

In the first week of April, Kathleen flew to Minneapolis, and we met with the pastor of my church. Because we were "more mature," we were to meet with him half the number of times of a regular marriage-counseling schedule. Pastor wanted to meet once alone with Kathleen, once alone with me, and twice with both of us. His goal for us was a marriage grounded in God, till death do us part. That was his take it or leave it mandate for performing the ceremony, given that we had been divorced before. His goal was our goal.

***

April 6, a Friday, was the first warm day of 2007. The snow was gone, the sun was out, and the temperature was in the low 60s. Kathleen and I celebrated by walking around Lake Calhoun. Sure enough, less than a quarter of the way around the lake, we saw Daniel wheeling towards us.

"I thought I would meet the two of you today walking around the lake."

How did he always know? I still couldn't comprehend that Daniel seemed to be in possession of my itinerary at all times. Daniel the prophet; I don't know how else to describe him. God's hand directed him as he showed up mysteriously at the most opportune times and bolstered my spirit.

"Welcome back to Minnesota, Kathleen. I heard from your husband-to-be that you'd soon be sharing your charm with us on a full-time basis. I pray that the two of you will be my friends as a couple."

"Your prayer is answered as we speak," said Kathleen. "You and Dave are my two favorite people in Minnesota…after Mitch, that is. You helped show me the Mitch I could love again. We will spend the time with you called for by a close friendship. I'll expect you at our house for dinner on a regular basis."

"You are generous, Kathleen. I look forward to food and fellowship on a regular basis. By the way, Mitch, I searched the web to discover more about your brother's new business and found something interesting. We have a mutual friend who works for the real estate agency Sam just purchased. You remember when we talked about Chris Jonas, the guy from my church who graduated from Washburn with you. He and I never talked about where he worked.

"If you don't have an agent yet, why don't you call him? He said he may have a surprise for you."

"We don't have an agent, yet, Daniel. I was going to call Sam for one. Now I don't have to. Thanks, I'll give Chris a call. It will be good to see him again after 42 years. Tell me what the surprise is."

Daniel laughed. "If I told you what the surprise was, it wouldn't be a surprise. You'll have to call Chris and find out."

We talked for nearly an hour. It was like a Sunday school class, with the topic of discussion being the April 6 selection from *My Utmost for His Highest* by Oswald Chambers. Daniel had the book in his wheelchair storage pouch. I listened quietly as Daniel and Kathleen talked about the cross of Jesus. My soul resonated to the message of salvation. As I paid attention to what they were discussing, the meaning of the cross came crashing down on me. In my mind I thought, "I must talk to Pastor soon and have him fill in the blanks of my understanding of salvation." I was ready to commit myself to being a Christian, but I wanted it to be a full understanding of what that would encompass.

As we departed and continued our walk, Kathleen said to me, "What a wonderful friend you have. Now I know what you mean by his being like a prophet. He was so perceptive and discerning, I thought I was talking to Oswald Chambers himself."

For the rest of the walk around Lake Calhoun, we tried to guess what Daniel's surprise might be. Perhaps it was a home in Tangletown with a special door right out of *The Doors of Tangletown*. Maybe it was a large house on a hill overlooking Lake Calhoun. Could it possibly be this? Was that a possibility? It was an exciting way to complete a walk.

***

We called Chris Jonas that afternoon. In a way he was thrilled to hear from his old classmate; in a way he acted as if he were expecting the call. More of Daniel's involvement? After a long discussion of what we were looking for, he asked us to come to his office in St. Louis Park the next morning for a tour of homes that may be of interest to us.

***

There we were, on the north side of Minnehaha Parkway, a few houses down from Nicollet Avenue, with the Nicollet Avenue Bridge just to the west of us. The house before us was a two-story Tudor Revival-style house that was constructed of white masonry and decorative half timbering, with vines covering the front of the house.

"What do you think from the outside?" asked Chris with a smile like the Cheshire Cat in *Alice's Adventures in Wonderland*.

Kathleen and I were stunned. This was my boyhood home.

"Is this the surprise?" I said with excitement.

"This is the surprise," answered Chris. "I predict you will have one of two reactions: either you will say you would never choose the house you grew up in, or you will say this is exactly what you want. I talked to both Daniel and Dave, and they felt it would be the latter. Dave said you could see a bond of your friendship right out the front door."

Kathleen and I exchanged brief looks as if we were reading each other's mind. We said in unison, "This is exactly the house we want."

The negotiations to purchase the house went smoothly. The couple selling was interested in letting the house go as soon as possible because he had been transferred to Chicago.

As I drove Kathleen to the airport on Sunday, I said to her, "I wanted to wait until today to declare to you the thought I had as we were leaving our new home, just in case I misunderstood what was revealed to me. Purchasing my parents' home is another bond in our lives. I realized it as we left the house and I looked west to see the scene of Dave's and my second bond. Second bond and second bond. God's ways are remarkable."

Kathleen responded, "Yes, Mitch, this is our second bond. I felt it too as we stepped out the front door."

I hugged Kathleen as we stood in the airport before she walked into the screening line. I would miss her greatly until we met again. I felt like a young man in love. In two months we would be husband and wife, until death do us part.

***

Monday morning early, I made an appointment to meet with the pastor of my church regarding salvation. I was primed. He was out of town Monday and Tuesday, so Wednesday morning was the first time available. I wrote out a few questions I wanted to ask. It was a short list. I felt like I was at the entryway of heaven, and the gate was starting to open before me.

Wednesday morning arrived with a bright sun and unseasonable warmth. I entered the front of the church and knocked on the office door. Pastor opened the door and gave me a hug. That was a good start. We sat in his office, on two wooden chairs facing each other. He opened our meeting in prayer, a prayer that was moving and set the stage for God's planned outcome for me.

Each question I asked, Pastor opened up a passage of Scripture and explained how it applied. After my list was completed, he had a list of his own, again using Scripture to present God's viewpoint on the matter. This went on for one hour.

When I stepped into his office, I was not a Christian. When I left, I was. God's Word instilled in me the faith of commitment that had been missing. April 11, 2007, was the most important day of my life. I could hardly wait to tell Kathleen. I flew to Chicago that afternoon and made a surprise entrance into her life.

Kathleen's reaction was not what I had expected. "You surprise me, Mitch. I thought you were a Christian by what you said and did, by the certainty of your spiritual insights. I never thought to ask you."

She never thought to ask me. What would I have told her? "Kathleen I'm not a Christian, though you may think I am." No, that wouldn't do. I believed in God as strongly as I believed in myself. I believed that Jesus Christ died for my sins. Yet, I sensed something was missing. I didn't know what. Dave said I needed to make a commitment in my heart, but it was like learning how to whistle. "You just keep trying and trying, and then one day you whistle," he said. I just couldn't put my mind around it until my heart was filled with the Holy Spirit.

"I sometimes believed I was myself, Kathleen. Dave helped me understand that you are not a Christian by what you do or say but by what you believe. By faith. Your life can be filled with goodness and compassion, but if it is not grounded in Christ, you are a branch that is not attached to the Vine. I had not fully accepted Him as my Lord and Savior. Now I have."

Silence hung like a curtain. Then the curtain opened, and Kathleen became filled to the brim with enthusiasm. She could barely talk. "*Now* I understand what happened! Isn't God amazing? He listened to my prayers from years back. I thought he had already answered them. I had assumed you were a Christian. I was wrong. Now I'm right. Isn't God amazing?

"Mitch, this must be our greatest bond. We will be husband and wife in the eyes of God, and we will both be bonded to Christ and bonded to each other in His name."

We held each other for a long time, tears streaming down our faces.

***

The day of the wedding arrived—June 30, 2007. It was a glorious ceremony. Dave was my best man and Michael, Jeff, and Daniel were groomsmen. Suzie was Kathleen's maid of honor and Jane, Dave's wife Cathy, and Kathleen's best friend from Chicago were the bridesmaids. The church was filled with some 200 attendees—church members, friends and acquaintances from Minnesota, and more people from Chicago than either of us would have expected. The friends I once thought were shallow had become closer to me than they ever were when I lived in Chicago.

***

We honeymooned in Beaufort, South Carolina, for two weeks. It was a popular destination that was both charming and relaxing. We rented a small house right on the Atlantic Ocean and spent the afternoons walking vast stretches of beach that lay before us. How wonderful it was to be in love in such a location. The Master Artist painted a landscape we would never forget.

EPILOGUE

Today, November 15, 2007, is exactly four months since we returned from our honeymoon in South Carolina. Fall is coming to a close with the trees bare and the ground covered with leaves. The afternoon sun is low in the sky, peeking through the trees in front of the Nicollet Avenue Bridge. The days are brisk and the nights cold. Winter will soon be here.

Thirty minutes ago, Kathleen and I were standing on our front lawn looking west at the Nicollet Avenue Bridge, the very arches of which Dave and I had climbed over when we were in high school. Kathleen said to me, "God has been involved in our lives more than I could imagine. He has given me more than I prayed for."

And so here I sit at a desk, completing the last page of my manuscript.

I have experienced a transformation that is as remarkable as a 5 ½-mile climb to the summit of Mt. Everest in the dead of winter:

1. One man's triumph over depression

2. Conversion from an agnostic to a Christian

3. An about-face from a lonely and desperate man to one with deep friendships

4. A transposition from being divorced and estranged from my children to being happily married with three loving children and their families

5. A monumental shift from being concerned only about myself to forgetting myself in the arms of God and His creation

6. A metamorphosis from the poverty of hollowness to the richness of new purpose and meaning

Dave was so right when he said it was never too late in the afternoon to make major changes in life. I am proof that earthshaking changes are possible even in the twilight of one's years.

Jane has been accepted into the William Mitchell College of Law in St. Paul. Her recovery from the tragic car accident eventually became 95 percent back to normal.

Our family in Chicago receives regular visits from Kathleen and me. Sam and Mary are now living in Edina, not far from where I used to live. Equality of Access is an agency that will be viable in perpetuity.

God is in His heaven and all is right with the world.

ABOUT THE AUTHOR

Patrick Day holds a master's degree in English Literature from the University of Minnesota and was a dean of instruction at a community and technical college for many years before turning to a career of writing and life coaching.

He and his wife Diane live in Buffalo, Minnesota, 30 miles west of Minneapolis. They have two grown sons.

COACHING FOR DEPRESSION

After reading *Too Late in the Afternoon*, you may wish you had a Dave Logan in your life to guide you through your own depression or the depression of a loved one, relative, or friend.

Patrick Day has an intimate knowledge of depression and is available to be your Dave Logan. Dave did not assume the role of a medical doctor, a psychologist, a counselor, or a pastor. Nor would Patrick.

Dave was a mentor to Mitch in understanding his depression and managing the healing elements of body, soul, and spirit. It's a lonely and difficult road to navigate the tumultuous journey of depression on your own. Patrick could be your partner and coach.

Call or e-mail Patrick Day for a no-cost discussion to see if he may be of assistance.

Patrick Day
pjdcoaching
pday@pjdcoaching.com
763-486-2867